THE STARS ARE A MILLION GLITTERING WORLDS

First published in 2025

Allen & Unwin Aotearoa New Zealand
Level 2, 10 College Hill, Freemans Bay
Auckland 1011, New Zealand
+64 (9) 377 3800
auckland@allenandunwin.com
www.allenandunwin.co.nz

83 Alexander Street
Crows Nest NSW 2065, Australia
+61 (2) 8425 0100

EU Authorised Representative: Easy Access System Europe, Mustamäe tee 50, 10621 Tallinn, Estonia, gpsr.requests@easproject.com

A catalogue record for this book is available from the National Library of New Zealand.

ISBN 978 1 991142 32 0

Cover images: Ruapehu maunga © Travel Pix/Alamy; mountain and lake © Victor Bordera/Stocksy; blanket © Mykola Mazuryk/Dreamstime

Cover design by Sandy Cull, www.sandycull.com
Internal design by Megan van Staden
Set in Tiempos Text
Printed and bound in Australia by the Opus Group

1 3 5 7 9 10 8 6 4 2

MIX
Paper | Supporting responsible forestry
FSC® C001695
FSC www.fsc.org

THE STARS ARE A MILLION GLITTERING WORLDS

GINA BUTSON

ALLEN&UNWIN
AUCKLAND • SYDNEY • MELBOURNE • LONDON

PROLOGUE

Ruapehu maunga, New Zealand, 2006

The slope stretches out in front of Thea, a pathway of moving lights. Jim and Penny are in front of her and Marcus is behind as they make their way through the snow up to the hut. There's no moon, but above her the stars are a million glittering worlds: dreams and memories cast wide across the clear dark sky. This is life. This is what her father had wanted her to experience, had wanted to share with her.

She can imagine him lovingly shaking his head, smiling and saying, 'I knew you'd love it, Thee.' Less than a year on, there are still so many times a month she wants to pick up the phone and call him, just to tell him something, to pass the time, to say hello — and then she realises that she'll never be able to do that again.

She thought she'd have more time. More time to tell him that she was ready to spend weekends on the mountain with him, learning to traverse icy slopes, to climb couloirs, abseil into snowy craters, to navigate cracks and seracs down a glacier and back to the hut. There were always reasons not to go on trips with him: tickets to gigs, plans with friends, too much study, her part-time job, then her full-time job and work events — but she always thought the time would come.

But time is like a wild goat: sometimes it stops and stares at you, an unblinking challenge; at others, it bounds off and no matter how fast you run, it's gone. Thea found herself, six weeks after her father's funeral, sitting in front of the bookcase at his house, running her finger along the spines of guidebooks and the thin folds of topo maps. She pulled a book from the shelf at random, flicked through the pages and saw her father's comments and markings scribbled in the margins. She stopped on one page: there in a blue ballpoint circle was a capital T. She slowly turned through the pages. There was another, and there was another. And in most of the guidebooks, there it was, just once or twice: a T to mark the routes and climbs he'd hoped to do with her. One day. When she was ready.

Sitting there, she'd felt the loss of him tumble down around her, all those unlived adventures and unsnapped photographs sliding away. All those stories of his time in the mountains that she only half-listened to and was already forgetting, memories fading like white breath on a cold day. She couldn't let that part of him, nor that part of who she thought she'd be, just disappear. Finally she joined the Mountain Sports Club and signed up for their Introduction to Mountaineering course.

At the time she enrolled, she hadn't realised that Marcus was one of the instructors. Marcus who, although much younger than her father, had spent the better part of the past decade climbing with him. He'd been in and out of their house over the years, planning trips and borrowing gear, often staying for a cup of coffee or dinner. Thea could hear her father in the way Marcus explained the difference between a true, pre-dawn alpine start and what he jokingly referred to as a city-slicker, post-caffeine alpine start; in the way he described clouds as 'the stuff of hopes and dreams — and sometimes disappointment and nightmares'; the way he told them to watch their feet, and the skies.

Being on the mountain always feels right to Thea, like she's exactly where she's meant to be. Yet all those course weekends felt like practice. *This* feels real. Tomorrow she'll climb the mountain.

Or maybe it's today. The trip from Auckland to the road end had taken much longer than it should have, with terrible traffic leaving the city, a last-minute grocery stop and dinner in Te Kūiti. By the time they reach the hut, today will have rolled over to tomorrow; tomorrow will be today.

Their boots crunch through the snow. A wind whispers down the mountain, rustling through their waterproof jackets and pants. She tries to catch hold of fragments of the stories her father told her about this mountain, spindrift memories breezing past. She remembers one about a plane that crashed on the Mangatoetoenui glacier. It took more than thirty years for the slow-moving ice to release the plane just six hundred metres from where it crashed. Some things take time. Those stories of his, his love of the mountains, have been churning underground across the years; they're part of who she is.

She follows Jim and Penny. Behind her, Marcus nudges her when she stops to stare up into the night sky. 'Come on,' he says, 'we've got a big day ahead and it's well past bedtime. Aren't you tired?'

'Exhausted,' she says. And she is, or should be. She and Penny were out late on Wednesday night — always a big night out on K Road — and she hasn't quite caught up on sleep. They were both yawning on the drive here. When they got out of the car, the bite of ice-tinged air woke her up, but she can feel the tiredness creeping back into her body as they make their way up the steepening mountain. It's like there's another body inside her, an internal shadow that with every step spreads farther into her limbs, tugging her downwards into sleep.

'I'm stoked you're joining us tomorrow.' Penny throws the words towards Thea over her shoulder. Before Thea can say anything in response, Penny adds, 'You haven't changed your mind, have you?'

'Ask me after breakfast. Or at least coffee,' Thea replies. Originally she was going to join the group going up the Whangaehu Glacier and back: the easier option. During the car ride, Penny, Jim and Marcus had convinced her to join them going up to Te Heuheu summit: the longer and more technical option.

'It'd be good to have an even number,' Jim had said as they drove through the chopped-up back of the North Island.

'You'll love it, Thea,' Marcus said. 'It can get a bit gnarly if it's icy, but it's great climbing.'

Thea had stared out the car window into the moving darkness of the King Country, wisps of mist settling into the crook of the land. As the black roads curved and rose towards the Central Plateau, she hadn't been sure that she was ready for a summit trip. Her ghostly face in the glass warned her that it would be challenging. But, caught up in the others' confidence in her, she decided it was worth a go. She had turned away from her dark reflection and back into the car. 'I do like a challenge,' she said brightly.

Now, walking up the night mountain, she remembers the photos on top of the bookcase in her father's house, gleaming white peaks against infinite blue skies. She wants that.

'Your choice,' Penny says, 'but if you don't come with us, you'll have to get a ride back with the others. The group that drives together climbs together. Or the other way round. No pressure though.'

Thea stoops to scoop up a handful of snow. She shapes it into a snowball and lobs it at Penny.

'That's enough, you two,' Jim says. 'We didn't come here to have fun.' Without looking at each other or saying a word, Thea and Penny both bend down, pick up a handful of snow and throw it at Jim. 'Hey!' He turns towards them, grinning. 'Watch it, I've got years more snowball experience than the two of you put together. You don't want to take me on.'

They continue up the mountain, laughing and talking until they see the shadow of Tāne Whakapiripiri, the club hut, crouched against the snow. The orangey outside light is a warm halo in the dark-white world. It makes Thea think of the lamppost in Narnia, a single light in the snow, a boundary marker between worlds. The group from the Wellington branch of the club arrived a couple of hours ago and they'll already be in bed, fast asleep. The four climbers approaching fall silent as they near the hut.

When Thea first stayed at Tāne Whakapiripiri, on the first weekend of the course, she wanted to text her father. *I thought you were hardcore. What happened to rustic huts and tents and snow caves?* Instead she'd said to no one in particular, 'This place is a palace.'

Marcus had responded. 'Palace might be stretching it,' he said, 'but it's pretty nice, right?'

For a mountain hut, it's luxury: on the main floor, there's an open area with a large wooden table and a couple of sofas, plus a kitchen equipped with pots and pans and other basics; two bunk rooms are wedged in the lower part of the building. Everything's a bit chipped and threadbare now, having provided shelter to hundreds of people over the years, popular for family-oriented club weekends where just being in the hut is the adventure, and a base for more extreme days out. The years of wear and tear only add to the sense of safety and comfort. Thea's already looking forward to sitting on the couch after the climb, looking through the big window back towards the summit and rewinding through the day, reliving the adventure and swapping stories.

'The Wellington crew are in the south room,' Marcus says, his voice low, 'so let's take the north room.'

Before following the others inside, Thea runs her eyes back along the trail of boot prints crisping into the snow until they disappear into the darkness, beyond the reach of her head torch. She could follow those prints back down the mountain. The snow would thin as she descended, rocks cropping out and scree dirtying the white as she reached the carpark where Marcus's car waits and her work clothes are folded neatly on the back seat.

She switches her head torch off and looks up once more, past the heavy darkness of the mountain to where the thickness of stars makes the sky milky-white. Time is slow and wide and deep; she feels like she can sail through it, light as a boat made of driftwood and dried leaves. In that moment, all her nervousness, all her uncertainty about tomorrow's climb, melts away. She breathes deeply, a smile on her lips, then joins the others inside.

☆ ☆ ☆

In the darkness of the hut, the turning and shaking of sleeping bags is slowly replaced with the soft rasp and sigh of sleep. Listening to Jim's snores, Thea doesn't think she's slept until she realises she's woken. The final group to arrive are quiet, unpacking their sleeping bags before they enter the bunk room, making as little noise and movement as possible, but it's enough to wake a light sleeper, or someone still trying to dampen doubts about the day ahead. Like slow dominoes, Penny rolls over with a muffled groan; Marcus shifts to face the wall; then Thea rolls onto her stomach, pressing her face into the folded fleece she's using as a pillow. Only Jim keeps sleeping, with a rhythmic in and out of breath. The room settles once more and, before too long, they're all asleep, dropping into exhausted rest, absorbing what they can from the shallows of the night.

Outside, the darkness slowly ebbs, swallowing stars as the sky changes imperceptibly from black to grey. Snow falls. Glaciers continue their crawling churn down the mountain. As the sky lightens, the broad top of Ruapehu cuts a dark seismic line between earth and sky, a line between now and then, between today and all the days that follow after.

PART 1

1

Panajachel, Guatemala, 2007

Sarah stands at the edge of the lake. A cluster of boats rises and falls against the jetty as the waves sweep in. A knot of men point at the lake, the sky, the boats. Sarah can't understand a word of what they're saying. Even if it's Spanish, she wouldn't have a chance, but she thinks it's probably K'iche' or the language beginning with T that she can't remember the name of. The men could be fiercely in agreement or arguing but, either way, it's not hard to tell that they're vigorously weighing up whether to cross the lake or not; whether to take these paying passengers who stand in two small groups — one of Guatemalans and the other of French tourists — across the chop of Atitlán, or whether to stay safely on the shore. She glances back towards the road but the van that dropped her off is long gone.

This is the part of travelling that Sarah hates: the actual travel. She loves being in new places — wandering through markets, running her hands over the feet of statues, gazing up at steeples and clock towers — but the getting there on sketchy roads or wild water makes her nervous every time. And when she has to do it by herself, it's next-level stress.

She can't help imagining buses careering straight over cliffs, plunging into whatever's sitting down below: scraggy plants, a rocky river, a farmhouse with children and chickens out the front. During those hours on the road, she's run the scenarios through her head: having to pull herself through a broken window and up a ravine; flagging down a car and explaining what happened with her few words of Spanish, frantic hands, and a body full of scrapes and grazes. Or, worst of all, not climbing out. Just like in Australia, they plant crosses by the roadside here. There's no reason why it shouldn't be her bright-coloured bus replaced by a white cross. She wonders what they do when a boat capsizes. Probably a marker on the nearest stretch of shore, but she can't shake the image of small white crosses bobbing upright all across the lake.

Even though it doesn't change the odds of disaster happening, travelling's so much easier with someone else. Someone to lend you change when the bus driver won't accept big notes; someone who speaks enough Spanish to buy snacks at the roadside; someone who might remember your name and where you're from, in case you do end up tipped sideways down a ravine. It had never been her plan to travel on her own. It was meant to be her and Hayley together, off on the adventure of a lifetime, but instead Hayley had got her dream job — and a boyfriend. When Hayley pulled out, tears sitting on the rims of her eyes as she broke the news, Sarah realised that she'd never really had to do anything alone; nothing major, anyway. It would be good for her to go out into the world and come back a braver, freer version of herself. She couldn't bring herself to do the trip through South America that she and Hayley had planned out with sticky notes all over a map stuck to Sarah's bedroom wall — she still hoped that they would do that together sometime. Instead, her eyes travelled to the top of the map and that small piece of land like a stalk sprouting from a chilli pepper, connecting South America to the north. Central America seemed like a much more manageable size for a person travelling on her own. She went back to the stationery shop and bought the adjoining map.

There are times like this, standing beside a dark, deep lake in the pouring rain, when she has to remind herself how good it's been for her to do this on her own. Truly, it *has* been good for her. And really, travelling alone has barely ever meant being all by herself. There's almost always at least one other foreigner, pack on shoulders and woven bracelets up their arms, heading in the same direction. Backpackers, she soon worked out, are all going the same way, wearing out foreign countries like threadbare carpet.

She'd like to stray more into the lush heart of Central America. The past week, up in the mountains and the caves, was a step off the beaten path, and she'd absolutely loved it. She'd like to explore more of the real life that she glimpses all around her outside the museums and tourist bars, but she wants to do it with someone else. And that's not *just* because she's nervous on her own. Sarah thinks of the wonderful people she's met along the way so far; how much she's laughed and learned about their worlds; the fun she's had; the friends she's made in dorms, on buses, at ancient pyramids, on rooftops with views of the bright Caribbean. Travelling's not only easier, but so much more enjoyable, with someone else. Someone to take photos with, someone to fall asleep against on long bus rides, someone to share a bed with. Someone like Chris.

☆ ☆ ☆

On the boat, the four Guatemalan passengers in front of Sarah drop to their knees. As she listens to the murmuring of prayer, the gentle rhythm and rock of the words, she wonders if it's a regular prayer, offered up to the life-giving lake, or if it's a prayer of panic, a life-preserver thrown out into especially rough waters. There's so much about this place she doesn't know, so much she's keen to learn. She's not seen anyone drop to their knees on a bus. Maybe it's a boat-specific fear. Maybe it's a lake-specific prayer. She scans for life jackets.

The small vessel bumps over the waves, a slash of bright blue against the dark water and sky. The waves throw water up from below and the rain pours down from above. 'San Marcos,' the boatman calls out, throwing a rope onto the gap-toothed jetty. Then Sarah's the only passenger left as they buck and sway through the grey chop to the next and final stop: San Pedro La Laguna. San Pedro, where Chris is waiting for her. Chris, the reason she's braved this surround-sound water and wind.

As she walks down the jetty, a boy who looks to be about fourteen or fifteen comes running out from under the cover of a building. '*Buenos días*,' he greets her, then continues in English, 'do you need a hotel? I can recommend several good hotels.'

'*Hola*,' she says. 'I'm fine, thank you. I've got a hostel.'

'I'll show you the way. Where are you staying?'

'The Xaman Ek.' She's hesitant with the pronunciation and when the boy repeats it with a slightly different intonation, she says it back to him, then repeats it again, silently, to herself. Her father talks about the tongue-memory and brain-memory of learning a new language. 'Say it, sound it, think it,' he told her when she spoke to him of her struggle to pick up Spanish.

The boy smiles. '*Venga*. Come with me. *No es lejos*. It's not far.' He takes Sarah's pack and leads her through the rain, along narrow lanes to a walled-off courtyard. At the end of the courtyard stands a three-storey turquoise building, a creep of blood-red bougainvillea up one side. The top storey is narrower than the two below. Its flat roof appears to be filled with the usual charmless clutter of TV aerials and functional junk. It's the space below that draws Sarah's eye: judging by the concrete balustrade, the lower roof area has been made into a terrace. If it wasn't for the torrential rain, it's exactly where she'd find Chris. He loves a rooftop bar or terrace. '*El Hostel Xaman Ek*,' the boy says, leading her up to the bar that also serves as reception.

The courtyard's almost empty; there's just one man behind

the bar, dressed in a US army-style cap and jacket, except the cap is blue and the jacket a faded orange. His white t-shirt spells out '*PAZ*' in blocky black letters. He talks briefly with the boy in Spanish, then leans in front of Sarah, cigarette clamped between his teeth, one hand cupping his stubbled chin.

'Hello, hello, hello,' he says with an American accent. 'Welcome to the Hostel Xaman Ek, where everyone is already checked out, but never leaves. Passport, please.' He glances at the cover of her passport, then flicks it open. 'Well, how do you do, kangaroo, if it isn't the lovely Sarah. I've been waiting for you. Yikes, that sounds like some kind of creepy, horror-movie thing to say, doesn't it? I promise you, this isn't the old bartender-in-a-deserted-hotel-who-turns-out-to-be-a-ghost trope, despite the eerily quiet surroundings.' He wiggles his fingers and looks around the courtyard with mock horror. 'I'm as real as any other loud American stumbling through Guatemala. My name's Michael,' he reaches out to shake her hand, 'and I've been told to expect you. Your buddies, sorry, your *mates*, are around here somewhere.'

Sarah relaxes. She's a bit confused, but she likes this man. Despite his mocking of the Aussie accent, he makes her feel at ease. 'You mean Chris?' she asks.

'You mean a loud and *somewhat* annoying Australian?' Michael stubs out his cigarette and picks up Sarah's pack, grimacing at its dampness.

'Loud, *maybe* a bit annoying, but loveable.' She laughs at the look on his face. 'He is! Really. Well, I think he is.' She's body-tired from the long day of travelling, but inside she's filled with the silvery flash of hundreds of slender fish through sunlit water, a shivery excitement. She can't wait to see Chris again.

When she heard about the retreat in the hills high above Lake Atitlán — a week of yoga, meditation and local culture, culminating in a *temazcal* and Mayan fire ceremony — she knew it was an experience she couldn't have anywhere else in the world and one she would take with her for the rest of her life. Falling in love with Mayan culture was one of the unexpected delights of coming to Central America. She knew it wasn't Chris's thing but mentioned it to him anyway, just in case. He'd looked at her and laughed that laugh of his she loves so much and confirmed that it most definitely was not his thing. Then he'd kissed her disappointment away and encouraged her to go alone. 'I'll ruin it for you if I go, babe, and this isn't something you should miss. Go without me and tell me all about it when you're done.'

'You'll be here when I get back?' she had joked, her arms clasped around his neck.

'Of course not. Time to move on,' he replied, his expression serious. 'But I'll let you know where I'll be.'

Yes, she had missed him like crazy, but she's grateful to him for pushing her to go by herself. For the first few days, she imagined him beside her, making jokes about the vegan food and cleansing juices, suggesting that instead of evening meditation they gap it and find a bar or somewhere private among the trees, and that definitely would've been its own kind of fun. But after a few days she became less self-conscious and allowed herself to be immersed in the experience. By the last day, she could feel the chanting reverberating through the ancient caves and into her, feel herself drifting on curls of incense-infused woodsmoke into the still air.

Michael leads her up two dark flights of stairs. On the third storey, he flings a door open and puts Sarah's pack inside the room. 'Now get yourself out of those wet clothes, then come back downstairs for a drink. Have a shower if you want, but be warned that they're cold. *Nada* hot water at the Hostel Xaman Ek.'

Sarah's surprised to see four beds in the room, two of which are clearly taken. She'd expected a private room, just her and Chris. And where is Chris anyway? She told him she'd be on the afternoon boat. Maybe the weather caused some delays, but she's not that late. She turns to ask Michael if he knows where Chris is, and who the other person sharing the room is, but he's gone, whistling down the gloomy hallway.

Although Michael seems to know exactly who Chris is, Sarah's relieved to recognise Chris's pack resting against the wall beside one of the beds. A couple of his t-shirts and the guidebook that he covered with the dust jacket from *The Book of Lies* sit on the bed. Resisting the temptation to have a look at the other person's stuff — just to satisfy her curiosity — she opens the door on the opposite side of the room. She was right: a tiled terrace fills the space. If the sun ever comes out, she supposes that it might be a nice place to sit, but today it just looks dreary.

None of this is the reunion she had imagined, but at least it gives her a chance to tidy herself up. She'd pictured herself lying on top of Chris, her hair cascading down so they were enveloped in the lingering scent of spicy smoke. He would tease her about having spirit hair, but he'd like it; he'd run his hands through it, tugging her gently closer to him, he'd *really* like it. But the smoke's been washed away by rainwater or lake water, Chris isn't here, and she's standing in a dorm room, her hair dripping onto the floor. She just feels travel-dirty rather than earthy.

☆ ☆ ☆

With soap-fresh skin and her hair smelling of apples, Sarah takes in the courtyard as she sips her lemongrass and ginger tea. It's made with real herbs floating inside the teapot. The rain has stopped, leaving the dregs of a grey day, darkening into night. A guaracabuya tree stands in the centre of the courtyard, multicoloured bulbs draped among its shivering leaves and twisted seed pods. A string of tattered prayer flags loops along the wall above a series of carved stone statues. The statues stand about waist high, imitations of figures carved into temples and ruins throughout Guatemala. She'll have to ask Michael which gods they represent.

At the table beside her, a Scrabble board lies open, a chaotic mess of tiles strewn across it, some placed on squares, some turned face-down, others stacked three or four high. It's got a Mad Hatter's tea party kind of vibe to it, if the Mad Hatter was a crazy drunken linguist. Sarah looks around before turning over one of the upside-down tiles. Z. She thinks of Michael's t-shirt and finds a P and an A to spell out '*paz*' in the corner of the board. If the players come back and notice it, she'll deny all knowledge. She thinks about what else to spell. *Vida*? Her name?

Then she hears his laugh. At last! Again, she feels the flick-flick-flick of tiny fish darting through her, quivering silver anticipation. She leaps up and races towards the entrance to the courtyard. 'Chris!' She wraps her arms around his neck and lets her body fall into his, arcing into him from the tips of her canvas shoes pressed into the ground.

He puts his arms around her, clasping her as though about to lift her like a dancer, but not following through on the action. 'You're here!' he says. 'How long have you been waiting? We went to the cash machine, then it started bucketing down so we took shelter for a bit. Sorry, babe, I thought we'd be back before you got here. Thought your boat might not even get across in this weather.'

Sarah can smell the beer on Chris's breath. Her face is close to his, but she feels too self-conscious to kiss him. There's a girl standing right beside him. She's tall and lean, with rich brown hair, chopped in a straight line between her chin and shoulder. She's trapped there, Sarah realises, only able to get past her and Chris if she turns side on and slides through the gap between them and the wall. Body still pressed into Chris, Sarah turns her head to this other girl. 'Hi, I'm Sarah.'

The other girl smiles, her lips pressed together. 'Hi, I'm Thea.'

☆ ☆ ☆

Sarah's got nothing against Thea, who seems quiet but nice enough, but she's disappointed not to have Chris to herself. She knows that Thea had tried to make an excuse to leave the two of them alone. It was Chris who had insisted that she stay. That's typical of him — he pulls people in, including all the strays. If he sees someone sitting alone in a hostel, or walking around a tourist site by themselves, he'll go up to them and start chatting. 'You're the Pied Piper of Mexico,' she'd told him in Veracruz, not long after they first met. They'd been heading to dinner along with a mixed bag of French, Swiss, German and English backpackers. He's great at gathering people together, but he always makes time for just the two of them. They'll eat with Thea, Sarah thinks, and then they'll slip away.

'How long have you guys been travelling together?' Sarah asks Thea, as they sit waiting for the food they've ordered. An image flashes into her mind of Chris waving goodbye from outside a different hostel as her shuttle to the retreat pulled into traffic.

'We haven't been,' Thea responds. 'Chris was here when I arrived. That was, what?' She looks at Chris. 'Three or four days ago?'

About half the time I was at the retreat, Sarah thinks. 'We met in Veracruz,' she tells Thea. 'I'd been in Central America for about a month. I was feeling so lost and homesick and then I met Chris.' She smiles at him and puts her hand on his forearm, pressing her fingertips one by one into the ropey muscles beneath his skin, like the way she's seen people push the little buttons on a piano accordion. 'Remember the time you walked over that ant nest then almost stumbled into a snake?'

Sarah turns back to Thea to tell the story, which reminds her of another adventure. The memories start gushing out of her until she realises that, although Thea's laughing and smiling, she must've had plenty of her own adventures without needing to hear about Sarah and Chris's. 'Anyway, tell me about San Pedro. And has Chris driven you crazy yet with his humming and those annoying songs he makes up?' Sarah does a brief imitation, humming loudly, chin pointing up, chest thrown out. Thea laughs again and her face is transformed. *It was* definitely *polite laughter before*, Sarah thinks.

'There's quite a bit to do here,' Thea tells Sarah. 'There's a yoga place. You can rent kayaks. There's a couple of hikes that I want to do. We've seen a few signs for movie nights and stuff. Not that we've done any of that. We've been really lazy — a lot of sleeping in and reading, too much eating and drinking. It's a good place to take a break from travelling, to chill out for a bit.'

'The beer's cheap. The food's good,' Chris adds.

'Have you signed up for Spanish lessons yet?' Sarah asks Chris. He shakes his head. 'Hey, that's why we came here.' She turns to Thea. 'We've been talking about finding a place to spend a few weeks studying Spanish. We did a one-week course in Oaxaca, which was nothing really. I heard about a place here that's run by a local cooperative. Chris was going to investigate while I was at the retreat.'

The next time Chris goes to get a drink, he gets distracted at the bar, talking to the barman — not Michael anymore — and a man who's been sitting on the same barstool all evening. Sarah smiles as she watches Chris leaning against the bar, so comfortable in his skin, so confident in himself. She draws her attention back to the table, about to ask Thea who the other guys are, when she notices that Thea's eyes are on Chris, too. For a moment she watches Thea watching Chris. 'Who's Chris talking to?' she asks.

'That's Hans,' Thea nods towards the man behind the bar. 'And that's Aksel. You won't see him before three in the afternoon. He's a cocaine vampire.'

'A what?' Sarah asks.

'Up all night and rarely seen during the day.'

'Is that a thing here? Vampires? Just kidding. I mean, cocaine, is it a big problem?'

Thea laughs. 'Not for some people — for a lot of people it's why they stay. Aksel's apparently been here about four months. Came for a few days, never left.' Thea pauses and looks across at Sarah. 'Hey, don't worry,' she says. 'It's not a problem. It's actually a really chill place to walk around.' Sarah frowns, digesting the information; she didn't really take in the town in the rush through the rain from the boat to the hostel. When Sarah doesn't respond, Thea speaks again. 'And, you know what, it always makes for a fun dance floor. There's always a super-high-energy vibe. Unless, you know, there's a group of vampire tourists, then they just suck the life out of the party.' She raises her eyebrows and laughs, and there's something in her expression that reminds Sarah so much of Hayley that she feels a flood of warmth towards Thea.

'You like dancing?' Sarah asks. 'Are there places to go out dancing here?'

'Yes and yes,' Thea says.

And with that the conversation shifts, taking loose twists

and turns, a comfortable ease in the back and forth of sharing stories of the people they've met, the things they've seen, of where they've been and where they're going.

'I wasn't even meant to be in Central America,' Sarah tells Thea. 'All those wasted Post-it notes,' she says with a laugh.

'You never know,' Thea says, 'maybe your friend will break up with the guy and come join you. You could still do the trip you planned.'

Sarah's happy that Hayley's happy, but it's definitely a thought that's crossed her mind many times. Before she left Australia, she kept looking for any sign that Hayley and Rob might break up. It's not that she wanted it to happen; it's more that, if it was going to happen, Sarah wanted to be sure that any plans she made could be stretched or changed to include Hayley. For the first few weeks, if she found herself walking around by herself, she'd imagine Hayley there with her. Back at the hostel, she'd check her emails thinking that maybe, just maybe, there would be a message from Hayley saying, '*I'm coming!!!*' Then she met Chris and the shadow of Hayley burned away under the white-hot Caribbean sun. Now, sitting here with Thea, she realises how much she's missed having a girlfriend around. It's a different buzz.

'How about you?' Sarah asks Thea. 'Why did you decide to come to Central America? Do you have your trip all planned out?'

'I hadn't planned to come here at all. Not that I really have a plan.'

Sarah waits for more but Thea falls silent. So Sarah laughs and asks, 'How on earth did you end up here?'

'It just kind of happened,' Thea says. This time Sarah holds the silence, looking at her expectantly. Eventually, Thea continues. 'I just wanted to leave New Zealand. I bought a round-the-world ticket, travelled through Asia for a bit, now here I am.'

'Are you travelling on your own?'

'Yep.'

Thea's holding something back. Normally Sarah would drop it, move the conversation on. Some people need longer to open up, and she's good at knowing when to leave gaps, when to change the topic, when to circle back with a gentle question. But she can't help thinking about those three or four days Chris and Thea spent together, and it's not helping that Chris seems to have forgotten her. Maybe they didn't actually travel here together, but maybe they met somewhere else beforehand. A cold snake of realisation slithers through her: just like her and Chris. 'So, what brought you to San Pedro?' she asks. *Who* brought you here? she wants to know.

'I just heard people talk about it as a cool place to come. Now that I'm here, I honestly think most of them were talking about the pizza and drugs, all the bars and stuff — which is fun. But it's also pretty magical without all that — the lake, the volcanoes . . . I just kind of ended up here.'

Sarah waits, she's *still* sure there's something else. 'Did you come here with someone?' she asks after a moment.

Thea laughs, then looks a bit embarrassed. 'It was actually the opposite. I came to get away from some people. We'd all been in Antigua together and it was fine, but they were starting to grate. When they said they were going to Quetzaltenango, I decided to come here. I know, I'm a terrible person, but there's only so much time I can spend with a group.'

Now Sarah laughs too. It doesn't sound like Chris has been inviting a chain of girls to join him here. 'We've all done that. People are great, but some people are so annoying!'

'Friends for a day, friends for a stay,' Thea says. 'But no more than that. The worst thing is, I really did want to go to Xela.'

'Xela?'

'Quetzaltenango. I don't know why, but it's also called Xela.'

Sarah mentally jots that down as something else she wants to find out about. 'So, are you still going to Xela? What's there?' Sarah asks.

'Probably. There's a trek I want to do.'

'Cool. What kind of trek?'

Thea waves her hand dismissively, as though batting away a fly. 'It's up a mountain.'

'Wow. Sounds intense,' Sarah says. 'Do you do a lot of trekking? Is that what you do in New Zealand?'

'No, not really.' Thea takes a sip of her beer and lapses into silence.

Trekking up a mountain *does* sound intense — and interesting, even if Thea makes it sound like nothing. She wants to know more, but the conversation is becalmed again. She's usually so much better at this. She's always prided herself on being good at reading people: being patient and knowing how to navigate them. It's like watching the skies and the sea when you're sailing, noticing the clouds on the horizon and the wind on the water, then quietly sliding into position when the time is right. With Thea, just when she thinks they're cruising, she finds herself hitting rocks. She tries again. 'What do you do in New Zealand?' Even as she asks, she hears Chris's voice in her head. *Babe, stop asking people about what they do at home. No one wants to think about normal life when they're travelling.* But for Sarah it's the opposite; she loves thinking about what people are like when they're around their friends and family. She loves that people have so many different sides to them, that they may be sitting in front of her wearing baggy blue fisherman pants, but at home they wear pressed woollen trousers, a crisp crease running down the front. She hasn't told Chris, but she *really* wants to see him in a suit.

Thea hasn't answered so Sarah nudges the conversation. 'For work?'

'Nothing,' Thea says with a slight shake of her head.

'Nothing?' Sarah asks.

'Nothing exciting,' Thea says. Then, after a beat, she adds, 'I'm a physio. But I quit to travel.'

Sarah doesn't understand what the big deal is, why the secrecy. It's an interesting job and she imagines Thea would be great at it: listening to her clients without interrupting, considering what they've said, then coming up with the perfect treatment plan. But maybe Chris is right, some people just don't want to think about home when they're travelling. She's about to say something when Thea puts her beer bottle down with a bang that startles them both. Thea's eyes widen and together they start laughing.

'Oops. Sorry, I didn't mean to do that,' Thea says, looking

more relaxed. 'Hey, do you want to go dancing tonight? There's a place that always has DJs playing.'

'Ohhh, I *do*,' Sarah says, and she really would have loved to, 'but I'm shattered.' While the tables around her have been sprouting empty bottles and glasses, Sarah's been drinking tea. The past week has been early starts and early nights, no alcohol, no anything that wasn't healthy. The laughter from around the courtyard's getting louder, jangling at her overtired nerves. Chris has been leap-frogging his way from the bar towards them, but has never quite made it to her side. Every time she catches his eye, he gives a nod, a smile or a twitch of his eyebrows in her direction, a promise of more to come. But each time he gets waylaid at a table, he just shrugs his shoulders, gesturing as though his popularity is out of his control.

Enough is enough. She came here to be with him and he hasn't spent any time with her at all. She needs to go to bed and she wants him to come with her. She wants to spend some time alone with him while she can still keep her eyes open.

She hugs Thea goodnight and makes her way to Chris. 'Bedtime,' she says, leaning into him and pulling his arm around her shoulders like a blanket. He's mid-conversation, but she doesn't care.

He kisses the top of her head. 'I like the sound of that.' His hand slides down from her shoulder to her hip. A gentle squeeze. *That's more like it*, Sarah thinks, wrapping her arm around his waist, closing the space between them, two fish-like halves of the yin-yang symbol slotting together. She's exactly where she's meant to be. *He's* exactly where he's meant to be.

2

Thea watches Chris and Sarah walk into the building, arms around each other's waists, tracking them until they disappear into the shadow of the stairway. She's on her own again. Except this time she's not the one walking away. This time she's not the one deciding to ditch someone because they've spent too long together, because they're getting close to that point where people start wanting to open up and pour their hearts and secrets out over tequila shots. She knows that Chris makes everyone feel special; he talks to people and really listens to what they have to say. She's watched him enough by now to see that it's not so much a gift as it is a game. Or a performance. He's done it masterfully tonight, flitting from table to table, not moving on until he's made each group of people laugh. But until this afternoon, she'd thought she was somehow different, that with her he wasn't playing the game, that with her he relaxed, and when he relaxed, small cracks started to show: tiny hairline fractures, but enough to let the darkness seep out.

She realises now that it's more that she had let herself relax, had begun to slowly open up. It turns out he's just another friend for a day, friend for a stay. No more than that. Of course he was only killing time until his girlfriend got here; of course, he wouldn't be interested in her when he had someone like Sarah.

She'll leave tomorrow. She just has to get through tonight. There's no one in the courtyard she really knows, except for Hans behind the bar, and Aksel, of course, sitting on his barstool as though he's holding the world in place. Hans is busy working and she doesn't have the patience tonight for Aksel with his drug-addled philosophy. She wishes she had a book or her sketchpad, but they're in the room and she can hardly go up there. What a nightmare. Luckily it's still early and she's not at all tired, but how long is she meant to wait until it's safe to enter? She's halfway to being drunk. Perhaps she needs to keep drinking until it doesn't matter anymore.

When they'd got back to the Xaman Ek and Sarah was there, rushing towards Chris and pouring herself into him like melted wax, Thea had tried to make her escape. She didn't want the introductions, the explanations; it was obvious enough what was going on, and she'd rather leave them to it. Sure, it would've been ridiculously early to have gone to bed, but she didn't think anyone would notice or care. But Chris, who seems to remember everything anyone's ever said, had insisted that she stay: 'You've just spent the past hour telling me how much you were craving the lasagne. Stay. Let's get some food.' And, if she's honest with herself, she read something into that. As soon as the food was ordered, she realised how mistaken she had been. Trapped at the table, she watched Chris and Sarah leaning in towards each other, talking like they had words to burn. She could practically see the sparks between them, as though they were throwing handfuls of sugar onto a fire. She watched Sarah tilt her head back, laughing at something Chris said, the light glinting off the three thin gold chains looped in different lengths around her neck and down the V of her exposed skin. Gold bracelets rattled down her forearm as she reached out, so comfortably, for Chris. Thea saw Chris almost purr under Sarah's touch, a tenderness to him that she'd never guessed he had. If Thea had to sit with them until she'd eaten, she resolved to smudge the edges with alcohol.

Then Chris had gone to the bar and had never come back and she could hardly leave Sarah sitting on her own. She felt a scratch of discomfort, or annoyance, like the itch of bed bugs crawling on her skin. Why had Chris walked away? She didn't think she and Sarah would have much to say to each other without him there. But maybe Sarah's used to Chris leaving her on her own; or maybe she's just really nice, because, after a bumpy start, it was as though Sarah could feel Thea's unease, knew what questions to ask, what facts about herself to offer up, how to find smooth waters.

Despite her resistance, before she knew it, Thea was sailing through the conversation. For a moment, she was back in Auckland, a world away in a past life of quick laughter and easy friendships. She'd known before she asked that Sarah would say no to dancing. Sarah's yawns were pulling her closer and closer to the table, her body falling in on itself so that Thea thought she might put her head down on the sticky tabletop and go to sleep. But she'd seen a snap image of them spinning and laughing, arms waving, shoulders shimmying, and couldn't resist putting the idea out there. She could see herself and Sarah being friends, if it wasn't for Chris; just like she and Chris could be something, if it wasn't for Sarah.

For the last few days, Thea had been kicking herself for not being bold enough to make some kind of move on Chris or, at least, make it more obvious to him that he should make a move. All the hours they'd sat across from each other, wasting time but getting to know each other, she'd thought about lightly hooking her fingers around his. When they'd lain on the picnic blankets spread across the lawn at El Jardín Café, eyes closed, faces turned up to the sun, she'd positioned her hand awkwardly out from her body, holding it unnaturally still to give him the opportunity to take it in his. Imagine thinking he could be interested in her, lying rigidly in the grass like a gingerbread person cookie cutter. She'd never have thought about making a move if she knew about Sarah. Not just to save herself the humiliation. She hardly knows Sarah, but she wouldn't want to hurt her like that. She saw the way Sarah tracked Chris as he bounced from table to table, and the lift and slump of her shoulders as he came close but never quite landed next to her. The way he makes a point of talking to everyone, of making everyone feel included, is what makes Chris so fun and charismatic, but honestly, is he a bit clueless, too?

He should've been with Sarah all evening. He should've mentioned Sarah to Thea before she turned up. Because he didn't mention her, did he? Thea tries to think back through their conversations. He must've said something. She must've been deaf to it because she's been too caught up imagining scenarios where they travelled together, hands clasped, fingers interlaced and lifelines pressed together. Or maybe she's just so far off his radar that he didn't think there was a need to signal to her that he had a girlfriend. She's been a fool to think the ease she felt with him, the things they have in common, was some kind of special connection. At least she didn't act on it.

Thea moves to sit in front of the Scrabble board, which is still strewn with tiles from their game earlier in the day. Head down, she absentmindedly rearranges the tiles into different words.

'It must be my turn.' Chris grins as he sits down, putting two drinks on the table.

Thea's surprised. It's been about twenty minutes since he and Sarah went upstairs. She hadn't expected to see either of them again tonight. 'You're back,' she says, then feels stupid for blurting out the obvious. 'Obviously. *In vino veritas,*' she raises her almost empty glass of wine at him. 'Where's Sarah?'

'Profound. I'm sure that's what the Romans meant. *In vino* stateth the obvious. Sarah's sleeping. She was out like a light.' He nods at the Scrabble board. 'Pick up where we left off?'

They both laugh at that because, in the few days they've spent together, this has become a running joke. They spend hours playing Scrabble or Rummikub or cards, then when they're hungry, they simply walk away, returning, often several drinks or maybe a joint later, to pick up where they left off — except they swap seats, taking up the other's hand of cards or rack of tiles, picking up where the other left off, a challenge in trying to remember what cards they had and how the other person thinks. Each time they sit down to play, they create a new rule. Half the rules make no sense or aren't remembered when they next sit down to play.

'What the fuck were we doing here?' Chris looks at the chaos of tiles, some upside down, some stacked on top of each other. 'Let's start afresh.'

Their game doesn't last long. It's the Spanish edition, with different letter distribution and values, making it less conducive to forming English words, and neither of them speaks Spanish well enough. For a while they play a hybrid English-Spanish version, having fun using the 'CH', 'LL' and 'Ñ' tiles and then they resort to putting all the tiles face up on the board and just forming words randomly. Their fingertips touch as they slide tiles from the jumble at the centre of the board onto the squares. *Maybe this is it,* Thea thinks: her last chance to hook a finger around Chris's while Sarah's sleeping. A small but firm link, a decision. She holds her hand there a moment, finger poised as though to push a button that could blow up the world. Then quickly she slides her hand back and busies herself with the tiles in front of her. She's got to stop reading signals that don't exist. CH-A-LL-E-Ñ-G-E. Thea spins the board round so that the word faces Chris, and sits back smugly.

'If you're so clever,' Chris looks at her, 'I challenge you to say that with Spanish pronunciation.' Between fits of laughter they take turns trying to pronounce the double L as a Y sound and the Ñ as an "ny". 'Like in "canyon",' Chris says.

'Like "gnocchi",' Thea says. She breathes deeply to stop laughing and holds up her hand. 'Right, let's be serious. Shh, stop laughing, we're being serious now. Shall we play a real game? The actual English version this time?'

'I've got a better idea,' Chris says, pulling a joint from his pocket.

☆ ☆ ☆

The rooftop is a jungle of water tanks, plastic barrels, a rusted satellite dish and other junk. In a corner, there are a couple of chairs, an upturned plastic crate with an ashtray, mug, pack of cards and book on top: a staffroom of sorts. Chris and Thea aren't meant to be up here, but it's easy enough to slip past the makeshift curtain and up the stairs. Unless they stand and lean against the concrete parapet, they can't be seen by anyone standing on the terrace that opens off the bedrooms below, anyone who might catch the sweet smell of smoke and look up, seeking to join in.

They sit without talking. Thea closes her eyes and enjoys the intimacy of the smoke and night-time sounds floating between them in the dark. 'Sarah's lovely,' she says after a while.

'Yeah, she's a good person,' Chris says.

The words fill up Thea's lungs. In smoke there's truth. *Sarah* is a good person. What's he saying about her? 'You're a bad person,' she says aloud. It's not what she meant to say. The smoke is pulling her brain apart, like fingers separating the segments of a mandarin.

She feels him glance at her, but she stays looking up into the night sky. 'I am my father's son,' he says, and hands her the joint.

'You're not a bad person,' she says. 'I didn't mean that.'

'I'm not a good person.'

She lets the smoke out of her lungs. *Neither am I.* He doesn't need someone broken. He needs someone like Sarah, whose goodness can seal up the cracks and keep his darkness in. 'Why didn't you mention Sarah was coming today?' she asks.

'I'm pretty sure I did.' Chris picks up the deck of cards and starts shuffling them. Thea watches, half hypnotised, as they're swallowed up in his large hands.

'We could've gone to meet her at the dock.' The riffling cards are making her eyes blur. Or that could be everything else: the beer, the wine, the hash, the night.

'In that rain?' He taps the pack of cards sharply against the book. 'I honestly didn't even think she was going to make it today. I thought they'd be mad to cross the lake in that weather.'

That's true. Thea's heard that people sometimes die on those boat trips across Atitlán: incidents involving a combination of rough weather, no life jackets, and people who can't swim. Locals die in boating accidents; tourists die swimming where they've been warned not to.

'Kerouac,' Chris scoffs, referring to the copy of *On the Road* sitting on the makeshift table. 'Of course.'

'Hey, I enjoyed that,' Thea says. 'Although I liked *Desolation Angels* more.'

'I liked it too. It's just that every second person you meet here is reading it. Just like every hostel and bar you walk into is playing Bob Marley. I'm really sick of "Buffalo Soldier".' He takes a drag on the tail end of the joint, 'Oh, and I preferred *Desolation Angels* too. It made me want to go and live on a mountain top.'

'I read it ages ago. Before I ever even thought about coming here,' Thea says. She almost adds *so there* and sticks her tongue out at him, but thinks better of it. It was the book's title that had made her pick it up, for the way it captured the despair she'd felt, how it conveyed the idea of a heavenly wasteland. 'Wanna go to Xibalba?' she asks, although she's not convinced she can move.

'I'd better stick around here,' Chris says, 'just in case Sarah wakes up.'

'Good idea,' Thea says.

'I was hardly allowed to read books when I was a kid. Well, not for fun,' Chris tells her. 'I practically had to sneak them home from the school library and read them after I had gone to bed.'

'What? But you love reading. Was it a religious thing?'

He laughs. 'No. It wasn't forbidden as such, just discouraged, or at least not encouraged. My dad had very firm ideas about how time should be spent. I played a lot of sport and the focus was always on training. Training and homework. Homework and training.'

'There were lots of books in our house,' Thea says. 'Although, actually, now that I think about it, at least one whole bookcase was just guidebooks, not *book* books.'

'What kind of guidebooks?'

'Mountaineering. You know, alpine routes and stuff.'

'Cool. So you're a mountaineer?' Chris asks her.

'No. They were my dad's.' Thea stands up and leans on the parapet. She doesn't know why she started this conversation.

'You didn't do family trips in the mountains?'

'No,' Thea says again. 'We used to go tramping a lot when I was little. Then I wasn't really interested in mountaineering when I was a teenager.' She hopes that's enough of an explanation to end the conversation.

'What about now?' Chris asks.

'No, not now.'

'He must be so disappointed in you, Thea!' Chris jokes. 'Of course, not as disappointed as my father is in me. You should climb a mountain with him when you get back to New Zealand.'

'I can't.'

'Why not? You've got legs, and I definitely can't see anything wrong with them.'

She pauses, weighing up which truth to tell him. 'He's dead,' she says. She keeps her back to him, staring out towards the dark lake. She knows how people react when she tells them that. It's even worse when they know her mum is dead, too. In the past two years, she's had to tread water through too many conversations about death; the grief, the loss, the guilt threatening to pull her under if she stops for a minute.

'I'm sorry,' Chris says, standing up and leaning beside her. She hears him draw a breath to speak again, but then the door to one of the rooms downstairs opens and three figures walk out onto the terrace. One of them is much taller than his companions, but all three look fit and muscular.

'US Marines.' Thea leans in towards Chris, talking quietly. This is another game they play, quietly observing other foreigners in bars and cafés, guessing their nationalities and making up stories about their lives.

'Oh yeah, gotta be,' Chris agrees, his head close to hers. 'Buffalo Shoulders and his soldiers.'

They stand there for a moment, shoulders touching. Then, without prelude, it starts pouring down, heavy raindrops slamming onto the rooftop, ricocheting off the plastic drums and tanks. Thea rushes towards the staircase. Realising that Chris hasn't followed, she looks back. He's jogging towards her, pack of cards and book in hand.

'Would a bad person do that?' she says, gesturing towards the book. It hadn't crossed her mind to bring it in.

He looks at her and grins, then reaches out into the rain and flings the book over the edge of the rooftop.

3

When Thea wakes the next morning, she's half covered by her sheet, the light blanket tangled at the foot of the bed and spilling onto the floor. She's relieved to see Chris is in his own bed, by himself. The hash was still playing tricks with her mind when she went to bed, sending shadow-shapes moving through the dark, and she thought she'd seen him floating from his bed into Sarah's. If anything did actually happen, she was oblivious to it. He's lying diagonally, face pressed into the pillow and turned away from her. She takes in his bare shoulders and back. He's got that rangy body type, the strength and confidence of long, loose limbs, tall enough to make her own height stand out less. She knows now that nothing will ever happen between them, but can't help imagining running her fingertips lightly down his spine. Instead, she lets her eyes skip down the knobs of each vertebra, from his hairline to the shoreline of the sheet across his hips. No harm in looking. Well, unless perhaps someone catches you looking. Standing, she glances over at Sarah's bed, but it's empty, the blankets smoothed up to the pillow.

Thea picks up her own blanket off the floor, trying to lay it across the bed so that the stripes lie straight, like Sarah's. She loves these blankets — hand-woven rainbows running through black cotton, colours pulled from nature in often unpredictable ways: the surprising pink from coconut shell or a disintegrating avocado seed; rich indigo blue rubbed from green leaves; an almost-edible palette of colour from tree-bark, insects, fruit and vegetables. Sometimes she lies in bed, just looking at the patterns, stories told in colours and symbols, histories as old as nature woven into cloth. She's slowly learning what the symbols mean: the cross represents the four directions of the winds in Mayan religion, as well as Christianity, of course; the double-headed eagle, half good, half bad; the green butterfly of hope. Sometimes she runs her hands along the undecorated bands in between the colours, as though her own stories were stitched there, hidden deep in the black dye.

She rummages in her pack and finds her sketch book, then opens the door onto the terrace. There's little sign of yesterday's rain; just a few small puddles where the pale pink tiles have cracked, and the hammock twisted up as though it's been drenched in orange dye and is ready to be wrung out. The buildings of San Pedro, all flat-roofed, square and concrete, are a paintbox of colour in the clean morning light. The lake is calm and dark silvery-blue, a subtractive mix of the sky above and the depths of the lake. And then there are the mountains.

It's not the view that she plans to capture now. The sketch book is Thea's travel diary, experiences recorded in pictures. The stroke of a pencil tip over the thick paper lets her capture moments in ways that words can't. She's brought both coloured pencils and charcoal and graphite with her. She prefers the hush of the charcoal and graphite on the paper, but sometimes she needs the coloured pencils to capture feelings: a blaze of yellow wonder, pale green loss, an ice-blue guilt. When she does write something, she plays a game with herself where she has to keep it to the same length and size as whatever would fit onto the back of a postcard.

Thea draws the outline of a hand and a broken mosaic of Scrabble tiles. She draws the tendons that look like they're about to break through the skin, the small dark hairs, and the square fingertips with their blunt nails. She's working on the shading across the back of the hand when she hears someone approach from the room behind her.

'Wow.' Sarah's voice is full of awe.

Thea snaps her book shut, holding it on her lap.

Sarah walks past the empty beer bottles, full ashtrays and other detritus of backpacker life washed up against the wall of the building. At the edge of the terrace, she extends her arms wide as though offering herself to the beauty of the world, or drawing it into her. She looks like she's on the deck of a boat about to break its moorings and drift off into the clean blue of the day, into the overlapping shades of the lake, the mountains, the sky.

'Amazing, right?' Thea says.

'What did you say last night? Magic? That's so true.'

Thea feels stupidly proud, as though the view is a gift she's given Sarah. She remembers when she first stood where Sarah's standing. The view had just as much of an effect on her, but instead of Sarah's bright wonder, Thea had felt like she was in a charcoal sketch, trapped on the wrong side of the paper, desperate to escape but utterly helpless to save herself. Although she'd spent all day travelling through the highlands, it was different seeing the landscape from a distance. The sight was no longer just of lonely winding roads; the form of the land was visible, a crocodile's back of dark green peaks ridged across the sky. Among those hills, she'd grown increasingly despondent and unsure of herself. With every change of bus on a dusty corner of another town whose name she didn't know, she became more uncertain of whether she was going in the right direction or anywhere at all.

By the time she got to the hostel, she was so relieved to have made it, but also deeply ashamed of herself. She was not the intrepid, independent traveller she liked to think she was. She was just like all the other backpackers who annoyed her with their loud English and guidebook recommendations, revelling in the novelty of being in a foreign country without realising that they're the foreigner. Although she hadn't eaten all day, she wasn't ready to go back down to the courtyard filled with its bright lights and faces. Instead, she went out onto the terrace, hoping to find a moment of calm, to watch the dusk fall into the lake and the world slowly darken into night. But the darkness was already there, contained in the three volcanoes standing sentry on the edge of the lake: Volcán Tolimán, Atitlán — and, so unexpectedly close that even in the dark she could've sworn she saw the shadow of people climbing it, the looming cone of Volcán San Pedro. It sent an ice melt sliding through her, the tumbling debris of her past. How could something so unapologetically itself, so distinctively a part of this place, remind her of somewhere so distant, of a time she'd come here to forget?

'You can imagine that jaguar god slinking through there, can't you?' A voice had crept out from the darkness behind her. 'Crossing over from day to night, between the world of the living and the dead.' The owner of the voice came up beside her and leaned down on the rail. He laughed. 'Jeez, if anyone at home heard me say that! Don't ever repeat that, OK?' He shook his head as though to clear the words away, then continued. 'A group of us are heading out for dinner. Coming? I'm Chris, by the way.'

Hard to believe that was just a few days ago. By now she's seen the volcanoes in all the changing lights and moods of Atitlán; she knows to expect them whenever she looks beyond the bars and cafés and above the rooftops of the town. They can still send an icy dread sliding through her, but she can see the magic in them, too. As each day goes by, she comes to love this view a little more, to feel more at home tucked under the shadows of the peaks.

'Hard to believe it was raining so much yesterday.' Sarah twirls around, running her fingers through the golden air. 'I've gotta say, I was a little bit down on the place last night, but now I want to go exploring. Have you had breakfast?' Thea shakes her head. 'Great, let's eat. I'm starving.' On the way past his bed, Sarah prods Chris. 'Rise and shine, lazybones. We'll see you downstairs.'

☆ ☆ ☆

Shortly after Thea and Sarah sit down, Michael appears beside them and places a couple of mugs on the table. '*Buenos días*, Kiwi,' he addresses Thea, while nodding his head in Sarah's direction. 'This one's putting you to shame. She's been up for hours.' He pours coffee into the mugs. 'How was yoga?' he asks Sarah.

'It was great.' Sarah beams at him. She turns to Thea. 'I want to do it every day, like at the retreat. I'm new to it, but I'd like to keep up the habit.'

Thea will be impressed if Sarah can do that in San Pedro. There are plenty of hippie vibes in this town, but they're mainly the drug-hippie kind of vibes, not earth-purity up-with-the-sunrise vibes. She'll be surprised, too, if Sarah keeps up her tea-drinking with Chris in the evenings. Still, maybe that's how the two of them work: Sarah does sun salutations every morning while Chris is sleeping, then is free to spend the rest of the day with him. Then night time rolls around and Sarah goes to bed to give Chris the freedom to do what he wants to do, what she might not want to see him do. Because she's sure there are things that Chris does that Sarah wouldn't want to see — or that Chris wouldn't want her to see. She gets a flash of memory of her and Chris on the rooftop. They didn't do anything wrong. But still.

Whatever their deal is, Thea could learn something from

Sarah. She used to run or work out almost every day, back before she went travelling. Even in her earlier travels, she spent most of the day on her feet, seeing the sights, or just walking through unknown streets. Here, when they go places, they stroll, they amble, never far. Most of the time, they sit. She has fallen in too easily with the pattern of Chris's days and nights, been too swept up in feeling connected to someone again, someone who seems to understand her, someone who seems to be like her.

'If the Kiwi hasn't already told you,' Michael says to Sarah, 'milk and sugar are over there.' He gestures to the side. 'Coffee's free for all our paying customers, so help yourself whenever you want. I know you've probably been told to drink eight glasses of water a day, but here, if you're thirsty, drink coffee. A hydrating eight cups a day. Or beer or mojitos — whatever, just don't drink the water. Don't brush your teeth with it. Keep your mouth closed when you shower. If you wonder why some people here look a little yellow-tinged, that'll be the hepatitis. Probably should've told you that yesterday.' As he walks away, not seeing the slight look of panic on Sarah's face, he calls over his shoulder, 'Don't get used to this, it's not table service. Order at the bar when you're ready.'

Chris joins them as they're ordering. 'Perfect timing,' he says. He turns to Michael. 'I'll have the—'

'Wait, let me guess . . .' Michael pretends to concentrate, as though peering through the swirling mists inside a crystal ball. 'The Xaman Eggs? Hangover breakfast.'

'He never gets hungover,' Thea and Sarah say at the same time, then look at each other and laugh.

'He's told you that, has he?' Sarah asks Thea, but it's Chris she's smiling at.

'Oh, yeah, only every morning.' Thea rolls her eyes.

'So predictable.' Sarah reaches up and teasingly tousles Chris's hair.

'I'm glad you're here, Sarah,' Michael says. 'I was just starting to think badly of Australians —' he glances at Thea, dramatically widening his eyes — 'if you can possibly believe that.' He turns back to Sarah: 'But you've saved your country's reputation.'

☆ ☆ ☆

'Show me around this town,' Sarah says, pushing her empty plate away and looking at Chris and Thea.

'I'll leave you to it,' Thea says, starting to stand up.

'What important business do you have to attend to this morning?' Chris laughs.

'I was thinking of leaving,' she says. She'd actually forgotten last night's resolve to leave until just now. It's the last thing she feels like doing.

'Leaving?' Chris says with disbelief. 'Don't do that. What a bad idea.'

'You can't leave,' Sarah says. 'I've only just got here. We're going to go out dancing.'

Thea's too tired to protest much, and now, sober but a bit hungover, she doesn't really want to leave. 'OK, I'll stay, but I'll leave you two to your exploring.' She's not keen to be the third wheel.

'No, come with us,' Sarah insists. 'Chris will just show me all the bars. I need someone to help drag him away.'

'Weren't you saying you need another book?' Chris says.

She knows they're being polite. She knows she should argue more, let them have time to themselves. And, really, she's not sure how much she wants to be around them, with their arms all tangled up together, leaning and draping as though they each need the other to keep themselves upright. But it's surprising how quickly she's grown accustomed to having someone to pass the time with. Sarah's enthusiasm is contagious, too. It makes Thea realise that, although she's been here for a couple of days, she hasn't really taken in the town. They've drifted from café to bar, but they haven't stuck their heads in any of the shops, or walked the path beside the lake. They haven't rented kayaks or gone to yoga. Sure, she could wait until they've left, then head in the opposite direction, but San Pedro's small, and she's pretty sure Sarah will want to see it all. She'll only end up bumping into them and having to make up a lame excuse for why she didn't join them earlier. She doesn't have the mental energy for that.

☆ ☆ ☆

With no traffic to speak of in the town and no footpaths, they walk down the middle of the road, drifting from side to side, looking at the shops selling clothes, jewellery and trinkets. 'Gringo Central,' Chris mutters. 'I don't think the locals are buying all these crystals and dreamcatchers.'

'Hey you guys, let's get one of these.' Sarah turns to the other two outside a place offering hair-braiding and henna tattoos. Her eyes are bright and she crackles with enthusiasm like a sparkler on a summer night.

'Sure, why not?' Thea says. It's not something she would do on her own, but that's just it — she's not on her own.

'I'll leave you to it,' Chris says.

'Come on Chris, it'll be fun,' Sarah enthuses. 'We could get something matching.'

'Love your enthusiasm, babe, but see, you shouldn't have pulled me away from all those bars. Maybe after a couple of drinks you could convince me to get a giant eagle on my back and a sleeve of tribal tattoos, but there's no chance when I'm stone cold sober. I'll meet you at Jimmy's when you're done.'

'Who's Jimmy?' Sarah asks.

'It's a bar,' Thea tells her.

'Of course it is. I should've known.' Sarah laughs.

Sarah and Thea flip through the books of designs. Sarah chooses a stylised turtle. The man who owns the shop tells them that the turtle represents the earth in Mayan culture. 'That's so interesting,' Sarah responds, nodding. Thea can't tell if she's just being polite or if this really is the first time she's heard the fact, even though it's kind of Mayan pyramids 101 stuff. Sarah says that turtles remind her of Margaret River, where she's from, and that she loves being in the water.

Thea's less certain about what to get. She pauses on a page of bird designs. Perhaps a flock of starlings, or whatever they are, taking flight across the back of her shoulder. 'A dove would be nice on you,' the shop owner says. 'They're the queens of the heavens, very feminine, very nourishing.'

Thea shakes her head. 'What about the owl?'

She's asking Sarah, but the shop owner answers. 'I think the dove is better for you. Or the butterfly. The owl is a symbol of death. When it hoots, it is an omen. But for gringos it is wisdom, yes? Or the night life.' He moves his shoulders quickly back and forth, out of time to the music playing on the shop radio.

'I'll get the owl,' Thea says, snapping the book shut.

Sarah gets her turtle inked on her upper arm, while Thea chooses the inside of her forearm for her owl. Then, at Sarah's insistence, they get near-matching designs on their hands, looping strings of golden bracelets around their wrists, draping into patterns across the backs of their hands. 'This is more like India, not Guatemala,' the man in the shop says, 'but very pretty. Pretty design for pretty girls.'

As the henna dries, they find Chris sitting reading a book, a beer on the table in front of him. Sarah holds her newly patterned hands in front of her face. 'Guess who?'

'Very nice, babe,' Chris says as she sits beside him. 'You're such a hippie.'

'Very *pretty*, according to the man in the shop. You look like you're enjoying yourself,' she says.

'Books and beer. It's my happy place.'

They sit and talk for hours. Chris and Thea introduce Sarah to their game of guessing where people are from and what they do. She makes them laugh every time, inventing whole stories, not just about each person, but about how they came to be travelling together. They talk about the things they'll do before they leave.

'We each get to choose one activity, and whatever each person chooses, we all have to do it,' Thea says. 'Deal?'

Sarah and Chris agree, with Sarah stipulating that it has to be something specific to the area. 'So you can't say "sleep in", Chris — or some other things that I know you might be thinking.'

'OK, OK,' he agrees. 'You're so strict for a hippie. What do you choose?'

'Swim in the lake,' Sarah says.

'Walk the Rostro Maya,' Thea says.

'Hash brownies at The Mota-Way.' Chris looks at Sarah. 'Before you say anything, they're apparently a San Pedro special. A top ten must-do.'

'I hate to admit it, but he's right,' Thea says. 'A lot of people have mentioned the brownies.'

Through the window, the lake shimmers a broad, deep blue. Thea looks down at the looping designs inked across her hands. She stretches her fingers, then clenches her hands into fists, then stretches them out again, moving her fingers as though playing a piano. She watches the henna beads and chains slide and roll across her knuckles and tendons. She's happy, she realises. For the first time in a long time, she hasn't had half her mind in a different time or place. She hasn't been mentally walking through the past, reliving memories or plotting out her next step, mapping an escape route. Here, on the edge of the blue caldera, verdant hills stretching out of sight, she's been thinking about nothing more than where she is right now.

She turns her attention back to the conversation. 'OK, let's sign up for Spanish School today,' Sarah is saying.

'*Mañana*,' Chris says.

'*No, hoy*,' Sarah replies. 'Come on, not everything can happen tomorrow.'

Chris tugs gently at Sarah's plait, using it to pull her towards him then kissing her on the cheek. 'You have too much energy. You need to give me time to prepare. Let's go *mañana*.' He kisses her on the mouth. 'To sign up.' He grins, flicking her plait around the front of her neck like a scarf. 'Then we'll start the day after that. *Pasado mañana*. Not everything can happen *mañana*, after all.'

Sarah rolls her eyes, shakes her head and smiles, all at once. 'Fine,' she says, 'as you wish.' She turns to Thea. 'Are you going to come?'

'Sure, why not,' Thea responds. *Mañana*, *pasado mañana*, it doesn't matter to her. She can see herself staying in San Pedro for a while longer. For just a flash, she sees herself never leaving, becoming one of the permanent gringo population, the people who have walked away from where they come from and who they were. She could stay here and live out a reinvented version of herself. Well, not forever. Probably not even all that long in the scheme of things, if she's honest. It would drive her mad, spending the rest of her life sitting around with people like Aksel, talking about seizing the moment, the power of now. But she could stay for long enough that when she leaves she feels like a different person. She could do that.

As she reaches out for her coffee cup, the large sepia eyes of the owl stare up at her.

4

'*Gracias*, Juan. See you tomorrow.' Sarah finishes up her Spanish lesson and heads back to the office building to meet up with Chris and Thea. As she walks, she mentally recites what they covered: *Yo vivo, tú vives, él vive, ella vive*... She recites it like a mantra, and then she smiles to herself because it really is like a mantra, it's so life-affirming: I live, you live, he lives, she lives . . . It's stuff she's covered before, but it's good to go over it again. They raced through the present and past tenses in the one-week course she and Chris did in Oaxaca, as well as numbers and colours and greetings. If they'd stayed there another week, they would have covered the future tense, body parts, and directions. Instead, they'd gone to Chiapas and then on throughout Mexico and into Guatemala, and Chris had joked that they had no future in Central America.

Somewhere along the way, Chris has picked up a lot more

than her. 'How do you know so much more than me?' Sarah asked him on their first day at the Escuela Huito after they'd done the test to put them in the right classes.

He'd rolled her plait around his fingers, coiling it towards her skull. 'You just care too much about getting it right.'

She does care, but that's not a bad thing; learning the language was a huge part of her plan to travel through South America and it still was for her changed itinerary to Central America. Two years ago, her father had started working at a health centre providing support for refugees and asylum seekers. Every day he lamented his lack of a second language, and went on to list all the things wrong with the Australian schooling system. 'Language is a bridge,' he'd taken to saying to Sarah and her brother, Arlo. 'You don't build a bridge from just one side of the river. We all need to become bridge builders.' He had started doing night classes to learn Burmese. Spanish seemed like it would be a lot easier to learn than Burmese. Sarah thought that maybe, if she started with that, she'd unlock the part of her brain that could pick up other languages.

While she waits for Chris and Thea, she flicks through a folder advertising homestays. It'd be good for her language to stay with a local family for a week, even if the thought of it terrifies her. At the moment, after lessons, all she does is go and speak English at the hostel with other backpackers or in a café where the staff, no matter where they're from, all speak English to make it easy for people like her. She's determined to learn enough Spanish to spend a few weeks volunteering somewhere. She wants it to be something real, where she actually has to use the language, something with children where her teaching degree will be useful and she could make a difference; not voluntourism where she would come away with only a bunch of photographs of her surrounded by smiling kids or standing in a marketplace holding a basket full of vegetables.

She's fine with it when it's written in her exercise book, lines and columns of tenses and vocabulary. She's fine reciting verbs aloud with Juan, or answering the questions she can predict, but she gets lost in the speed and tangle of it out on the streets. Real-life language doesn't come in rows and columns, sitting still on the page until she's ready to start. It feels more like trying to cross the road in Mexico City. While Chris strides confidently through the language, she freezes at the lanes of verbs and nouns racing towards her from either side, words ripping around a corner unexpectedly. And that's the problem: she's been too reliant on Chris; too scared to get it wrong and not be understood. It doesn't even make sense to her; she *loves* meeting new people and can chat comfortably to anyone in English. She needs to be more courageous. She puts the homestay brochure down as Chris and Thea approach from their lesson at the picnic table under the grove of trees. She doesn't expect Chris would do a homestay, but Thea might. She'll think about it and ask them later.

'*Hola chica,*' Chris greets her, slinging his arm around her shoulders. They walk back through the office area, out into the alleyway and onto the street. '*Tengo hambre,*' Chris says as they turn downhill.

'You're always hungry.' Sarah leans into him. 'One day we should turn left instead of right. Have lunch in the *pueblo*.'

'*Mañana*?' Thea suggests.

'*Pasado mañana,*' Chris says.

☆ ☆ ☆

They get into a rhythm. Coffee and breakfast, then up the hill for Spanish lessons, then back down for lunch. At the hostel, they sit in the courtyard or on the terrace, passing the afternoon in slow time. Sarah studies her Spanish lessons, then walks around the group of shops and cafés by the lake, finds someone to talk to in the courtyard, or does yoga on the rooftop. Thea usually does a bit of revision, then sketches or reads, and often joins Sarah on her outings around town. Chris reads or sits talking and playing cards with other travellers. Afternoons blur into evenings. Sometimes they sit for hours at the Xaman Ek; sometimes they venture out to one of the bars where movies are shown, projected onto a screen drawn down against a wall, or where DJs play late into the night.

The two weeks of Spanish lessons they signed up for end. Thea enrols for another week. Chris decides he's done enough. Sarah considers stopping, but imagines her father stacking nouns on top of verbs, big chunks of language stretching out across a divide. She thinks, too, of travelling to Argentina or Chile with Hayley one day — probably just for a short holiday, a girls' trip while they leave their partners at home — and being able to navigate for them both through foreign streets and menus. Besides, Chris is in no hurry to leave San Pedro and has encouraged her to keep going to lessons. 'It's just not for me, Sarah. I've had enough of being forced to do drills of any sort. But this is something you really want to do — don't let me hold you back.' So she continues to walk up the hill with Thea each day, after kissing Chris goodbye, if he's awake. 'See you later, lazybones.'

'*Hasta luego, guapa,*' he responds, and she shakes her head at the fact that, even when he's half asleep, Spanish comes more naturally to him than it does to her.

On the last day of class, Sarah and Thea leave the school. They haven't committed to another week yet; they're going to think about it over the weekend. 'I've barely seen Chris lately,' Sarah tells Thea. He hasn't been awake the last few days when she's headed off to school. She's left him sprawled out, face-down on his bed, the sheet shucked off his body. He's spent every night this week at Bar Xibalba, heading off when Sarah and Thea go to bed and coming back in the darkest hours of the night. It's kind of what she likes about him — this bad boy edge, his careless disregard for — what? She's not quite sure — following rules? What other people think? Whatever it is, he's not like her usual boyfriends, not that she's had many. She probably wouldn't dare to go out with him at home, where her friends would judge and her parents would disapprove. It thrills her. The downside, though, is that they've become like those tiny figures on a German weather house, the sun woman and the rain man, never out at the same time. She's got to change that. She misses him — no, more than that, she craves him.

Sarah loves the dynamic that she, Chris and Thea have; it makes her feel like part of something special. Thea's reserved. She's often the quiet one in a conversation; sometimes to the point where Sarah thinks she's tuned out, disinterested, but then she'll suddenly say something, and it's always funny or insightful or somehow gets you thinking, and it's clear she's been following every word. At first, Sarah thought that Thea was just being polite, hanging out with her only because she was with Chris. But after a bit of tacking and gybing at the start, it's plain sailing; more than that, it's effortless, invigorating even.

Thea seems genuinely keen to join Sarah on her rambles around the shops, to walk to the dock and watch the boats offloading fresh arrivals to San Pedro, to sit in El Jardín and talk for hours. The more time they spend together, the closer they get. Sarah loves having her around. Much as she loves Chris, he likes what he likes and can't be convinced to do things he doesn't want to do. He can be such a boy, and Sarah's realising more and more how important girlfriends are to her. Even so, this week things have started to feel out of balance; Sarah's spending more time with Thea than with Chris, and when she is with Chris, Thea's often there. Sarah needs to focus on Chris for a bit. 'Maybe I'll take a week off lessons,' she says to Thea, 'so Chris and I can go away somewhere for a night or two.'

Now that she's thought it, that's exactly what she'll do. She skims back through conversations she's had with people at the hostel, thinking of places she and Chris could go. She loves talking to people about where they've been, and keeps a list at the back of her travel diary of all the places people recommend and why. There's a place two Swiss girls raved about that's been lodged in her mind ever since: a place in San Marcos where you can sleep in a treehouse overlooking the lake. It's exactly her kind of thing. She loves the idea of falling asleep and waking up in the treetops. She pictures herself and Chris, a mosquito net cascading down from the ceiling, lightly cocooning them. There's a traditional sweat lodge there and an outdoor oven where you can make your own wood-fired pizza. She thinks that Chris would like it too — who doesn't like a treehouse? She'll just describe it to him more as a Robinson Crusoe kind of thing. She won't mention that it's the bird's-nest vibe that makes her want to go. San Marcos would be perfect too; it's close enough to San Pedro that Chris would hardly feel like he was leaving.

Thrilled with the idea, Sarah grabs Thea's hand and pulls her out of the lane the school is on and around the corner onto the road back down to the lake. She wants to run down the hill so she can tell Chris about her plan, but she hasn't ever seen anyone run in San Pedro and doesn't want to draw attention. She thinks that if she did run, all the stray dogs in the town might chase after her. She hates those dogs. They're always slinking along the walls, silently watching her. She's never seen them run either, but she suspects they just need the excuse to give chase, to growl, to sink their teeth and lock their jaws.

Thea nudges Sarah and points. 'Is that . . .?'

Sarah's seen them too. Chris, together with Aksel and Hans from the Xaman Ek, at the bottom of the hill. One of the village dogs is trotting along beside them. 'What the . . .?' Sarah trails off. She's always assumed Chris spent the hours that she was at school sleeping and mooching about at the hostel.

'Should we catch up to them?' Thea asks.

Sarah makes a sound of indifference. If Chris has been in the village, he could've met her at the school. They could've walked home together, maybe had lunch at a *comedor*, something she's been suggesting for ages. 'No. Leave them to it.' Feeling Thea's gaze flick towards her, she softens what she's said. 'No rush. Fine for your long legs, but it's too hot for me to walk any faster.'

☆ ☆ ☆

Chris isn't in the courtyard of the Xaman Ek when Sarah and Thea return. Aksel's settled down on his usual barstool and Hans is talking to Michael in the storeroom behind the bar. When Sarah asks, Aksel tells her that Chris is upstairs. She doesn't know why it bothers her, but she can't shake off her annoyance that Chris didn't meet her at the school and now isn't waiting in the courtyard. He knows exactly when classes end. She doesn't like this sense that he's slipping away from her, and needs to do something about it. She turns to Thea. 'Hey, I've just realised, if we're done with school, that means no homework, no revision. So . . .' she continues, 'I might find Chris. You won't be needing to go into the room for a while, will you?' She smiles sideways at Thea.

Upstairs, Sarah dumps her bag on her bed and heads out onto the terrace. Chris keeps reading as she comes up behind him, putting her hand on his shoulder and forcing him to move his book out of the way as she lowers herself onto his lap. Her legs dangle over the arm of the chair. 'School's out.' She kisses him. 'Thea's gone off somewhere for lunch.' As they kiss, Sarah twists her upper body into his, pressing against him. 'We saw you on our way home. What were you guys doing in the village?'

'Did you just? You should've said hello.' Chris slips his hand under her long skirt as he kisses her. The flat of his palm glides up her leg, pulling the hem of her skirt to reveal her ankle, her calf. She reaches out a hand to smooth it down, but it only lifts again as Chris steps his fingertips one by one along the inside of her thigh.

Each press of his finger pads into her skin sends a quicksilver thrill through her. 'We should go inside,' she says, turning her head to scan the terrace while he kisses her neck.

'Shh,' Chris says.

She's never been like this with anyone else. The only time she'd ever had sex at her house was when her parents were out. Not just out for the day, but out of town with no chance of coming home early. With her ex-boyfriend, she'd insisted that he move his desk chair in front of the door whenever they were about to have sex, even though he was adamant none of his housemates would ever barge in. But with Chris, she lets him pull her along like a riptide. First it was when they showered together. Then there was the time down by the lake, when no one was around, except two kayakers cutting across the bay, far enough offshore not to see or hear, but really only a few paddle-strokes away. Maybe it was just the nature of sharing rooms with other people, she thought. They had to grab opportunities when they could. Maybe travelling on her own *has* made her a freer, braver version of herself, even if it's not exactly what she had imagined. That doesn't matter; it's just great that she's embracing new things, going with the flow, letting herself change. But, really, she knows it's just Chris. She's surrendered to his current. He could take her anywhere.

She falls into him, unable to kiss him any longer, just concentrating on breathing into his shoulder as quietly as she can. Then, electricity humming and sparking between them, they stand and he leads her into the room and onto his bed and she doesn't even care that they're right next to the door.

☆ ☆ ☆

That evening, Thea tells Sarah and Chris that she's going to Livingston for a few days with a couple of other people from the hostel. 'Snap decision. I decided while you guys were . . . busy . . .' She laughs awkwardly. 'Figured that if you're going on a romantic getaway, then I'm going on an adventure.'

'We're not actually going away,' Sarah tells Thea. Thea looks confused and opens her mouth to say something. Before Thea speaks, Sarah jumps in. 'It was just an idea. Now's not the best time, but we might go in a few days.'

Lying in bed that afternoon, Sarah had suggested the San Marcos getaway to Chris. He said no, before she'd told him all the details. She hadn't had the chance to tell him about going to sleep to the whispering hush of the treetops, of waking to sun filtering through the leaves and the mosquito net stirring languidly in the morning breeze. Chris wants to stay in town this weekend because there's a party on at Bar Xibalba. 'There's always a party on,' she'd said with a laugh. But this was big, he'd assured her, one they wouldn't want to miss. She had to agree that, even though days shouldn't matter when you're travelling, Saturday nights were still the extra-crazy nights; the dance floor always more packed than on other nights, limbs looser, smiles wider. They'll go to Xibalba tomorrow night, then afterwards, when they're in a sluggish comedown, she'll tell him more about the place in San Marcos where they can lie chrysalised high among the leaves and sky. There's plenty of time to head there later in the week.

Sarah knows that Thea wants to ask something else. She can see her forming the question in her mind, deciding whether or not to voice it. In the end, Thea doesn't ask anything, just suggests that they join her. 'Only problem is, it's a very early start tomorrow. Actual early, not just San Pedro early.'

Sarah's tempted. She loves the sea and the thought of being back on the coast, of being away from San Pedro with its volcanoes biting into the sky, is hard to resist. But, then again, with Thea away, she and Chris will have the room to themselves. She can talk to Michael about making sure that it stays that way, at least until Thea gets back.

☆ ☆ ☆

The next morning, Sarah sleepily smiles as Thea tiptoes across the still-dark room. She waits a minute after the door closes to make sure Thea's not coming back, then slips out of her own bed and into Chris's, sliding her body next to his and waking him up. Livingston has been added to the list in her notebook, but staying here, in San Pedro, in this room, this bed, his arms, was definitely the right decision.

They spend half the day climbing in and out from under the covers as though they were on holiday at the beach, in and out of the water all day long, nothing else to think about. She luxuriates in having Chris to herself and is thrilled that he's content to be with just her.

Then it's dark again and they're up, restless to get moving, to laugh, to dance, to be among a hundred other moving bodies. The courtyard is lit up, the coloured lightbulbs threaded through the guaracabuya tree like beautiful, magical moths. From the bar, Sarah watches them hovering above Chris and all the people he's gathered around him. Each bulb's an aura, Sarah decides. Or a delicious fruit. If she planted the pill that Chris gave her in bed just before they came downstairs, it would grow into something like this. It already is. She can feel it stretching her limbs; a wondrous fruiting, flowering tree growing and glowing inside her, colour exploding in her joints, taste of sweet delight in her brain. Standing under the tree, hands spread, head thrown back, Chris reminds Sarah again of the Pied Piper of San Pedro, or perhaps some kind of prophet, about to lead them who knows where. She laughs to herself and bounces on the balls of her feet, eager to join the others, to taste her floating aura-fruit, to follow Chris.

As they walk from the Xaman Ek to Bar Xibalba, the group sways, spreads out and closes in, like a clump of seaweed moving on the tide. A dog weaves in and out among them, anticipating the staggering feet of drunken foreigners and avoiding getting kicked. Sarah feels a surge of love towards the dog. The path turns sharply to the left like a dislocated finger. It leads into a vacant lot planted with maize. On either side, the plants are contained by the remnants of concrete foundations, what remains of someone's house or business. The green stalks rise above the partygoers' heads. Long leaves bend and brush against Sarah's bare shoulders. Then suddenly they're out the other side, and Bar Xibalba's there in front of them, like an idol to be worshipped. There's a hand-painted banner across the entrance: 'Welcome to the Crisis'.

Chris was right. There's a different level of madness inside the bar tonight. The music is louder, the room is darker, the lights that flash through the darkness are brighter, more erratic. The crowd absorbs her and Chris, lifts them, tumbles them towards the bar. The drinks put down in front of them are as bright as butterfly wings. Sarah feels the liquid fluttering down her throat. A whirlwind of coloured wings moves inside her, flittering under her skin and in the soles of her feet. She tugs Chris's arm, pulling him towards the staircase to the rooftop where the dance floor sings to her, but he's anchored to the bar with Aksel, Hans and a couple of other guys. Their wide mouths are moving, teeth glinting, but she can't hear anything above the music, just rounds of laughter discharging above her head. She drifts away from them, floating through the crowd, up into the night air.

Dancing reminds her of being home, among her friends. It's something she's always loved doing. First, when they were teenagers, too young to go out, she and Hayley would spend

Friday and Saturday nights dancing in one of their bedrooms. Sometimes they'd organise what they called raves, but that was just a term they used to get their friends and classmates around to Hayley's parents' garage, where they could turn up the music without complaint. As soon as they were old enough to get into bars and clubs, she, Hayley and a group of girlfriends would head into town and spend hours on the dance floor. She has a stab of longing for her hometown friend. She hopes Hayley is enjoying her job. *At least she still has a job*, Sarah thinks, now that the world is crashing and companies are shedding staff like dead leaves.

She loses herself in the music, letting her mind slip away from Hayley and feeling a flood of warmth for the people she's with tonight. 'Friends for a day,' as Thea says. She misses Thea too. Then the music intensifies and she catches the rhythm bouncing off the shining faces all around her. Friends for a stay, a night, a song, a beat; Sarah's just so happy to be surrounded by love tonight. She dances until finally the group she's with decides it's time to head back to the hostel. 'I'm going to find Chris,' she tells them, hugging them all goodnight.

The crowd seems even wilder now down in the main bar, but perhaps it's just that the dancing has sobered her up. She squeezes through the gaps between bodies and ducks under arms, then sidesteps as someone stumbles backwards into her. She heads past the bathroom to the small space outside that's really just a storage area but has been decorated with fairy lights and spray-painted with large cartoons. Chris is standing on top of a keg, facing a man of similar height on top of his own keg. They're trying to push each other off. '*Hola, chica, qué tal?*

Bueno?' He glances at her as he grapples with his opponent, then loses his balance and jumps off. Another guy jumps up onto the keg in Chris's place.

'I'm tired,' she tells him. 'Wanna head home?'

'I'm wide awake. I'm gonna stay,' he says, looking over his shoulder and bouncing as he speaks, like a boxer getting ready to go back into the ring. 'I'll see you in a bit.'

'Can you walk me home?' She waits a beat then adds, 'The others have left already.'

'You'll be fine.' He cups her face with both his hands. 'It's not far.'

'I don't like walking by myself through the maize, not in the dark. And the dogs scare me. Please, Chris?' She hates herself for saying it. She wishes she wasn't so scared of everything. She wishes she was more like Thea, who Sarah can imagine in one of those around-the-world-alone yacht races, unfazed by mountain-high water and towering icebergs. But she's not. At the start of yoga class, when the teacher invites them to set an intention — for the practice, for the day — Sarah tells herself she'll 'be courageous'. She often sets herself 'small acts of courage' or 'quiet acts of courage' — things that no one else would notice, but which, for her, are moments that make her feel like she's growing. This whole trip has been a series of quiet acts of courage. To soften the blow of pleading with him, she reaches for Chris's hand and tangles her fingers in with his, adding, 'I'll make it worth your while'. And it works, because he turns back towards the bar, telling the guys that he'll be back, and tugs her towards the door.

Chris swings their joined hands wildly back and forth as they walk down the lane. 'You *are* wide awake,' she says. 'What's your secret?'

Chris doesn't look at her. 'Don't ask me to reveal my secrets, babe. I'd have to tell you a little white lie. Or sell you a little white line.'

Sarah stops walking. She tugs at his arm to get him to turn to her. 'What do you mean, Chris?' she asks, although she's got a pretty good idea what he means. Since the time she and Thea saw him walking down the hill from the village, she's tried to ask him about where he and Hans and Aksel go while she's at school. The first time he made a joke of it and the second time he teased her about how good she was, how much she loves rules.

Now he just puts a finger to his lips, and leans in towards her. Just when she thinks he's going to kiss her, he reaches up and grabs one of the stalks of maize, bending it down to brush against her cheek. She squirms away from the pointed, papery leaf tickling her ear, batting at his arms but not wanting to move too far away from him in the dark. 'Stop it.' She laughs. 'Chris, don't.'

'No chance of having sex in the corn, then?' He raises an eyebrow at her as he takes hold of her hand again. 'You're no fun.' Then they're out of the maize and they pass only one stray dog lying asleep in the shadows, which doesn't stir as they go by. Within moments, they're back at the entrance to the courtyard of the Xaman Ek. 'You can take it from here, sleepyhead?'

'Aren't you coming in?'

'I'll be back before you know it.' He kisses her, stays until she's at the door to the building, then turns away. She can track his movements halfway back to the bar as he hums and sings his way through the dark. A dog barks nearby, and then there's nothing but the muffled bass from Xibalba.

☆ ☆ ☆

Chris had come back sometime around sunrise and slid into Sarah's bed. She slept for a broken hour or two, clinging to him so she didn't fall out the other side, before surrendering her bed to him. She got up, tried to detox with some yoga on the rooftop, went to El Jardín for breakfast, then walked around down by the lake. When she got back, Chris was finishing his own breakfast in the courtyard. He pushed his plate away and declared it time to go back to bed.

Come early afternoon, they're lying on Sarah's bed again, their legs criss-crossed over each other. 'Do you think we'll be OK with this global financial crisis or whatever they're calling it?' she asks him. 'I mean, the value of our dollar has dropped a *lot*. Do you think we should be heading home?'

'Nah, we're better off here.'

'Good,' she says, turning so that her cheek presses into his chest. 'I'm not ready to go home yet.'

'I'm never going home.' They're silent for a while, then she feels Chris turn his head. 'Don't worry, hippie, I've got a plan.'

'Oh yeah, what's your plan?'

'My plan is to never go home. Let's stay here forever.'

'For a little longer, but not forever. We have to leave sometime.'

'Do we though?'

'Yes! *Claro*.'

'OK, so tell me about this place in San Marcos,' he says, gathering up her loose hair in his hand. As she talks, he slowly twists her hair until she feels the roots pulling at her scalp. She tells him all the details that she wanted to tell him earlier. He lets her hair go so that it fans out across her back. 'Shall we go, then?'

'Are you serious?' Sarah lifts herself up on her elbow so she can look into his face.

'*Claro*. Let's go—'

'Don't you dare say *pasado mañana*,' she cuts him off.

'*Hoy*. Oi, don't you interrupt me,' he teases. 'Let's go *hoy*. Today.'

'Really?'

'*Sí, claro*. Let's go. Up you get, lazybones.' Chris nudges her towards the edge of the bed.

She's reaching down for her clothes when she groans. 'I'd better check the price. Now there's this financial crisis.'

'*No hay problema, señorita*. My treat.'

She tries to argue with him, or at least get him to agree to let her check the price first, but he's now a bullet in forward motion, throwing clothes onto his body, into a bag, and pulling her up from the bed.

They make arrangements with Michael to store their stuff in the *bodega* next to Thea's stuff, then head down to the *embarcadero*.

As they approach the lake, Sarah can see two black-clad officers talking to a pair of women. For just a moment, she imagines that the officers have emerged from the lake, the way that eels slither out of water and over land at night. She laughs to herself. *This place is getting to me. This trip is exactly what I need.* Even so, she glances at the police car parked outside Jimmy's, not pleased to see it, but taking some comfort in the ordinary shape and purpose of it.

Sarah drops in behind Chris so they can squeeze past the car onto the jetty. 'I hope no one's drowned,' she says. She looks around for any sign that the boats aren't running today, but a man catches their eye and asks them where they're going. He directs them to a boat with no indication that anything's out of the ordinary.

They sit on the vessel as it cuts out across to San Marcos. 'Where are we going anyway?' Chris asks, his arm around Sarah's shoulders. 'What's this amazing place with the pizza oven called?'

She looks up at him, her smile smothering her laughter. 'Dreamcatchers,' she tells him.

'Of course it is.' He shakes his head.

'Too late to back out now.' She bumps against him with her shoulder, then turns her head up so that she can feel the sun and the wind skimming over her face. Their backs are to San Pedro as the boat flies over the water. She feels lighter and lighter the farther behind they leave the town.

5

Thea is sitting in the courtyard when Sarah and Chris come in, straight off the boat from San Marcos. She watches them smiling at each other, arms locking them together. Chris whispers something in Sarah's ear and she tips her head back and laughs, then shakes her head at him. They're like a binary star, orbiting each other, pulled in by each other's gravity to create a single bright light. Thea got back from Livingston a few hours before and had been looking forward to seeing them again. Watching them now, the way they move as one, she feels like an outsider. They'll probably tell her they've made plans to head off. They'll move on to somewhere else; they'll meet new people, make new friends, then move on again, happy just to be in one another's company. She had been planning to tell them about Livingston — about how the river and the ocean blend together and lap at the legs of the bright, wooden stilt houses; about how it feels like some kind of balanced tug of war between the encroaching jungle and the windswept sand. She'd been savouring the idea of telling them about the deep, uncovered concrete pit in the plaza where three large crocodiles circle round and round, and about the two tourists who stood on top of the ledge for a photo. If she tells them about how captivating and surreal Livingston is, they'll go there and she can't follow them to a place she's just been. Besides, they're too wrapped up in their own adventure story to want to hear about hers. Thea lowers her head, staring down at her book without taking in the words. She doesn't want them to see her and feel like they have to sit with her.

Then they're at her table, smiling at her and pulling out chairs to sit. Chris helps himself to her guacamole, scooping a heap of it onto a tortilla chip, which Sarah then plucks from his hand and puts in her mouth. Chris pulls at the scarf looped around Sarah's neck in playful reprimand. 'Don't worry, we ordered more,' he says to Thea.

Sarah reaches up to her scarf, hooking her finger between the fabric and her neck to loosen it.

'That's new.' Thea points to the scarf. It's bright green with an orange and pink pattern running through it. 'Very nice.'

'Thanks. We bought it today at the market in San Marcos. It's actually a belt. A — what's it called?' She looks to Chris.

'A *faja*.'

'A *faja*,' Sarah repeats. 'We bought a few. And these.' Her hair is loose and she pulls it back just enough to show off a gold earring, a dangling sun; then in the other ear, a shining silver moon. 'Chris tried to stop me—'

'Such a hippie.'

'—but I love them. You'd love it there, Thee. We should go back sometime.'

As they eat dinner and catch up, the courtyard darkens to night. From behind the bar, Michael switches on the coloured bulbs looped through the tree, calling out '*Feliz Navidad!*' as he does so, just as he does every night he's working.

'What are we going to do tonight?' Sarah asks.

'We could watch a movie,' Thea suggests. '*Scarface* is playing at Xibalba.' She suddenly feels embarrassed, wondering if the 'we' was meant to include her. 'I mean, you could go to that. You probably want some time to yourselves.'

'Oh no, we're sick of each other.' Chris looks at Sarah, puts his arm around her, and they both laugh.

'We've missed you,' Sarah says. 'Of course we want to hang out with you. You have to tell us about Livingston.'

☆ ☆ ☆

They tread the well-worn path past the dogs, through the maize, to Xibalba and up onto the rooftop. The rooftop is half-covered, half-open to the night. Partway through the movie, Sarah whispers into Chris's ear. Thea keeps her eyes on the screen, but can't help hearing their conversation. Chris's voice is a low rumble, quiet, but no attempt to whisper. 'It's two minutes, three minutes max. Probably one minute if you run.' Thea can't hear Sarah's response, just Chris again. 'When has one of those dogs ever done anything to you? All they do is lie there.' Tony Montana's on the screen, soulful dead eyes and unbuttoned shirt, gold chain resting on his chest. 'Babe, I want to watch this. You'll be fine.'

Sarah says something else to Chris, then leans across him to tell Thea that she's leaving, 'I'm exhausted, and this is too violent for me. I'm going to have an early night.' Thea's about to offer to go with Sarah. The movie's old, there's a lot of shooting and not much else. If Chris insists on staying, then she'll walk home with Sarah. But Sarah smiles at her and turns away before she can say anything. Sarah squeezes Chris's shoulder as she stands. Thea settles back, eyes on the screen, the heat of Chris's upper arm beside her.

It feels odd to sit in the dark, with Chris but not with Sarah. Something's up between them, an asteroid belt of tension that wasn't visible earlier on. She should've gone with Sarah, checked she was OK. But she seemed all right, didn't she? Chris is focused on the movie. Thea is distracted by the warmth radiating from him, filling the small gap between them. For just a moment — just briefly — she imagines moving closer to him, slouching down to rest her head on his shoulder. She'd never do it. She's a terrible person for even thinking it. It's just been so long since she was close to anyone; so long since she felt like there was someone in the world looking out for her, their warmth hers to share.

She hadn't realised until she saw them again how much she

missed Sarah and Chris while they were gone. They've started to feel like family of sorts, and she'd forgotten how comforting it is to have family around.

When the film finally ends, there's a moment of darkness when the screen snaps to black and before they switch on the fairy lights. In that moment, Chris turns to Thea. 'Drink, Kiwi?'

She should go back to the hostel. 'I think I need one after that,' she says, and starts to stand.

'Stay,' Chris says. 'I'll go.' And he's springing up, sliding between the other movie watchers, and slipping down the stairs.

Thea watches him leave. She should follow him downstairs, tell him she's changed her mind, and head back to the Xaman Ek. Instead she stands and wanders to the corner of the rooftop. The bass from the bar thumps its way up the stairs. She leans against the parapet. From here, you can see the different shades of darkness of San Pedro, the lake, the mountains, the sky; layers of shadow in the night all stacked up on one another. It's completely different from Livingston. There it was all river and sea, sandy roads and flat skies, Garifuna and Afro-Caribbean vibes. In Livingston, the sea stretches out into broad blue possibility. In San Pedro, the mountains circle in and keep you here, hard up against the sinkhole of the lake.

There's something about coming back to a place you've been before when you're travelling; a strange sense of homecoming. Thea loves the adventure of travelling, the moving on from place to place, the twists and turns of foreign languages; but sometimes she finds herself searching for a piece of home. It might be a song played in a bar; a book she's read before; or a familiar t-shirt worn by another backpacker passing by. On low days, she finds herself looking for these things, never learning that they don't bring comfort. The homesickness and sadness that follow almost overwhelm her every time, an avalanche of memories of the people she's lost, their futures sheared off in great crushing blocks, pale scars of absence left in their place.

Thea pulls her focus in closer, away from the dark peaks of sky to the rooftops then to the street below. She sees Chris coming out the front door. She's about to call down to him, but something stops her. If he's going to go back to Sarah and just leave her here, then fine, she's not going to look desperate by crying out to him. She watches to see if he's even going to turn and look up before he heads off. He doesn't, but he doesn't walk away either.

Instead, he goes up to a couple of guys leaning against the wall of the bar, smoking. Chris stands, his back to Thea, shoulder to shoulder with one of the men. The shorter of the two gives Chris something. Chris glances down at it then reaches into his pocket and hands whatever he's taken out to the guy. Then he shakes their hands, bends down to rub the head of a dog lying in the shadow of Xibalba, and turns to go back inside. Another person stops Chris before he re-enters the building and a similar exchange takes place.

This is new, Thea thinks to herself. She knows that Chris visits the house in the *pueblo* that is known as 'Alice's restaurant' because of the range of things on offer. Thea's never been, but Chris has described Alice — the gringo name for the Tz'utujil woman who runs the operation — to her: 'She's tiny,' he said, holding his hand out flat below his rib cage. 'She looks like any other *abuela* in her *huipil* and *corte* but she sells every drug under the sun and negotiates like the most hardened Wall Street slimeball.' As far as Thea knows, Chris has bought only weed, coke and a few pills from Alice's restaurant — and she has to admit that she's benefited from some of those purchases. But she realises now that she doesn't really know half of what Chris gets up to.

A minute or two later, he's back on the rooftop, his fingers gripping two shots of tequila in one hand, two bottles of beer in the other. He puts them down on the wooden shelf that lines the inside edge of the parapet, then leans beside Thea, his arm brushing against hers. 'Have you read any Murakami?' he asks. She hasn't. 'This place reminds me of *Hard-Boiled Wonderland and the End of the World*.'

'Sounds interesting,' Thea says, straightening up and moving a fraction away from him. 'Is this the end of the world?'

'No, this is hard-boiled wonderland.'

'I'll have to read it,' Thea says, then raises the shot glass that Chris hands to her. 'To Wonderland.'

'To the end of the world,' Chris says picking up the other glass. They stand in silence for a moment, looking towards the lake, letting the burn of the tequila settle. 'Now here's to Wonderland,' Chris says after a while, taking a small bag from his pocket.

'You've been to see Alice,' Thea says, wondering whether to ask him if he's now dealing to other tourists.

'Mmhmm,' Chris says absentmindedly as he wipes the bottom of an ashtray against his jeans. He peers at the surface in the dim light, seems to determine that it's clean enough and places the ashtray upside down on the wooden shelf. 'You should come sometime,' Chris says as he leans over to carefully shake the white powder out of the bag onto the upturned bottom of the ashtray. 'I think you'd like her. She's got a wicked sense of humour and she always serves that white drink that you like.'

'*Horchata*?'

'Yeah, that's it. Her sister, Maria, runs the local weaving cooperative. You should check that out too. They do it all in the *pueblo* — the dyeing, the weaving. It's your kind of thing — you can watch colours being made.'

Thea listens to Chris in amazement. It's easy to think of him just sitting around doing nothing — another day, another beer, another beer — and then he comes out with something like this. You turn your back for a moment, and he's somehow met everyone, learned some local custom or piece of history, picked up the language. She watches him roll up a fifty *quetzales* note. *But, yes, he also does stuff like this.*

Chris glances up and must see something in her expression. He laughs. 'I know, I know, we've reached a new low, Thea. A dirty old ashtray and fifty Q note. Desperate times.' He straightens up, reaches out to take her hands and starts dancing, pulling her into him and pushing her away again. 'But it's so much fun. You know it is.' Grinning in the shadows and leaning in towards her, Chris reminds Thea of a cartoon devil sitting on her shoulder. 'Come on,' he taunts her playfully, 'let's have some fun.'

Several hours later, they walk back to the hostel. Chris throws his arm around Thea's shoulders as they turn up the slight rise back towards the Xaman Ek, his hand squeezing her upper arm. A dog slides past in the shadows. 'Did the trip to San Marcos inspire you to leave San Pedro?' Thea asks him. They're going to leave, and she'll have to wish them well and wave goodbye.

'I'm never leaving, Kiwi.'

'Really?'

'I've got a job at Xibalba.'

'What, you're going to work at Xibalba for the rest of your life?'

'It's not a forever job, but I figure I'll ride out the financial crisis here.' He pulls her in closer, his palm spread over the back of her neck, and steers her through the entrance into the hostel courtyard.

Thea wonders if Sarah knows. Aloud, she asks, 'Then what?'

Chris raises his free hand skyward, an operatic gesture towards the sleeping hostel '*Qué será*, Sarah! Wake up, Sarah!' He turns back to Thea and shrugs. 'Who knows? The future's not ours to see, Kiwi.'

☆ ☆ ☆

The next morning, Thea wakes feeling restless and uneasy. Last night, spending time alone with Chris, felt wrong. Or, more to the point, it felt a bit too good. She resolves to do something different, not to slip back into the habit of sitting around all day drinking coffee until it's time to drink alcohol. She thinks of the must-do activities that she, Sarah and Chris came up with a little while ago. They've got to start crossing things off or they'll never leave. She corrects herself: she's the one who has to leave. She can't keep being a clunky third wheel.

She finds Michael restocking the fridge behind the bar, and perches on one of the stools on the other side of the counter. There are a few people sitting at the tables scattered around the courtyard, but it's too early for Aksel to have planted himself on his usual seat.

'*Buenos días*, Kiwi,' Michael greets her while continuing his work. 'What's the plan for this gorgeous day?'

'I was wondering about walking the Rostro Maya,' she tells him. 'Have you done it?'

'Sure have,' Michael says, closing the fridge door and turning to lean on the counter-top in front of her.

'Can you do it on your own or do you need a guide?'

'Have you been buying crystals at the market?' Michael asks her with mock suspicion. 'Reading the tarot? Really getting into the San Pedro spirit of things?'

'What? No.' Thea laughs, confused by the non-sequitur.

Michael wipes his brow with an exaggerated gesture of relief. 'I thought for a moment you could read my mind: I'm going up the Rostro Maya this afternoon, once I finish up here. I can be your guide — as long as you don't mind a side trip to the cemetery first.' Michael explains that he walks the Rostro Maya every year on the anniversary of his partner, Pete's, death. He tells Thea how Pete had grown up in both New Mexico and Guatemala, split between countries and parents. Pete had done the hike whenever he'd been in Guatemala for his birthday. As a boy, he'd followed his father up the trail to the lookout. The last few years, Michael and Pete had walked the track side by side. 'Now I'll do it for him,' Michael says to Thea.

'I don't want to intrude,' she says.

'The company will be beautiful.'

'Sarah and Chris will probably want to come,' Thea tells Michael, hesitation in her words. She knows Michael isn't Chris's biggest fan. 'We kind of made a pact to do it before we leave San Pedro.'

There's a pause before Michael responds. 'The more the merrier,' he says somewhat brusquely, pulling a packet of cigarettes from his shirt pocket. He lights a cigarette and moves from behind the bar into the courtyard, where he starts straightening chairs and clearing tables. Thea turns around on her seat to watch him. Neither of them speaks for a while. Thea is about to suggest that she, Sarah and Chris go some other day when Michael speaks again. This time it's as though he's reading her mind. 'Truly, truly, it's no intrusion. Me, I'm not so amiable, but Pete, he loved being surrounded by people — it's why we ended up here.' He spreads his arms to take in the hostel's courtyard, cigarette in one hand, an overflowing ashtray in the other. 'He led me to Paradise,' he says dryly, then adds, 'Give me an hour or so and I'll be ready to go.'

'Thanks, Michael,' Thea says, pulling her gaze away from the ashtray and shaking off memories from the night before. She hops down from the barstool and heads off to tell the others.

Although it's short notice, Sarah and Chris are both keen to do the walk, which is only about four hours all up. 'You guys get yourselves sorted,' she says. 'I'll grab us some snacks.'

When Thea gets back from her quick trip to the shops, she puts the small packet of biscuits and bag of nuts in her daypack, which is waiting on her bed. As she's walking down the hallway, past the doorway to the bathroom, she sees Sarah at the sink, splashing water on her face. She goes in to check if Sarah's ready. Sarah straightens up and meets Thea's eyes in the clouded mirror. Her face is blotchy.

'What's wrong?' Thea asks Sarah. She tentatively puts her hand on the other girl's upper back, wondering what could have happened in the short time since she went out.

'It's nothing,' Sarah says. 'Chris and I had a fight. He's not coming with us.' She smiles but is obviously upset. 'It's dumb, I know, but I suggested we could finish with a swim in the lake. You know, cross at least two things off our list — maybe even all three. I just thought . . . Never mind.' Sarah wipes the back of her hand across her eyes, readjusts her scarf in the mirror, and smiles again. 'It was a stupid idea.'

'It wasn't a stupid idea,' Thea says. *It's just,* she thinks to herself, *that it wasn't Chris's idea. Or, perhaps more accurately, it wasn't his decision.* Thea really admires Sarah's energy, but she's seen that sometimes her enthusiasm grates on Chris. Sarah can jump too quickly from an idea to a decision, putting a plan in place before Chris has even agreed to the concept. It's clear to Thea that Chris hates being told what to do, that he doesn't like it when he has no choice in a matter. It's better to let him decide things for himself. But Thea doesn't think it's her place to tell

Sarah about her own boyfriend and, in any case, doesn't know how to do it without hurting her feelings. Instead, she gives Sarah a side hug, her head resting against the other girl's, and simply says, 'His loss.'

Sarah gives a small nod, but then she says, 'I *know* he'd enjoy it though. I'll ask him again.'

Thea turns Sarah to face her. 'Leave him, Sarah. I'm going to kill time in the courtyard until Michael's ready. Join me. Chris knows where to find us if he decides to come.' She hopes that Chris doesn't come. It'd be good for Sarah to do something without him. And she knows that Michael would prefer it if Chris wasn't there. And, well, if she's honest with herself, she thinks she needs to keep her distance from him, too.

Sarah nods again. 'True,' she says, then adds. 'Or he can just go by himself. *Pasado mañana*.'

Thea glances at Sarah. She's looking at the ground but Thea sees the corner of her mouth twitch. After a second, Sarah catches Thea's eye. They burst into laughter.

In the courtyard, the friends find a table in the shade. 'Teach me how to draw something,' Sarah says to Thea. She gets a few sheets of scrap paper and a pencil from behind the bar. Before long, they're helpless with laughter as they look at Sarah's attempts.

'Hey!' Sarah lightly slaps Thea's arm. 'You said anyone can learn. You said it's something that can be taught.'

'Maybe I'm not a very good teacher,' Thea says, picking up Sarah's sketch of one of the statutes in the garden. She mock frowns, turning it on its side and upside down. 'This is culturally offensive, you know,' she teases. 'Maybe even blasphemy, if you can use that term for non-Christian gods.'

'OK, I don't want to be one of those tourists who ends up in the news — you know, like that girl who danced on top of a pyramid in Mexico, or those people who carve their names into the Colosseum.' Sarah plays along. 'How can I fix this before I get deported?' Thea gives some instructions, but it's not long before she's almost crying with laughter. Sarah puts down the pencil and pretends to be offended, but can't help laughing too. They feed off one other until they're gasping for breath and begging each other to stop.

Just as they're gaining control of themselves, two police officers enter the courtyard. They don't talk, but it's like they have choreographed their walk through the tables, each forming one half of a figure of eight, crossing over in the middle and meeting at the bar. Thea and Sarah fall silent. Thea feels Sarah give a small shudder, as though shaking off an unpleasant thought. Thea doesn't blame her; she's got nothing at all against the police, but there is something a little sinister about these men. Dressed all in black, in military boots, and with guns strapped to their thighs, the officers look like shadows that have broken free and taken on a life of their own. They nod at Hans behind the bar, then turn and walk back out.

When they've left, Michael comes out of the building where he's been watching from the doorway. He holds a small daypack by its straps. 'Why were the police here?' Sarah asks him.

'Probably investigating a crime against art,' Michael says, picking up Sarah's drawing and grimacing. 'They're just making their presence felt since the shooting,' he continues. 'We don't see them for months and months — and don't get me wrong, I'm not complaining one single little bit about that — but then something like a shooting happens and they come and shake up the gringos for a bit. We'll get a daily dose of joy from Guatemala's finest civil servants for a week or two, then all will be *tranquilo tranquilo* again.'

'Hang on.' Sarah and Thea exchange a look, then turn back to Michael. 'Shooting?'

'You need to fill in some gaps for us,' Thea says.

'Right, you were both off touristing when the news broke.'

While Thea had been in Livingston and Sarah had been dancing the night away at Xibalba, a local man was shot in an alley behind the plaza in the village, not far from the Spanish school. The news had reached the Xaman Ek the next day, arriving like one of the stray dogs from the village, carrying rumours like fleas. Michael had listened to the speculation as foreigners washed down corn chips and guacamole with beer. Gang wars. A love triangle. A long-standing family feud. Something political. 'Probably something to do with Alice's restaurant,' Michael tells them now.

Thea thinks back to the night before. She wonders how much Sarah knows about Chris's activities. Sarah's no fool — she knows about Alice's restaurant and knows Chris is a customer. Still, Thea suspects that Chris largely keeps his shady side from Sarah; he probably thinks he's doing her a favour, but maybe it's that hint of danger that draws Sarah to him.

Michael interrupts her thoughts. 'Right, if you're ready to

stop the art lesson — and I think you should — let's go. *Vámonos,*' he says, zipping up his backpack.

'Is it safe?' Sarah asks, her mind clearly still on the shooting.

'As safe as it ever is, *chica,*' Michael says.

'And you're *sure* it's OK if we go with you?' Thea asks one more time, although with Chris's absence she's more convinced by Michael's assurances that they're not intruding.

'Absolutely. I've got a picnic packed. As delicious as it is, you can't leave me to eat it all by my lonesome.'

Thea and Sarah follow Michael away from the Xaman Ek and the enclave of restaurants and bars clustered by the lake. They walk up the hill, past the Huito Spanish School and into the village proper — the petrol station, the churches, the post office, police station and other government buildings; all the trappings of regular, working life. There are no yoga studios or kebab shops in this part of San Pedro. It feels to Thea as though they've found a hole in the beaded, feathered net that traps foreigners close to the lake. As they cross the centre of the plaza, groups of locals sitting at the edges, she wonders who wove that net. Have the tourists created a comfortable haven for themselves, a familiar bit of home, down by the lake? Or is it something that the locals have cast over them to keep them from wandering through everyday life, practising Spanish on men waiting for the bus, taking photos of the *abuela* with most sun-creased face and broadest smile, bringing drugs, guns and death into the village?

As they walk through the *pueblo*, Thea keeps an eye out for the weaving cooperative that Chris mentioned.

She also watches Sarah, checking she's OK as they pass a

group of police officers, a reminder of the shooting. Thea soon stops worrying, though: Sarah looks happy and carefree. 'I can't believe I haven't checked out the village before,' Sarah says. 'All that sitting around the hostel is killing me. I'm going to start exploring more.'

'Here we are,' Michael announces. They pause at the entrance to the cemetery, standing in the gap in the concrete wall, the iron gates propped open. Thea's walked past Central American cemeteries on her sightseeing strolls through towns and villages and has often been tempted to go in. She's never felt comfortable enough to do so, though — it feels wrong to be a tourist in another country's death rituals and mourning. But now that she's here with Michael to visit Pete, it doesn't feel so disrespectful. She follows the others through the gate and into the paved labyrinth. Instead of plots dug separately into the ground, each with its plaque laid into the earth, the graves are built above ground, one on top of another, encased in concrete. They form small towers on either side of the path.

Reminiscent of the houses in the *pueblo*, the blocks making up the towers are painted different colours — a patchwork of pastel pinks and greens, bright yellows and blues. But here, each concrete square is a doorway to the afterlife. Pablo Lorenzo García. Rosaria Maria Rodríguez. Hagen Juan Córdoba. Hand-painted names and dates indicate whose body was sealed behind each cemented square and when. On many, a photo reminds the world of who the person was when they were alive: their gentle smile and dreamer's eyes, their beloved face. Jacinto Pedro Maria Herrera. Eva Carmen Catarina Escobar. Candelaria Ana

Maria Vasquez. It's a village occupied by the dead.

The tomb they've stopped in front of is lemon-yellow. There is no photo, just a brief epitaph painted in sloping black letters: Peter Pablo Horado Barrios. 21 August 1976 – 21 August 2006.

'*Feliz cumpleaños*, Pete,' Michael says.

Thea and Sarah stand in silence, just behind Michael. 'Did he want to be buried here?' Sarah asks. When Thea had asked Sarah and Chris if they wanted to do the walk — and the trip to the cemetery — she had shared with them everything that Michael had told her about Pete. 'He wouldn't have wanted his body taken back to the States? You didn't want that?'

'That was his home, but this was just as much his home. In the end, he chose to live here. In the end, he chose to die here.' Michael touches his fingertips to Pete's painted name. 'Now I'll stay here, too,' he says, leaning forward to kiss the grave.

Sarah lightly places her hand on Michael's shoulder before she and Thea wander off to give him time alone with Pete. They walk slowly between the tombs, silently taking in the melted candles and dried-up flowers, turning this way and that to avoid family members visiting their loved ones. They drift their separate ways, lost in thought.

Thea tries to read each name, to think about the person who had lived, and all those they left behind. But there are too many: death piled on death, lives stacked from the ground towards the sky. She suddenly sees herself on a gently sloping lawn, yellow patches among the green, a mound of earth heaped up in an oblong, dry and cracking in the summer heat. It surprised Thea just how long it took for the earth to sink back to flatness, for the grass to grow over a newly dug grave. Months after her dad died, the outline of his death was still clear. Even on her last visit before travelling, she thought she could see the shape of the cut in the earth, a slumped rectangle in the lawn. *But of course that's right*, she thinks now. She knows that death isn't something buried and forgotten. It leaves phantom limb aches and recurring nightmares.

Even the oldest graves here have a frame of artificial flowers and melted wax, showing that people are still honouring relatives down generations. She imagines her own parents' plot as a plain green blanket, grass grown back to life in her absence, no adornment or trinkets of remembrance. Perhaps her father's widow, Magda, visits from time to time to trace his name with her fingertips and leave bunches of the blue hydrangeas that he loved. But Magda lives in Wellington now, close to her sister and nieces. Instead of wide-swept west coast skies carved by gannets, Magda now looks out onto grey-green hills sliced by the white wing of a wind turbine, a view Thea's only seen in grainy photographs sent by email.

Thea thinks again of her father's funeral — not the actual service, but the planning of it, when she didn't know how to ask Magda, 'But what about you?' Both Magda and Thea were always clear that Magda was Andy's wife, not Thea's stepmother. There was no animosity in that, just a statement of how it was. Thea's known Magda for almost as long as she knew her own mother and she loves her dearly. She feels terrible that she didn't have the courage to ask Magda how she felt about Thea's mum and dad being buried together while she was left to make her own way through the years with no place waiting for her when the time came. It felt right to Thea to have her parents lying in a shared grave, but that doesn't necessarily mean that it was the right thing to do.

All Thea can really remember about her mum's funeral is running off to climb a tree by the low fence surrounding the graveyard. She refused to come down, telling her dad she was a baby bird and she lived in the tree now. He sat on the grass, leaning against the trunk. After some time, he started talking, wondering aloud if he should find some worms to feed the baby bird or if baby birds preferred ice cream. It was only at her father's funeral — the memory exhumed as the ground was opened up to lay her father above her mother — that Thea realised he'd missed his wife's wake to buy Thea an ice cream.

She may not remember much about her mother's funeral, but she remembers growing up without her, those years when it was just her and her dad, long before he met Magda. She remembers the sympathetic whispers when she went back to school and the kindness of her friends' mothers when she went around to play or stay the night, the way they always baked cakes when she was there, the way they tucked her in, smoothing her hair and kissing her on the forehead before she went to sleep.

Thea wears each death she's known like a layer of skin, a tailored sorrow, each particular pain building up to make her who she is: Motherless. Fatherless. Friendless. She wonders, if she were to peel it all away, back through the layers and years, who she would find.

After some time, Michael appears beside Thea. His presence pulls her back to the current moment. 'You OK?' she asks him.

He nods a couple of times, lips pressed together, then says, 'It's always nice to have a chat. I miss our chats.' He nods again, as though lost in thought, then turns his focus back to Thea. 'All right, let's go track down the Aussie.'

They wander a little way to find Sarah. Michael is still subdued as the three of them make their way towards the exit, but as soon as they leave the cemetery, he switches back to the jovial person that Thea has grown to know. 'Next stop, Rostro Maya,' he says, slapping his palms together as though cleaning them of dirt. 'You might know it as the "Indian's nose" hike, but let's aim to eradicate that oh-so-slightly-offensive name. When I say "next stop", we can of course rest before then, if your hearts, legs, or stomachs so desire. Your friendly tour guide will accommodate your wishes. And I won't even awkwardly hit you up for tips.'

☆ ☆ ☆

Thea, Sarah and Michael sit under the crucifix at the top of the Rostro Maya. Michael pulls out containers of food: beans, chicken and rice, still warm from the morning kitchen; soft corn tortillas, wrapped in foil to keep them fresh and pliable; small loaves of banana bread; and a whole pineapple, pulled by its spiky dull-green hair from the bottom of Michael's bag.

'Pete and I were up here for sunrise on his birthday last

year,' Michael tells them. 'He told me that he wanted an early start because he had some business to attend to in San Juan later in the day. I didn't think anything of it. He often had to talk to officials to get permits and what not for the Xaman Ek and it could take hours. *El gobierno guatemalteco* makes an art out of paperwork and bribery. He told me to head home. It's not helpful having a gringo waiting in the queue with you. He said he'd see me later.'

Michael had gone back to the Xaman Ek to prepare a private celebration for that night, hiding small presents and scraps of paper with things he'd written for Pete around the room. Pete hadn't returned.

'Poor old Pete, he always had his struggles.' The words rest in the air, like the little bugs that hover and vibrate above the surface of the lake, then Michael speaks again. 'It's much too easy to get hold of pills in San Pedro.'

Thea wants to ask him if he feels responsible — or, at least, whether he feels like he could've stopped Pete from dying, if only he'd done one thing differently. She imagines Pete in a hotel room in San Juan, and no one there to stop the cold, slow creep of death down the hall towards him. She doesn't want Michael to feel bad; she just wants to know if anyone else feels like her.

Michael lights a cigarette and lies back, inhaling and exhaling smoke with his eyes closed. The narrow shadow of the crucifix cuts across his face and torso.

Thea and Sarah walk the short distance to the lookout. They gaze out at Lago de Atitlán. Today it's a blue-green Wonderland mirror, boats skimming across the surface like dragonflies. Much in the way statues of saints line the walls inside churches, settlements sit all around the lake: San Pedro, San Juan, San Pablo, San Marcos, Santa Clara La Laguna, Santa Catarina, San Antonio Palopó, San Lucas Tolimán. And also there, always there, woven through the small bays and high into the ancient hills: the red thread of the east wind, the black of the west wind, the white north wind, and the yellow wind from the south, blowing across the mountain tops and rippling the surface of the lake since the time before conquistadors, saints and tourists.

Sarah looks towards San Pedro. 'I didn't realise until today how big the village actually is. When we were there, I was thinking how much of it there is to explore,' she says. 'But from up here it looks tiny. There's so much more to see out there.' Thea watches Sarah as she gazes out at the horizon. Her body is contained, arms tucked into her sides, each hand lightly holding an end of her scarf, pulling it gently downwards. She looks so small against the vastness of the country laid out before them but, as she stands there, it seems to Thea that Sarah's drawing it all in towards her, her head slowly turning to take in all the mountain tops, all the places she hasn't been. After a moment's silence, Sarah continues, talking quietly. 'We can't become like them, Thee. All those coke addicts, just spending the rest of their days partying in someone else's country, getting more and more dysfunctional.' Thea follows Sarah's gaze, which has come back to rest on the blocky rooftops of San Pedro.

'You'll never be like them,' Thea says. 'For a start, you don't do coke.'

'But if I stay here,' Sarah starts. She pauses, then speaks again. 'It's one thing to be a tourist, passing through places without seeing anything. That's bad enough, but that's what travelling is when it all comes down to it. It's another thing again to live in a place but not really live there. It's been fun, but I can't imagine staying long enough to think this is normal.'

'Permatourists,' Thea says.

Sarah half-laughs. 'Yeah, permatourists.'

'Where do you want to go?' Thea asks her, looking from the rooftops of San Pedro out across the lake.

'Anywhere. I just want to go somewhere else.' Sarah turns to look at Thea. 'Where do you want to go?'

'Anywhere but home.'

A statue of the Virgin Mary averts her eyes. She watches the maize growing at her feet, arms spread towards the green stalks as though gesturing for them to rise, though there are iron rods and crumbling concrete where her hands should be.

6

The next evening, Sarah sits with Chris on the terrace, her feet in his lap, a book in her hand. She should be enjoying this time together, but she can't relax. Her mind keeps wandering from her book to their relationship. They never see each other in the mornings now. Their waking lives overlap only from mid-afternoon when Chris wakes up, until sometime in the evening when he heads to Xibalba. Every day feels like those days when the ghostly moon rises in the last hours of daylight, the dying golden light and the rising silvery night existing together for a brief lapse of time.

Sometimes she joins him at Xibalba, but he's so often working and, even when he's not, there's always someone coming up to talk to him; or he's taking off with someone else, coming back and going again, a flickering figure under the strobe lights.

She puts her book down and sits up. 'Let's leave, Chris,' she says, leaning in towards him. '*Pasado mañana.*' She grins. 'You can't object to that.'

'Why leave?' he says without looking up from his own book. 'Things are good here. There's a financial crisis out there in the big wide world, but here I'm making money.'

Sarah pauses, weighing up the approach she wants to take. Eventually she says, 'You could pick up bar work anywhere.' Then, as the idea latches in her mind, she continues enthusiastically, 'That's what we could do. We could keep travelling, but stay for a week or two in some places and get jobs at the hostel or whatever.' She's met plenty of people who work in hostels in exchange for free meals and accommodation. It's not the long-term volunteering she had in mind, but it's a plan for now.

'That's a way of saving money, not making money,' he says. Sarah's imagined Chris in a suit, but for the first time she visualises him at a desk, in a glass tower high above a harbour. It feels more real than her previous daydreams — it's like a premonition of her future and, even though she never thought she'd end up with a corporate type, it excites her. There's something commanding in this version of him, and she can't help but find that sexy. She's always assumed her life partner would be a tradie, just like her father and her brother are. But Chris stretches the horizons of her experience and expectation. Being with him makes her believe that she can keep reinventing herself. And it's not that she's unhappy with herself — she loves her life — it's just that, for the first time, she can see endless possibilities of who she could be, so many different worlds that could be hers. The excitement of all that lies ahead hums within her. They just have to move on from here, leave the Xaman Ek and Xibalba behind, get away from Hans and Aksel and all the others, start living the life that could be theirs.

When she and Chris first met, she'd been so excited to learn that, like her, he was travelling the whole way through Central America. That very night, as they moved closer and closer towards each other, they plotted out all the places across and down the isthmus that they wanted to go. 'To Panama,' they'd agreed, then made out in the dark corner of the hostel rooftop. But they've never really talked about what happens after Panama. What happens to *them*, that is. Right at the start, Chris mentioned that he was on his way to London, and that still seems to be his plan — eventually. After all this time they've spent together and how close they've become, she just wants to be clear about how *she* fits in. She hasn't wanted to admit it to Chris, but she's pictured the two of them living in a flat in London: a few years spent rugged up against the dreary grey and drizzle, joking about missing the sun and Vegemite, crossing off European cities weekend-by-weekend. And then? And then back to Oz, of course.

She pictures weekend barbecues back home. For her family, that means sausages wrapped in bread, throwing a frisbee across the lawn, Arlo blasting music on the stereo, various friends stopping by, dropping beers into the ice-filled Esky in the shade. From the way Chris talks about his family, she imagines food laid out on white platters, fridge-chilled wine served in glasses, guests by invitation only.

She can see herself being part of that, living in Sydney, with professionally manicured nails, passing nibbles around at Chris's family barbecues. For a few years, at least. It'd be another layer to the geology of their relationship, another version of herself. But she can't imagine settling down anywhere but WA. She's imagined Chris in Margaret River, even Perth as a compromise. He'd like it if he tried it, she knows he would.

'I've got a good gig here, babe.' Chris interrupts her thoughts. 'If I keep it up, we can go and stay at a couple of those fancy eco-resorts you talk about. A luxury getaway every now and then.'

She puts thoughts of the future to the back of her mind and tentatively steps towards another conversation she knows she needs to have with Chris. 'But making money at whose expense?'

'I don't know, Sarah, whose?' He puts his book down on the low table in front of them and looks at her. 'Certainly not yours. I haven't heard you complain about the free meals and occasional party favour.' She can feel her throat thicken with the threat of tears and hates herself for it. He's right, she's happily let him pay for drinks and meals. She had become increasingly suspicious, and then uncomfortable, with the way he's making money but has never outright raised it with him. His job at Xibalba isn't the problem. 'I'm just giving people what they want,' Chris continues before she can find her voice. 'It's not like I'm forcing anyone to buy drugs. I'm basically just saving them a walk up the hill.'

That's technically true, Sarah supposes — from what she's heard, anyone could go to Alice's restaurant and buy whatever they want. Obviously it's not that simple, though. But she doesn't want to argue with Chris again. She smiles softly at him, giving his hand a gentle squeeze. 'We said we'd make it all the way to Panama. Remember?'

'Chill, babe. We'll get there. No rush. *Qué será, será*, Sarah.' He pulls his hand away from hers and wraps it around the neck of his beer bottle. In his other hand, he twists the cap around and around between his fingers and thumb, its serrated edge biting into his skin.

Sarah leaves her hand resting on her lap, within reach if Chris chooses to reach out and hold it. After a period of silence, she says, 'I've actually bought a bus ticket. To Xela. For you, too.' The words start slowly, then tumble out. 'Thea and I bought them this morning. There's a mountain she wants to climb. It's the highest mountain in Central America.'

'Tajumulco,' Chris says. 'Thea's talked about it.'

'That's the one. Thea wants us to go with her.' Thea had only said that Sarah should accompany her, but that's not important. Chris only needs to get as far as Xela; once he's left San Pedro, she's sure she'll be able to get him on a bus south. And this time they'll take all their stuff with them so there's no reason to return. She's been reading about Xela in the guidebook since Thea mentioned going there. It's one of the more detailed sections and she's read it several times, softening the edges of the paper as she pores over information on the history, the nightlife, volunteer organisations and more. Within those few pages her horizons expand.

Going to Xela isn't just an escape route. Now that Thea's

put the idea in her head, Sarah's really excited about climbing the mountain. She's never done anything like that before; never thought she could. Walking the Rostro Maya made her understand why people seek out the world's highest peaks. The freshness of the air and the open views had thrilled her, but Thea said that Tajumulco would be so much better — 'It means "above the clouds",' she had explained.

Sarah had visited the internet café and looked at images of people standing on top of Tajumulco, arms wrapped around themselves for warmth, the mountain casting a perfect triangular shadow behind them. She wants that photo, wants to be one of the people standing above the clouds, peering through the gaps as they race by to see the land stretched out below, to look out across where she's been then turn to where she could go next. She wants the freedom of all that air and space around her. Thea assured her it's not actual mountaineering. 'It's just a trek,' she said. 'It'll be strenuous, the altitude might make it tough, and it'll be cold at the top, but you don't need any gear, just a few extra layers.' Sarah's pleased it's not proper mountaineering — she's definitely not ready for that, and probably never will be — but she's surprised to find that the thought of it doesn't absolutely terrify her.

'Climbing mountains isn't my thing.' Chris brings Sarah tumbling down from the heights. 'You go. I'll wait here.'

Sarah wants to say a hundred different things. It's not just about the mountain. It's not just about moving on to a new place. It's something they can do together; it's about forming a memory. She wants him to see, like she can see, the two of them looking back through their photos, or having drinks with friends, in a year or maybe five, recounting the time they climbed the highest peak in Central America. She thinks of Michael and Pete and how, despite the tragedy, Michael has a tangible way to honour their love. There must be some kind of comfort in that — a pilgrimage of sorts back to a special place they went together.

'You get to the summit at sunrise,' she tries again. The excitement of that burned deep inside her. She imagined the orange sky rippling around her and Chris, sunlight bouncing off the clouds. It would feel like being part of the sunrise, like being immersed in the orange essence of it. It would be a photo to frame and hang on the wall at home. 'It means you have to start walking really early in the morning, like the middle of the night, so that's perfect for you,' she tells Chris. 'It's not like you have to wake up for sunrise, you could just stay up all night.'

'Enough, Sarah.' Chris's words are loud, their impact heavy like a slab of granite toppling over. He's never spoken to her so forcefully before. 'I said I'm not going.' He picks his book up from the table and starts to read.

Sarah freezes, her gaze fixed on Chris, but his eyes are focused on his book. She waits, but when he turns the page and keeps on reading, she stands up and walks over to the edge of the terrace. No one's ever made her feel as special as Chris does, but sometimes she feels like her very presence annoys him. She turns to go back inside. 'I'm going to get something to eat,' she tells him as she heads back towards the building.

'Come here.' Chris grabs her wrist as she walks past and

pulls her down into his lap. 'I'm sorry.' Grasping the back of her head, he kisses her in between his words. 'It was very nice of you to buy me a bus ticket.' His hand slides between her shoulder blades. 'I'm just tired. And I don't want to get on one of those buses for as long as I can avoid it.' He pushes her hair back and kisses her neck. 'And I definitely don't want to climb a mountain.' She tilts her head, exposing more of her throat to him while he continues to talk. 'You go with Thea. The two of you will have a much better time without me bitching about everything.' His lips are soft on her skin while his thumb presses firmly against her collarbone.

They sit, wrapped together, kissing and talking as the sky around them becomes more mountain-black than blue. Sarah won't mention the Tajumulco hike again but she still wants to go *somewhere* with Chris. San Pedro's been fun, but she never would've stayed this long if it wasn't for him. Buying a bus ticket out of town was almost like breaking some kind of fairytale curse. Almost. She just needs to find the *exact* right words to say to break the hold that the town has on him. 'Tell me about where you live in Sydney,' she says, her head resting in the space between his head and shoulder. Gazing upward into the night, she tries to find the line between the volcanic peaks and the sky above. 'When you go back to Aussie are you going to live in the same place?'

'I've told you, Sarah, I'm never going home.' She can hear the impatience creeping back into his voice; the trickle of stones down a mountainside before a landslip. But she's getting impatient, too.

'You're not seriously planning to stay here for the rest of your life?'

'Nah, I'll leave eventually. Then it's London. I've told you that.'

'And then?'

'And then, what? Why all the questions?'

'Never mind,' she says. They've argued too much lately. 'I won't ask any more questions.'

'Good,' he says, giving her hair a playful tug, 'because I have to go out for a while and I don't think you should ask me what I'm doing.'

Sarah walks downstairs and out to the street with Chris. She says goodbye to him then goes back into the courtyard to join Thea and a group of other backpackers.

'Is everything OK?' Thea asks. 'You look upset.'

'It's nothing,' Sarah tells her. 'Chris doesn't want to climb Tajumulco. He doesn't even want to come to Xela.'

'Come without him,' Thea says, repeating words Sarah's heard before.

'I think he'll change his mind,' Sarah says. 'He just needs a bit more time.'

'He's had enough time. Come on, Sarah, come with me. You can always join up with him later. You've done it before.'

'I love him, Thee. I don't like being away from him. I missed him so much last time.' All that's true. She's also scared of how long she might have to wait for him to join her. She might even have to come back here. She remembers arriving in San Pedro and seeing Chris and Thea walk into the Xaman Ek together. If she goes away without him, he might find someone else.

Thea looks like she's going to say something, but she doesn't. Sarah can guess what it might be — another one of the things Thea has said to her before. Thea's right: maybe she shouldn't worry if he follows her or not. Maybe it's only a matter of time until they go their separate ways. Whatever will be, will be, as Chris would say. But, no, she doesn't want to let what she has with Chris — what they *could* have — slip through her fingers. She can't imagine being on her own, not now that she knows this feeling of belonging with another person; knowing you're part of a pair, even when they're not right there beside you. She doesn't want all this time she's spent sitting around in San Pedro instead of exploring this amazing continent to be for nothing.

He changed his mind about going to San Marcos; she just needs to keep trying.

☆ ☆ ☆

Two days later, Sarah and Thea are in the village, in the street just off the plaza where the buses stop. It's a riot of colour, noise and activity, which would usually make Sarah nervous, but this morning it just makes her head hurt. They had a bigger night than usual the night before, one last hurrah before Thea heads off to Xela. 'Not a farewell party,' Thea had said. 'Let's call it a "see ya later" party. I hate goodbyes. I refuse to do them anymore.' Then, earlier in the day when they stood beside a sleeping Chris and Sarah had reached out to shake him awake so that he could see Thea off — like he'd promised he would — Thea had stopped her. 'Don't wake him,' she said. 'Just tell him he owes me a beer when we meet up again.'

Sarah tries to ignore her headache and concentrate more on her surroundings. Five buses are lined up in the street, like a string of Christmas decorations. They're all old US school buses, but instead of the uniform yellow, each has its unique personality painted onto it. Bags, baskets and boxes are passed up to the drivers' assistants, who secure them to the luggage racks atop the buses. Arms reach through the narrow sliding windows, exchanging cash for food and drinks. A different soundtrack blares from each bus, the music clanging in overlapping waves as they walk down the row to Thea's bus. It's mainly red but there's a bright green stripe down the side. A silver foil banner with '*Jesús El Señor*' in pink block letters shines in the windscreen.

For a moment, she imagines getting on the bus with Thea. In her mind, she fast forwards to the mountain top, throws her arms out wide and her head back in triumph. She almost laughs with the thrill of it. But before the mountain top there's a long slog uphill, and before that, hours of winding roads on an overpacked bus. The buzz of excitement seizes up like rusty brakes. Staying in San Pedro for so long, she's blissfully forgotten the nightmare of bus trips. She feels guilty leaving Thea to travel on her own, even though Thea's told her she enjoys staring out the window for hours — 'a moving meditation', she'd called it, and they'd both laughed at that. But getting on a bus hungover? Even Thea's got to dread that.

Sarah's queasy just thinking about it.

'Do you hate me?' Sarah says to Thea, looking at the ground between their feet. 'Leaving you to do this on your own? Saying I'll join you, then piking? I'm sorry I'm not coming.'

'Of course I don't hate you,' Thea says. 'It was time for me to stop being the third wheel anyway.'

Sarah looks at Thea with a small smile. She doesn't tell her that she and Chris are moving to a private room that night. 'You weren't. I'm really going to miss you.'

Sarah and Thea both have tears in their eyes as they hug. 'I'll see you soon, OK?' Thea says as she pulls away from Sarah.

Sarah nods. 'Definitely. We'll see you soon. Travel safe.' She wipes her eyes with the end of her scarf.

Then Thea's climbing up the stairs onto the bus. Sarah tries to keep her eyes on her as she walks down the bus, but Thea finds a seat on the other side, so there's no prolonged goodbye through the window. Sarah's wondering if she should wait until the bus drives off, regardless — a final wave even if Thea doesn't see it — or if she should walk away, pretending that her friend's not really leaving. The decision's made for her as the driver blasts the horn and steers the bus out onto the road. 'Bye Thea,' she says quietly. As the bus heads up the hill and around a corner, a trail of music and dust in its wake, Sarah feels the loneliness shudder through her. She already misses her friend. She misses her family. The longing to be with them, back on the deck at home or on the beach, almost knocks her to her knees.

She takes a deep breath in, then out. She lets the feeling of it travel through her, down to her toes. If she's going to stay here, she's going to make the most of it. 'Little acts of courage,' she tells herself, and turns back towards the plaza.

7

Three days after leaving San Pedro, Thea's on top of Tajumulco. She stands apart from the other members of the trekking group, watching the sun rise. She breathes deeply. She wants to stretch her arms out wide, reaching for the open space, but she's embarrassed. It would feel like she was posing for one of those motivational posters people put on office walls: *Nothing's impossible. Reach for your dreams. If this tiny blue-eyed kitten can do it, so can you.*

In the van ride to the start of the trek, their guide, José, had told them that the Mayans believed — and, as she understood it, Guatemalans still believed — that if you approached Tajumulco with fear or uncertainty, it will punish you for your doubt. You might get sick. You might get lost. 'Approach with faith,' José had said, 'and the mountain will look after you.'

With José's words in her head, Thea had stood on the steep cobbled street leading to the start of the trek and reminded herself that she had done more technical walks. Hours tramping with her dad up muddy hillsides, soaked by rain, using tree roots to haul herself up steps cut by a man who must've been well over six foot tall, had conditioned her for more rugged terrain, for longer days. Tajumulco wasn't a technical climb: no crampons, no harnesses, no ropes, no snow, no ice. But at over 4200 metres, it was higher than anything she'd climbed before — about 1400 metres higher than Ruapehu. Thea had been seized with something close to panic, the slice and cut of shame. Doubt lodged in her mind like a splinter of ice. *I can't do this. I shouldn't be here. José's wrong,* she thought. *It's got nothing to do with faith and certainty; no one can control a mountain. And, worse than that, even if the mountain does look after you, you're at the mercy of the people you're with. That's the real danger.*

Then she had breathed deeply, knowing it was too late to pull out. Instead of trying to shake the doubt, she looked up towards Tajumulco and murmured a greeting. '*Buenos días.*' As the other members of the group took photos, she silently asked the mountain for permission to climb.

Now, standing at the top, above the clouds, she thanks Tajumulco. It wasn't so long ago that she thought she'd never climb another mountain. She'll probably never put on crampons and a harness again, probably never climb another snow-covered peak, but this — looking out into the wide openness, wrapped in the power and beauty of nature — *this* she's missed more than she realised. For at least this moment, she feels like she's exactly where she's meant to be.

Clouds of orange fire bump across the sky, a cold wind pushing them off to the horizon. The sun burns from deep tangerine to the pale lemon of an acid drop. Thea wishes Sarah were here to see this, to feel this freedom, the stretch of adventure in all directions. They could stand here, together, spinning, arms pointing outwards from their bodies like arrows, and when they stopped, that's the direction they would go. Thea's not surprised that Sarah didn't come to Xela. There was a moment when it might have happened — when Thea was talking about the trek and Sarah lit up with the idea of standing on top of Tajumulco, swimming in a fiery sunrise — but she knew before she boarded the bus that the dark magnetic pull of the lake, of Chris, was too strong. She truly believes that Sarah would love this, and she truly thinks that Sarah should leave San Pedro. But if she's really honest, one of the reasons Thea tried to talk Sarah into joining her is that, after months of being so resolutely independent, she hadn't wanted to leave by herself, to set off on her own again. If she and Sarah hadn't bought the bus tickets together, Thea doesn't think she would've left. But once she had that ticket and had announced to everyone that she was leaving, she couldn't stay. If people asked her why she wasn't going, what could she have said? 'Because I have a friend again'?

The volcano casts a pointed shadow over the land stretched out below. She turns in a slow circle, looking across at all the places she's been on this trip — her eyes skimming along where she thinks the Mexico-Guatemala border must be — and all the places she's yet to go. Thea watches as the sun continues its ascent up the sky and the shadow shifts by degrees; an ancient sundial slowly marking time. It points her west, towards the coast.

When she's back down from the mountain, Thea moves quickly, making up for the lost time in San Pedro. She heads to the coast, not due west, but south, down into El Salvador where the land breathes salt air through palms and mangroves. She doesn't stay anywhere for more than three nights, no particular route in mind, just deciding on her next destination the night before she leaves.

Thea and Sarah exchange emails. *We'll catch up to you in a week or two. Maybe Costa Rica — we can go swimming with the turtles!!! xx*, Sarah's first message says.

Turtles sound great! See you there xx, Thea responds.

Days pass. *Tell me about the big wide world out there*, Sarah writes.

Tell me the news from San P, Thea writes back.

They pick the best parts of what they're doing to share with each other. Thea starts expressing herself with a poetic honesty that until now she's kept to herself, words in a sketchbook. She tells Sarah about surfing in El Salvador and driving back from the beach in the back of a ute, salt-drenched and sun-tumbled. *Growing up on the west coast, I've seen the sun set into the sea all my life, but this was something else. It was like the world got turned inside out and the sky was the lava at its core.*

Sarah writes how she's spending more time in the village. *I'm back in Spanish school. I go to classes in the morning while Chris is sleeping, then head back up there in the evenings when Chris is working — finally going to those free salsa lessons and cooking classes and stuff that the school puts on.*

Thea describes the ruins of Copán. *Trees growing out of stones. I sometimes forget that people, not time and nature, carved those temples.* She talks of long bus journeys and nights in hostels, of marketplaces and cobbled streets.

Sarah tells Thea how she's exploring the streets around the plaza more. She sends a photo of the weaving cooperative — no message, just the subject line *Found it!* She describes the preparations for El Día de la Independencia in the village up the hill — *They're putting up blue and white ribbons and banners everywhere, Thee. It's like they're decorating the town with strips of sky* — and the complete lack of recognition of the occasion down by the lake. *No one even knew it was Independence Day and no one could be bothered watching the parade so I went alone then stayed to watch the fireworks. It was amazing. I can't believe everyone else missed it.*

Sarah's message reminds Thea what a fucked-up place San Pedro is. She'd fallen into its trap. For weeks she saw only the rainbow swirls on the surface, and not the dark oiliness underneath. She was content to enjoy the good times, to pretend the rest of the world didn't exist. She would've been one of those people, dancing under the criss-crossing laser lights in Xibalba, instead of walking up to the village to watch the glittering starbursts of colour in the night sky. Indeed, why celebrate a nation's independence while you're lazily colonising it with hash brownies and pizza? In the settlement by the lake, everyone was running from something — sometimes real, often imagined.

She'd seen it with backpackers, where people's problems grew in size the more they travelled because they thought it made them more interesting. There's a fucked-up version of 'me' in 'problem'.

And yet, in a way, San Pedro had started to heal her. She had brought her problems — her screwed-up version of herself — to town. And there she'd made friends, she'd laughed, and she'd realised — finally — that she needed to move on. She's not ready to head home, not ready to face up to who she was, to what she's done, but perhaps she's ready to discard some of her guilt and sadness. Perhaps that's the magic. You go to San Pedro to wash away your problems. The trick is to get out, washed clean, not to swim with those who have gone there to drown.

☆ ☆ ☆

For three days Thea doesn't hear the news. First, there's a message from Michael saying that he needs to talk to her. He doesn't say why, and she can't imagine what he's got to say — perhaps some gossip she no longer cares about, but she likes him; he was one of the people she grew closest to while in San Pedro. So, the next day, she slots the ill-fitting headphones over her ears and sits down at a computer in the common area of El Barrio hostel. Michael sighs heavily, the hum of distance filling the space until he talks and changes the world.

'I've got to tell you something,' he says. 'It's about Sarah.'

When he speaks, his words are dull and muffled. Thea can

picture him, face in his hands, as though he's channelling the words through the feathered serpent folded back and forth on itself on the thick silver ring he wears. She waits, not wanting to let her mind race ahead, as though if she can stop her thoughts, she can stop his words.

'I'm sorry. It's not good news.' He pauses. 'It's the worst news, *chica*, the very worst.'

When he tells her Sarah's dead, she feels both absolute disbelief and a deep, raw knowledge that it's true. Sarah is dead.

As though trying to make sense of the tragedy for her, Michael fills Thea's silence. 'She was found in the lake. Just the wrong time, wrong place, everyone's saying. Things have been really crazy here — crazier than usual. Maybe it's the GFC, but here's been a lot of trouble in the *pueblo* lately. A gringo was stabbed last week. There was a raid on Alice's restaurant. Who knows, maybe the Mayan calendar is right and the end of the world is drawing nigh.'

Thea tries to focus on Michael's words, tries to form some words of her own, but suddenly she just needs to get away from the computer. She knows he's not being flippant, she can feel the weight in his words, but still. She staggers outside. More than anything, she wants to run. She wants wide open spaces, endless stretches of sand and sky. She wants to be somewhere without people, without words, where the cries of wide-winged birds slice through the air. Instead she walks the grid of streets of Comayagua, trying to untangle what Michael told her, but Michael hadn't told her much. Sarah was found in the lake. Thea stares up at the yellow-white tower of Iglesia de La Merced and can't stop herself from filling in the gaps. She imagines it was the weedy part of Atitlán, where there's no real edge between land and lake; where water slowly hardens to ground as the reeds and rushes thicken. The bit that isn't far from Xibalba, within the pulsing range of the bass, but beyond the reach of lights; where the bars and parties fade out, and the narrow track up to a group of houses and round the long way to the village begins.

She leans against the wall of the church, resting in the deep shadow the building casts over the plaza. She imagines Sarah face-down in the lake, her plait falling over her shoulder into the water like the waterlogged ropes that tie boats to the jetty. She pictures Sarah's long, pale orange skirt — the one she bought in San Pedro with Thea — clinging to her legs, her green scarf floating out from around her neck. The image is as vivid as if Thea was there. She can see Sarah being lifted from the lake by faceless hands, the water rushing off her as though from a fishing net dragged back up above the surface. Thea gasps for air.

She goes back to the hostel and sends a message to Michael. It's a message full of disbelief, but apology too — for running off, for not asking him how he was coping. First Pete, now Sarah. She pictures him behind the bar at the Xaman Ek and wonders what this means for him. Will it fall to him to talk to the authorities? There will be an investigation. There will be things to arrange. Tragically, he's been here before, must have some idea of what to do, how to help a body through the paperwork between life and death. She tells him she's coming back to San Pedro.

She knows she needs to message Chris — Skype him, if she

can. What are the right words to say? How do you start that email? In the end, that's all she writes: *I can't imagine* and *I don't know what to say*. A series of helpless half-sentences. She worries what he'll do — how he'll cope, how he'll deal with the shock and other emotions. She wants to say something, to tell him not to do anything crazy, but instead ends her message: *I'll come back as fast as I can.*

As she's searching for flights and buses, a message from Michael comes through. He gently lets Thea know that Sarah's body is already on the way to Guatemala City, where she'll wait, wherever bodies in Guatemala City wait, for her father and brother to arrive to take her back to Australia. Then there's a break, a breath of white space, and in the next paragraph, Michael's quivering rage comes through: *They couldn't get rid of her fast enough. They investigated for a whole fucking day, maybe two, then case closed. No evidence. Just labelled it the act of a desconocido and washed their hands of it. They think we're all hippies and druggies here and we get what we deserve. Not Sarah. Sarah didn't deserve this. She deserves justice.* Then another line break and Thea can almost hear Michael draw a breath to calm himself. She breathes deeply herself before reading on. *Did you know that one of the translations of Atitlán is 'the place where the rainbow gets its colours'? I think Sarah would like that. Rest in beautiful peace, Sarah. Que ella descanse en paz.*

Thea's filled with rage. There's nothing poetic about Sarah dying. Fuck rainbows and finding beauty in tragedy. She thinks of the dark waters of the lake lapping at Sarah, leaching the colour out of her skin, taking whatever evidence there was and sucking it down to its silty depths. But even as her body trembles with fury, Thea knows it's not Michael — or the lake — she's angry with.

Still, she wants to write back, to list her questions and demand answers. What exactly happened to Sarah? Who did it? Why? Michael won't have the answers to her questions, though. And, even if she stood on the shore and screamed at it, Atitlán would never tell her what it knows. It's just so unfair. So fucking unfair. Thea knows the unfairness of death too well, is too familiar with the weight of unanswered questions. Grief is heavier than anger and it pulls her into its dark centre.

She thinks of Sarah's brother and father making the long trip from Australia — the unbearable powerlessness of sitting for hours on a plane, pacing around an airport, waiting to catch another plane. Rushing to get there — but for what? Rushing to meet the rest of their lives without Sarah in them.

It's Chris she's angry with. Livid. It's Chris who needs to answer her questions. Where was he when Sarah's life was being torn from her? Why was she down by the lake on her own? And where is he now? Did he travel with Sarah to Guatemala City or leave her to be escorted only by strangers? She was scared to travel on her own. Thea can't bear the thought of Sarah lying in a cold drawer in a foreign city, all alone. Not just any city. Guatemala City, the unavoidable centre of the web of buses criss-crossing the country, but so infamous for its high rate of crime — of murder — that foreign travellers minimise the time spent there, jumping from one bus and straight onto another, all without leaving the walled compound. Or, if there's really no other choice, taking a taxi to a hotel to hole up in for a night, then into another cab in the morning and straight back to the bus station. Guatemala City is the last place Sarah would choose to go. She supposes that the danger can't touch Sarah now, but she's still furious to think that, while Sarah lies there, Chris might be drowning his sorrows — or snorting them — in Xibalba. He didn't even bother to let her know. If Michael hadn't messaged, would Chris have even told her?

She doesn't share the news with anyone at the hostel. No one there knows Sarah. People might be running from problems back home, might show them off to you on long bus trips, like patches stitched onto their backpack: this is my breakup; this is my alcoholic mother; this is me escaping privilege; this one is from my brother who doesn't love me; this one represents my brother who loves me too much — but no one wants to be confronted with the here-and-now tragedy of the death of a backpacker.

She gets drunk, surrounded by other travellers, until she can't handle the lightness and loudness of their laughter anymore. In bed, she lies in the darkness, shivering even though it's a warm night. She shakes and shakes with all her unshed tears and unscreamed anger until she's hollowed out.

The next morning she reads an email from Chris, sent in the middle of the night. *I keep thinking it's not true. It can't be true. I'm in Guatemala City. It's absolutely fucking awful. I'm heading home soon, thank the gods. Let's talk later.*

That afternoon, Thea takes a bus to Tegucigalpa then straight on to León in Nicaragua, putting another country between her and San Pedro.

The following day, Chris leaves Central America; not onward to London but back home to Sydney.

☆ ☆ ☆

Weeks stack up like graves. Thea travels through Nicaragua: León, birthplace of the nation's poets. Managua, where she sits in an internet café off the Plaza de la Revolución and writes an email to Chris. Granada, where she gets a response. Ometepe, a volcano in the middle of a lake. San Juan del Sur, where a colossal statue of Jesus overlooks the beach and a giant concrete turtle swims over the painted pavement at the entrance to town. She's acting out a charade, joining other backpackers to look at cathedrals, waterfalls, coffee farms; laughing when everyone else laughs and smiling for photos. No one notices that she's just a papier-mâché version of a carefree traveller, made of layers of grief and guilt and blame.

Each place becomes a sketch in her book, a coloured rectangle, with the name of the place and the date at the bottom. On the back of each page she writes a line or two of text: postcards to Sarah. The emails between her and Chris are intermittent but grow in length as time passes and he settles back into life in Australia. Sometimes she has to walk away partway through reading his emails, sometimes several times, serialising them into manageable chunks, giving herself breaks to control her rage. He talks about his grief, his guilt, his anger, but never writes about what happened. He blames himself, but doesn't tell her why. She always waits before responding, walks for hours and hours until she can trust herself not to type out her own anger to him. At him. She knows what it's like to blame yourself for another's death. He doesn't need to hear her fury. She wants to ask him what happened, but doesn't want to make him relive details of something that causes so much pain. It's not a kindness; it's a penance.

But eventually the scenarios and details she imagines become too much. She writes to Chris with a newfound determination. *Have they found out who did it? Michael says it's all gone quiet in San Pedro, like it never even happened. He says the police left after a few days. I get the feeling he's been told not to keep asking questions. Have they told you anything?* And then, after typing and deleting and retyping the question several times, she adds, *What actually happened?*

His answer comes quickly, while she's still sitting at the computer. *I don't know what happened. No one will tell me. Or no one knows. I'm so fucking furious. All I know is that they found her in the lake. I should've been there. If I was there, it would never have happened. I'm so angry at myself for not being there.*

Thea responds immediately, asking what she's wondered ever since Michael told her the terrible news. *Why was she down by the lake? What was she doing there?* What she really wants to ask is why Sarah was on her own, why Chris wasn't there.

She was just out exploring, I think. You know how she liked to wander around and just enjoy being in a place. Apparently all this dodgy shit had been happening in town, but no one told us. If she'd known anything about it, she would never have gone anywhere on her own. If I'd known, I never would've let her walk around by herself. I was working. I didn't know she'd wandered off by herself. I hate myself. I can't even stand the thought of Xibalba now. Man it was good to see the back of San Pedro and that whole fucking country.

It's not an answer, really. She still doesn't know what happened, but when all is said and done, perhaps that's not important. Knowing how Sarah died, or by whose hands, won't answer *why* she died; there's no answer to that — or, at least, no answer that will make Thea feel any better.

Chris writes how no one in Sydney understands. *It's just gossip to them. Scandal. They have no idea how I feel.* But when Thea suggests that they arrange a call because *she* knows how he feels, he says, *I can't do another call. Sarah's friend Hayley Skyped me the other week. I don't even know how she tracked me down but she did and it was awful. She wanted to me to relive every moment with Sarah and she told me her whole life story. It was unbearable.* And then, *It's destroying me. I'll never be the same. I just can't talk about it anymore, Thea. It hurts too much.*

Thea doesn't care about Chris's pain. She cares about Sarah. And Hayley, and Arlo, and Sarah's parents, and the wide ripples of Sarah's existence. She goes to a lake just so she can scream underwater. Afterwards, as she's sitting on the shore, short of breath and drying slowly in the sun, her anger ebbs, a slow shallowing out. She understands the burden of death, the sleight of hand of blame. She shares with him what she knows of grief.

She moves on, to Costa Rica, which is rich with rainforest and sparkling stretches of sand. Chris's emails start to tell of his move from Sydney to Melbourne, his flat, his job, his weekends: the slow drip of normality into the pool of tragedy. Thea tells him about zip-lining and shares stories about her fellow travellers that she knows will make him roll his eyes and laugh. She doesn't swim with the turtles. Their lives continue. They both see ghosts. In marketplaces, in city streets, in dreams.

Thea notices all the things that are running out — her money, the year, time, the land. She lets herself be pulled down the isthmus like slow-moving water down a drain. It's December when she gets to Panama City, the narrow link between two great continents. She hasn't thought beyond this point. She just hears the echo of Sarah's words, 'We said we'd make it all the way to Panama.'

Her round-the-world ticket expires in less than two weeks. She can extend it, but not without cost, and her money's running low. The world is still gripped by the GFC, and she knows it's time to head home, find work, make a life. It's the sensible thing to do, and surely there's still work for physiotherapists in a financial crisis? People get injured, and people get old, no matter what the state of the economy. But heading home means falling into empty spaces, crevasses in a landscape once held together by family and friends. It means facing up to reality and living some version of the life she once thought she'd have — a job, a place to live, things to fill up evenings and weekends. She's not ready. But she can't imagine retracing her steps back north up the isthmus, revisiting places she's been before, as though trying to unwind the events of the past months.

South America lies within tantalising reach. Stretching east to west for weeks and north to south for months, it offers endless possibilities to drift in a suspended reality. But between here and there, there's an expanse of blank space on the map — the Darién Province, where the Pan-American highway literally stops in the middle of the jungle. Flights are too expensive on the dregs of her savings. With that option gone, the guidebook reads like a choose-your-own adventure novel — pick a path between danger and sickness at sea or along the rivers. Parts of Thea's trip have been adventurous, with a certain carelessness for personal safety, but she knows she's not that intrepid, or quite that reckless. She's not ready to head home, but perhaps she'll never be ready. Maybe now's as good a time as any.

She takes the first step towards home: she opens the email chain from Magda. She's been ignoring Magda's messages since she heard about Sarah, as though telling someone from her life outside Central America will underscore its permanence. It won't be a memory that she can pack away like an ugly souvenir; it will be another experience forever inked onto her skin. But Magda's emails are piling up and she knows it's unfair of her to leave them unanswered; in fact, unread. The first message is just Magda's usual check-in, responding to Thea's last email and sharing some of her own new life in Wellington. Then there are a couple of gentle nudges from her: *I haven't heard from you for a little while . . . Just thought I'd say hello . . . I hope you're having fun . . .* until *I hope you're OK?* And finally, *I'm worried about you darling, please get in touch.* Thea checks how many minutes remain of the time she's paid for at the internet café then clicks 'Reply'.

She sits back, drained — exhausted, but there's relief in it, like taking your pack off at the end of a long day in the hills and, although it's still filled with all the things you've carried, the weight has been set aside for a time. She lets herself think about the grey-green blue-grey textures of home.

There's one more place to go before she heads back to New Zealand. She wants to stand beside Sarah's grave and say goodbye. She wants to visit Sarah's family and let them know how much she talked about them, how much she missed them. She can't tell them about Sarah's last moments, but she can tell them about her final weeks. It's not much, but perhaps it's something to give a tangibility to that last bit of her life lived out so far away from them.

There are international flights to Sydney or to Melbourne. Of course, she chooses Melbourne. She sends Chris a message to let him know she'll be passing through. She doesn't mention her plan to visit Sarah's home town. There's no need to bring up ghosts when he's starting to sound settled. She'll fly in to Melbourne, catch up with Chris; fly across to Perth and bus down to Margaret River, say goodbye to Sarah; then — at last — home to Auckland, to unpack the past.

8

Melbourne, Australia, 2007

As soon as she steps off the Sky Bus in downtown Melbourne and sees Chris, Thea feels that same electrifying bolt of attraction that used to crackle through her in San Pedro. It burns off the jet lag. She'd been hesitant about seeing him after all this time and, more than that, nervous about seeing him in his regular life. She wonders if he'll have time for her — he must have lots of friends in the city. She's been looking forward to hanging out, but maybe he's just offering her a couch for a few nights out of politeness. But by the time they get to Chris's flat, they've slipped into the ease of days when they had nothing more to worry about than where to go for dinner; it's as though seeing each other in a different country has deepened their friendship, the kilometres acting in place of years.

Night after night, they sit on the couch in Chris's flat, rehashing memories and old jokes, talking about books and the random things that flow through their thoughts. Talking about everything but Sarah. She's there in the room with them, though; from time to time, Thea feels the air dip, as though Sarah's just perched herself on the armrest beside her.

This Chris — who stays up late, a drink in hand, a story to tell, who lifts the mood of a room when he walks in — is a flashback to Guatemala. Sometimes Chris's housemates join them, sharing meals, sharing stories, and making Thea feel like she's part of the life that they all have together.

In the mornings the housemates tiptoe around her, getting ready for work as she sleeps tangled under a sheet on the couch. Often Chris is already gone by the time Thea wakes up, and this other Chris — who works in an office all day, who runs before or after work, who cooks healthy meals — is someone to get used to. It's like seeing his reflection in a teaspoon. Thea likes this version. If he can settle back into normal life, perhaps she can do it, too.

During the days while Chris is at work, Thea passes hours walking around Melbourne, through the botanic gardens and past large brick and stone buildings. One day she walks through the inner suburbs, another day she pushes through the city rush. Wherever she is, she notices physiotherapy clinics, imagining herself into days crammed with appointments and rushed coffee breaks. She takes the tram to St Kilda and sits beside the ocean, looking out to where she thinks New Zealand must be. She pictures the expanse of grey sea stretching out for miles until it washes up on the flat black sands of Muriwai. She imagines stepping out of the sea and walking with sandy feet up the road to the house where she once lived. When Chris works late, she sits in the small courtyard of his flat, watching bats drift like flakes of ash against the darkening sky.

After she's been in Melbourne for a week, Thea turns towards Chris while they're sitting on the couch, just the two of them, and says, 'I was thinking of going to Margaret River. I want to see Sarah's grave. I thought I'd see her family, too, maybe her friend Hayley.' She says it like it's something she's considering, a plan that's just forming in her mind; she doesn't tell Chris that her need to say goodbye to Sarah, to send her off in a way she couldn't while drifting through Central America, is the reason she diverted through Australia.

'Do you really want to put yourself through that, Thee?' Chris asks her.

'Well, obviously I'd rather not. But I need to.' Beyond words she wishes that there wasn't another grave for her to visit, but since there is, she can't ignore it. She doesn't know how to explain it properly, so she fills the pause that follows with words that sound right but aren't really an explanation. 'I haven't really said goodbye.'

'Sitting by a grave and saying goodbye isn't going to magically make you feel better,' Chris says. 'It doesn't close a door on everything.'

'I know that,' she responds. She holds that knowledge bone-deep. 'But it feels like the right thing to do.'

He huffs, a note of dismissal breathed into the air. 'If you must. But to see her family?'

'It's the right thing to do,' she repeats. It's more than that. Sarah's future was ripped from her family. They don't get the chance to be proud of her for all the things she was yet to do, all the ways she was going to change the lives of other people. They don't get to watch her children play with their cousins at family picnics, to wipe ice cream off their faces or tell them bedtime stories. They lost all of her future, but they also lost the tapering-off months of her present. They got a phone call now and then, emails and perhaps a postcard, but they didn't get hours of sitting across a table from her, or walking up and down a hill, arm in arm. Thea wasn't there at the very end, but she can tell Sarah's family the stories behind the photographs on Sarah's camera; she can tell them where she bought that skirt, this scarf, those bracelets; she can tell them about how much Sarah smiled and laughed and danced in the weeks before she died. Thea can fill in some of the gaps for them, bright brushstrokes of happy memories. Or maybe it's not for them; maybe it's just something she needs to do for herself.

'I spent a couple of days with them in Guatemala City.' Chris looks down. 'With her dad and brother, anyway. It was horrible.'

'I can imagine,' Thea says. At least, she can imagine a version of it: A foreign city. Your girlfriend dead. Meeting her family for the first time. The sense of being so absolutely adrift, but at the same time trapped, no way to get out.

'No, I mean, they blamed me, Thee.' He looks up into her face. 'They thought it was my fault.'

It was your fault. Thea can hear the whisper of those words. What are the right words to say in response, to break the repeating echo through time? It wasn't your fault? Thea breathes in, to collect the words inside her, but all she says is, 'They were upset.'

It doesn't really matter what she says, Chris talks on as though she hasn't said anything. 'They said it was my fault that she died. It was my fault she was there in the first place. It was my fault that I didn't protect her.'

It's true that Sarah was there because Chris was there; she may never have gone to San Pedro, and would never have stayed, if he hadn't been there. She doesn't know why Sarah was at the lake, by herself, at night. It's not like Thea thinks women shouldn't go places on their own — both she and Sarah did that all the time — but it seems so unlike Sarah to roam alone along the dark lakefront. Thea couldn't bring herself to ask Chris in an email why he wasn't there with her, but it's something that she still wants to know. She steadies herself to ask now, but when she meets his eyes, the watery uncertainty she sees there tips her off balance. She's never seen him cry, never even thought to imagine it of him, although that seems stupid now; of course, he's cried. She wants to reach up and wipe away his tears before they fall. She wants to reach out and hold him close so she doesn't have to see the sadness pulling his face into unfamiliar shapes. He had no idea what would happen when he told Sarah to meet him in San Pedro; he couldn't predict how tragically it would all turn out; he would have done everything differently if he had known.

She doesn't reach for him, but she does say, 'I'm sure they didn't mean it. People say all sorts of things they don't mean when they're upset.'

Chris gives a series of tiny nods, almost a tremble, his eyes fixed on his hands clasped in the space between his knees. Thea thinks again of reaching out to him, of putting a hand on his. Then he looks back up, at her. 'They might blame you, too,' he says. 'You left.'

She can't believe he said that. It's like he's picked up his drink and thrown it in her face then coolly leaned back as though nothing happened.

The truth is, Thea does blame herself a little. She did leave. She knew that Chris was busy working, that Sarah was getting restless, had talked about exploring more. If Thea had stayed, Sarah wouldn't have been on her own, walking up and down the hill between the Xaman Ek and the village, wandering along the streets and paths of San Pedro, finding ways to pass the hours by herself. Perhaps Sarah was right — Chris would've left soon anyway; he just needed to warm up to the idea, to make the decision on his own. Perhaps Thea should have been more patient. Maybe she should have been more insistent. But it's not her fault. It's not. Chris stayed. Chris was there. It was Chris who wasn't looking out for Sarah.

Chris must see the look of shock on her face, the anger in the breath she draws. Before she gives voice to it, Chris speaks again. 'It's not what I think. I'm only saying what they might say. I don't want you to get hurt.'

There's truth in his words. Perhaps Sarah's parents read through Sarah's emails after she died, trying to make sense of what happened or to reclaim those last months and weeks of their daughter's life. What would they have seen in Thea's messages to Sarah? Did she ask if she was OK? Did she tell her to be safe? Did she discourage her from going to dark and empty places by herself? Or did she encourage her to get out more? Suggest places to go? She could go back and check those messages, but she's scared of how careless, or worse, her words might have been.

Maybe Sarah's family will blame her, but Thea needs to take her guilt to them. If they choose to wrap it tight around her until she can't breathe, then so be it. Most of all, Thea needs to throw it in handfuls on Sarah's grave. If she's truly honest with herself, she's not sure that, in normal circumstances, she and Sarah would have been friends — or, at least, she's not certain that their friendship would have lasted through the years or even months. She imagines it diluting, once they parted, getting weaker the farther they went from San Pedro until it was washed away completely in the vast Pacific Ocean on their separate journeys home. But there's a difference between people drifting apart and the sudden tearing of someone from your life. She didn't realise she would miss Sarah so much until she was gone. She needs to tell Sarah she misses her. She needs to tell Sarah how sorry she is.

There are memories that Thea's kept unexamined for months, pushing them down deep underwater until she's strong enough. She can feel them now, a thousand tiny air bubbles rising to the surface whether she's ready or not. A reminder that hidden things still exist. She casts around for something solid — the here and now of a glass in her hand, the armrest against her hip, Chris's thigh against the sofa cushion.

She rests her eyes on the bend of his knee, the small dark hairs breaking through the skin. Then she pictures, underneath the skin, the bones and ligaments. She recites them in her mind — the patella, the femur, the fibula and tibia; the lateral and medial collateral ligaments; the lateral and medial meniscus. She feels the dip in the sofa as he shifts his weight, rolling onto his hip and resting his elbow on the back of the sofa, facing her. She breathes and internally recites the muscles of the upper leg: the sartorius, the rectus femoris, the vastus lateralis and medialis that make up the quadriceps. His knee moves close to hers. She moves inwards, onto the muscles of the groin: the obturator, gracilis, pectineus, and the four adductor muscles.

'Stay,' Chris says, leaning in towards Thea.

His knee bumps hers. The light touch of skin against skin. Then the hard pressure of bone against bone, as he leans closer. His knee braces against hers as the rest of his body angles in towards her. He runs his hand through her hair, once. He kisses her.

She's frozen in place, but beneath her skin everything's buzzing, excitement conflicting with doubt, opposing forces causing chaos in her stilled body. His eyes, so close to hers, still damp, are seeking an answer. This is wrong. She knows this is wrong. 'I'll only be gone a few days,' she says, her lips still touching his, her surprise unspoken. 'I'll be back. My flight home is out of Melbourne.'

'Stay here,' he says.

Does it matter if this is wrong? She'll be gone soon, back to New Zealand. This is nothing, this doesn't have to mean anything. She lets the excitement ripple through her. They're connected now at the lips, a hand, a knee.

'In Melbourne,' he says. He kisses her again and doesn't stop. Their bodies are pressed together now. A hand to a face, reaching around to the back of a head, through hair. A leg crossed over a leg. Chris pulls her down on top of him. They're joined from ankle to hip to chin, even when they roll to lie side by side, facing each other, then over again so that he's on top of her. Thea can no longer identify the specific points at which their bodies touch.

The ghost of Sarah leaves the room.

☆ ☆ ☆

Four days later when they're lying in Chris's bed, the morning sun bright on the sheet, Thea brings it up again. 'You could come too,' she says. 'To Margaret River.'

'You can't just turn up there, Thea. Not at Christmas time.'

'No, I know,' she says. 'But after.'

'What? You're gonna be like "Happy New Year. I'm here to remind you of how shit last year was"? I think you should stay away. Let them move on with their lives.'

Thea knows that turning up at Christmas time, a reminder of someone's dead daughter, sister, niece, grandchild, like some kind of Dickensian ghost, is not a good idea. She doesn't need Chris to tell her that. She knows too well what it's like to spend the festive season without your loved ones, how hard it will be for them just to get through this year. But would January be too bad? There's never going to be a good time. If she goes now, she's inflicting fresh pain. She's a face they don't know, a reminder to Sarah's family that at the end there were parts of Sarah's life they didn't know. If she waits — what? a year? two? five? — it's insulting that she didn't visit sooner. She should've gone when she first arrived.

She didn't expect Chris to be so opposed to the idea, but if Sarah's family blamed him, maybe they were crueller than he's saying. She shouldn't have tried to make him go with her; of course he wouldn't want to do that. It's just been so great hanging out with him, so nice to have that feeling again that there was someone in the world who understood her. Maybe going over the Christmas break isn't such a bad idea after all: if she goes while he's visiting his family, it takes the pressure off. 'I think I'll head there anyway,' she says to him. 'I need to go somewhere for Christmas, so I'll spend a few days at the beach then visit on one of those empty days between Christmas and New Year's Eve.'

She hasn't told Chris but, while she's been spending time with him in Melbourne, trying to work out a plan to visit Sarah's grave, her round-the-world ticket has expired. She wasn't all that worried — it's always been possible to get a cheap flight across the Tasman. Just — as it turns out — not at Christmas, or at the last minute. There'll be some kind of New Year's sale; she just needs to stay until then and cross her fingers that domestic flights are affordable. Thea isn't in a hurry to get back to New Zealand. Magda invited her to spend Christmas in Wellington, and she's touched by the gesture but, as much as she loves Magda, Magda's family is Magda's family, not Thea's. She'd rather be by herself than feel alone surrounded by someone else's relatives. Going to

Margaret River gives her a good reason to say no to Magda.

'Stay here for Christmas,' Chris says to her, brushing his thumb against her lips, pulling her bottom lip down. 'In my bed.'

'What? While you're away? It's not a hostel, Chris. Your flatmates mightn't be so keen on that idea.' Chris's housemates have been amazingly welcoming and tolerant, and she's tried to be a good guest, but they probably don't want her hanging around if Chris isn't there.

'You'll have the place to yourself. Min and Angie will both be away. You can walk around in nothing but tinsel, or whatever your traditions are.' He trails his fingertips over her bare skin. 'I'll only be gone a few days. My limit with *la familia* is about two days, four if you allow for travel on either side, but even that's a stretch. Min's throwing a New Year's party in a warehouse by the river. We can go to that then head off camping for a few days. Sound good?' He shifts his weight so he's closer to her, grasps her chin and kisses her. His hand moves down, over her breast.

It does sound good. It sounds better than she had ever imagined. 'Sure, why not,' she says to him, as his fingertips walk farther down her body and he slides down under the sheet beside her.

☆ ☆ ☆

After Christmas, Chris is back from Sydney and they're out for brunch at the local café. They've pushed their dirty plates to the side to make room for the newspaper they're reading. Chris is reading the world news. Thea has been flicking through the weekend Lifestyle supplement, looking for the crossword, but has paused on a page advertising cheap flights to Western Australia. Her eyes flick to the blue-yellow ad, a picture of a woman underwater, swimming among bright tropical fish, the yellow sand like sunshine beneath her. She hadn't meant to linger on the image long enough for Chris to notice, but when he speaks, she looks up and sees his eyes resting on the page.

'Come to Tasmania,' he says.

She's caught off-guard by his words, her fingertips pinching the corner of the page, about to turn it. The effect is as though she's lifting it up to show him. 'What? Camping?' she asks.

'To live,' Chris says.

'What?' She half-laughs, turning the page over.

'I'm moving there.'

'What? When? *Since* when?'

'I've been thinking about it for a while, but I only just decided. I told you, too much time with the family and I try to get as far away as possible.' Chris explains that his firm is setting up a new division in Hobart and has asked him if he wants to transfer to the new office. 'Seriously, it's a great opportunity. It's a promotion. Exciting work too.'

'I had no idea you were thinking about moving. Why didn't you mention it before?' There's a lot she wants to ask but needs a moment to sort through all her thoughts. He's only just arrived in Melbourne and now he's leaving. He was practically in San Pedro longer than he's been here.

Chris ignores her question. 'Come on, Thee, come with me.

You'll love it there. The landscape's wild — mountains, lakes and beaches and all that stuff you love. A third of the island or something is national park. There are even vineyards if you want to be more sophisticated.'

Thea's heard about the cram of wild beauty in Tasmania. You can't grow up with a father like hers and not know about the peaks that jut out across the island, as though all of Australia's mountains were packed into one corner and pushed out to sea. Or not know about the towering stacks of dolomite that people climb while the sea crashes up against the rock in foaming white and birds swoop past. Tasmania is where her parents spent their honeymoon, camping on the central plateau. As a teenager, Thea had endlessly hassled her dad about it. 'I can't believe you took Mum to Tasmania for your honeymoon. What a treat. How romantic, Dad.'

'Your mum loved it. She said Tasmania was shaped like a human heart. So we pitched our tent as close to the centre as we could. How's that for romantic?' Even as a teenager, Thea had to admit that her parents looked wildly happy in the photos — her mum kneeling by a camp stove, the orange tent behind her no match for the fiery sky stretched to the edges of the frame; another of her parents, arms around each other and smiling, as though they were unaware of Barn Bluff looming like a tombstone behind them.

It was on that holiday that her father had come up with his plan to climb the one hundred and fifty highest mountains in Tasmania. Thea had no idea how many he'd actually crossed off before he died. All she remembered was their running joke that continued even when she was much too old for it: every time he went on a trip, he told her that he was off to visit Janet. 'Who's Janet?' she would ask on cue. 'You know,' he said 'our friend Janet the Gannet.'

Sitting in the crowded café with the clatter of crockery and cutlery, Thea is suddenly back at the tākapu refuge on the cliffs of Muriwai. 'Let's welcome the tākapu home,' her father used to say to her at the start of every season, as the birds came in off the Tasman, back from the rocky islands off the coast of Tasmania and Victoria where they spend half the year. 'Look, that one's new,' he'd say, pointing at one particular bird among the many. 'The one with the yellow head. Say hello.'

'Is this their home or is Australia their home?' Thea had asked.

'Both places are. You might do that when you're older. You might fly off somewhere far away for a while. And that will be your home when you're there, wherever you are. But I hope my little gannet will always come back home to Mum and me.' Thea would spread her arms out wide and run off up the path away from her dad before turning and sprinting back to him, dive-bombing into his open arms.

'OK Mr Tourism Tasmania, I'll read the brochures later,' she says to Chris. 'But important details first — like, when are you going?'

'Couple of weeks. I have to give two weeks' notice on the flat. The sooner I get over there, the better. I want to be there from the get-go. New year, new city, new role.'

She still can't believe he hasn't mentioned it until now, but she supposes he needed to be sure about inviting her before he said anything; his head must be as muddled as hers with what's happening between them. Thea is ashamed — ashamed of both herself and Chris. It's been just over three months since Sarah died. It feels so much longer, but it's been no time at all. Thea thinks again of distance standing in place of time. There are countries between her present circumstances and Sarah's death, so much land and water. If Sarah were here, now, on this continent, Chris wouldn't be with Thea. But she can't help it. For all his faults, Thea thinks she loves him. There's no one who makes her laugh like he does. There's no one who gets her like he does. He understands her need to keep moving from place to place, drifting like a piece of shipwreck on ocean currents, and he doesn't need to ask why. He knows that some people have things that they're not proud of, things that they don't want to talk about. If she doesn't have him, who does she have?

There was something between her and Chris before Sarah arrived, a natural attraction that would have flourished if Chris hadn't been with Sarah. She's sure there was. Although she'd a hundred times rather have Sarah with them still, if every tragedy has to have a silver lining, this is it. And Thea's not entirely sure about this next part, if she were to dwell on it, but she thinks Sarah would be happy for them — in the circumstances as they are. Sarah was all about happiness and wouldn't want her friends to punish themselves, to deny themselves their own happiness, because of her. Of course it would all be different if Sarah were still alive, of course it would, but she's not and now the living have to move on as best they can. And, in any case, it's done now.

They've already betrayed her, nothing they do can change that. Wouldn't it be worse if it was all for nothing?

In those few weeks leading up to Christmas, Thea had been starting to get a feel for Melbourne: its imposing gothic architecture; the weight of an immense, dry continent stretching out behind the city in one direction; the tidal tug of the sea in the other. She had started imagining what it would be like to call the city home. But now, with Chris announcing he's moving away, Melbourne feels empty and edgeless: a vast sprawl disappearing into the dusty land around it. It's just another place she's visiting; just another place she'll leave.

When it comes down to it, she can't think of a reason not to go to Tasmania with Chris. Her life is already packed up. There's no need to head home — her ticket has well and truly expired. Her funds are obviously even more depleted now, but while Australia hasn't entirely escaped the global financial crisis, it's doing better than other places. There's probably more chance of getting a job in Tasmania than in New Zealand. Even if it doesn't work out with Chris, it'll be fun. She's got nothing to lose.

'So, whaddya think? Are you going to come with me?' Chris entwines his fingers with hers across the table. She's silent, the thoughts still flipping through her mind. 'I need you, Thee.' Chris squeezes her hand and leans towards her.

'Sure, why not?' Thea says. And then they're laughing, caught up in the delight of a new place to go, a new adventure, a future together. They start making plans. He tells her about his job, about Hobart, the history, the festivals. She tells him about her parents' honeymoon, and her dad's unfulfilled lifetime goal. They talk about potential road trips across and around the island.

'Let's head home,' Chris says, slapping the table with his free hand and standing up, his other hand still entangled with Thea's. 'Let's check out ads for houses to rent. Let's find you a job. We'll pick up something on the way home to celebrate.' He lets go of her hand and pulls her whole body in close to his to kiss her. 'It's going to be great,' he says. 'A whole new life.'

He's right, Thea thinks. It's a fresh start, but one in which they'll have each other. Western Australia will always be there. Once she's settled in Hobart, and Sarah's death isn't so raw, she can make a trip across the strait and across the continent to sit by a grave beside a river.

☆ ☆ ☆

The next few weeks are a flurry of activity as Chris packs, Thea writes her CV and applies for jobs, and they jointly look through rental listings. They decide to get a place for just the two of them. Thea questions whether they should find a room in an existing house so they can make friends — neither of them knows anyone in Tasmania — but, 'You know how annoying other people are to live with,' Chris says to Thea. 'What was it you always said? "Friends for a day, but no more than that"?'

'That was when travelling. Living with people is different.'

Chris points out that they'll soon be meeting people through work and other things. Then, 'Imagine a whole place for just the two of us. It could be Christmas all year round — every day you could wear nothing but tinsel.'

'I don't know where you got the idea that I do that.' Thea laughs.

'In my head,' he tells her. 'It's an image I definitely have in my head. Let me tell you about some of my *Chris*-mas traditions,' he says, grabbing her and pushing her up against the kitchen bench.

☆ ☆ ☆

And then Thea's saying goodbye to a place she's never really been as she watches Geelong recede into the distance from the car ferry. She watches the wide stretch of the sky and the broad plane of the sea layered on top of each other, separated only by a thin slice of flat land. In her short time in Melbourne, Thea's come to love the vibrancy of the city, the café-stuffed laneways and restaurant-filled nights, but she's never got used to the flatness of the place. The thought of Tasmania excites her, with its bush-clad mountains, rocky towers and the sea in all directions. She looks for a moment longer at the mainland, picturing Sarah standing on the shore. She turns her back and gazes out across the Bass Strait in the direction of Tasmania. She forgets that ghosts can cross water and that hidden things still exist.

On the long ferry ride, she alternately brushes up on human anatomy and physiology, preparing for the job interview she's got lined up, and studies the large fold-out map of Tasmania with Chris, tracing the drive they'll do the next day. Tomorrow they'll slice right through the heart of Tasmania, driving from Devonport to Hobart, putting a sea and an island between Melbourne and their new lives.

Midway through the journey, Thea goes out on deck for a break. Arms braced against the railing, she leans into the salty space between a place she's left behind and the place she's going. All around her, water stretches towards unseen land. Above, a single gannet coasts across the clean blue sky.

PART 2

9

Wellington, New Zealand, 2015

Thea pulls herself through the water, arm over arm, legs kicking. The harbour is glass-still on the surface but underneath jellyfish drift through the water like untethered moons. She tries to avoid the white-purple shapes as they pulse out of the dark sea into her orbit. The gelatinous slide of them against her skin makes her shudder; at least they don't sting. It's what else might glide through the depths, unseen but still there, that keeps her close to shore when she swims alone. Although she tries to focus her mind on the smooth in and out of her breath, she can't help thinking of the dark wave of a stingray shadowing her, the slow rippling inhale and exhale of its fins.

She glances up to sight the pontoon, adjusts her course, and puts her head back down. When she gets there, she pulls herself up onto it, windmilling her right arm to loosen her serratus anterior while she turns in a slow half-circle to take in the city. As a child she used to look at postcards and think that Auckland and Wellington were twin cities, skyscrapers stacked around the harbour. As she grew older, she often heard Auckland compared to Sydney, and Wellington to Melbourne. She can see that, but Wellington reminds her more of Hobart now. Both cities cling to rugged hills, buildings gripping against the tumble into the sea, people braced against weather that sweeps up from Antarctica. She feels both at home and homesick here.

Turning back towards the beach, she sees Magda. Her arm is raised above her head, an exaggerated wave to catch Thea's attention. Thea smiles: Magda's long cobalt blue skirt is enough of a beacon. She waves back before diving off the pontoon and swimming to shore.

'Good swim?' Magda asks as she hands Thea a towel.

'Always,' Thea replies. 'Good walk?' she asks Magda.

'Always,' Magda replies. 'Coffee?'

'Always,' Thea replies and they both laugh. They wander back along the beach to the changing rooms where Thea gets dressed while Magda orders the drinks. They sit at one of the small tables facing the playground and the sea.

Thea passes her phone to Magda, opened on a property listing. 'This is the one Chris is looking at today,' she tells Magda. She takes a small sip of her coffee then sets it aside and leans forward to look at the photos as Magda scrolls through. 'It looks nice,' she adds, although she doesn't know why she said it. It's obviously nice, all sleek surfaces, polished like the harbour on a still summer's night. It looks like something from a magazine, like somewhere they could host Christmas drinks.

She's told Magda this part of the truth: that after all these years of living in Tasmania, they've finally decided to call it home. 'We should've have done it ages ago,' she says to Magda now, repeating the words that she and Chris have said to each other several times.

It's true, financially it would've been the sensible thing to do. But who knew that a year or two would become eight. 'I'll just do two years there. Max,' Chris had said when they were planning for the move. 'It's less hierarchical, so I'll be doing work I wouldn't get the chance to do in Sydney or Melbourne. Fuck photocopying and proofreading for two years.' Thea can't remember now if she had such a fixed timeframe in mind. She was just letting each month sweep under her and, before she knew it, the cyclical swell of a year had passed, twelve months washing by just like that. Once the first year had been and gone, the others flowed on almost without notice. Now, all these years later, she can look back and see how far time has carried them from where they started.

'It's beautiful,' Magda says as she gives Thea back her phone. 'You'd love all that light.'

The part of the truth that she hasn't told Magda is that she's not entirely sure she wants to buy a house. She's not certain that she's ready to call Tasmania home in such a permanent way. But that sounds wrong, even when she just thinks it to herself. She loves Tasmania and has made herself a good life there. She loves her work. She's got a fantastic circle of friends and, at the centre of the circle, two of the best friends she's ever had. Thea had met Liz and Kirra when she was new to the island, still in travel mode and readily striking up conversations with strangers — at the pool, in her art class. They'd come into each other's lives at just the right time, and had fallen into a quick friendship, first over drinks, then weekend walks and, before they'd known each other very long at all, they'd organised a weekend away with plans for more to come. Aren't friends what make a place a home?

She glances down at her screen, still open on a photo of the main living space. She could be happy there, for a while, in that room with large windows looking out across a patchwork of rooftops towards the sea. And, in any case, a house is just a house. Houses can be sold. She flicks to the next photo.

She's not convinced she wants to buy a house with Chris.

That's another part of the truth she hasn't told Magda. She's hardly ready to admit it to herself, and is definitely not ready to say it aloud. But if she's honest with herself, it's what brought her here, back to New Zealand. She came to see Magda, of course. But she also came to give herself space with this thought, to see if it keeps drifting past or if it settles into permanent orbit.

'It looks more Chris's style than yours,' Magda says, as she watches Thea.

Until she's clear in her own mind, Thea doesn't want to hear what Magda thinks she should do. Or not do. She's never quite known what Magda thinks of Chris.

When Magda's come to visit, Thea's sometimes walked into a room and seen Magda and Chris laughing like the greatest of old friends — it's not unusual for Chris to find ways to crack people up — but she's also caught Magda observing him the way you keep an eye on a cat sunning itself in the same room as the Christmas ham. She's not sure what to make of it but she does appreciate having someone look out for her, especially since Magda's technically not even family.

Although Magda's come to Hobart several times over the years, more often than not they've met in Sydney or Melbourne, enjoying a long weekend of art galleries, restaurants and cafés. Chris doesn't join them on those trips but he always surprises them with tickets to a show, or a voucher for a spa treatment, or something else that neither Thea nor Magda would arrange for themselves.

And every year, Magda invites them to spend Christmas in Wellington. They've never taken her up on the offer. Thea doesn't think Magda's ever really expected her and Chris to accept, but she appreciates how Magda makes a point of always letting Thea know she's welcome. Welcome anytime, not just Christmas; Magda has made that clear, too. 'You don't even need to let me know you're coming,' Magda has said to her in the past, holding both of her hands and looking her in the eye. 'If you just turned up on my doorstep unannounced, I'd welcome you with wide open arms. You can stay as long as you need. You know that, don't you?'

It wasn't until more than a year had passed after getting together with Chris that Thea met any of his family, and that was only by chance. She had ducked out from the clinic one day to get a sandwich, and had seen Chris sitting at a table outside a restaurant with a grey-haired man. She smiled and waved at Chris, but hadn't wanted to interrupt, assuming it was a work lunch of some description — a colleague or a client. The other man must've caught the greeting between them and asked Chris who she was. As she was walking away, she heard her name called out. She turned and followed the quick flick of the older man's wrist back to the table.

'So you're the mythical Thea,' the older man had said, standing up and holding his hand out to her.

'This is my father, Bill,' Chris said, also standing.

Thea tried not to show her surprise. She had no idea that Chris's father — Invisi-Bill, as she called him when talking to Liz and Kirra — was in Tasmania. She smiled and shook his hand. He was the kind of man who made you feel like you should add 'sir' to the end of your sentences. 'Nice to meet you,' Thea had said.

'Join us, Thea. Cath and I have heard all about you but we were starting to think you didn't exist. Have a seat.' Bill gestured at Chris's chair. 'Chris, find a waiter. Get us moved to a bigger table.'

'I can't stay,' Thea had explained, but sat as Bill sat back down.

'So, Thea, you're not a fan of Sydney?' Bill focused his attention on her and Thea felt a pulse of shock as she looked into amber eyes just like Chris's.

'I like Sydney,' Thea said, trying to work out where the comment had come from, where the conversation was going. 'It's a beautiful city. I haven't spent much time there though, and not for years.'

'We would've shown you around if you'd come for Christmas. Taken you to Bondi, Taronga Zoo, the Opera House.'

As far as Thea was aware, they hadn't been invited to Chris's parents' place the previous Christmas. She and Chris had been excited about having their first Christmas together, just the two of them. They'd spent a small fortune on nice food and had a picnic at the beach, popping the bottle of bubbles on the sand before carrying it into the sea to drink. 'To keep it cold,' they agreed. She still remembers it as one of her favourite Christmases. Not just because it was theirs alone, but because they were at their best — shimmering with a carefree haze of happiness, at ease with each other and not thinking beyond the day they were in.

Bill had gone on to talk about how much better Sydney was than Hobart — how much warmer, how much more beautiful, how the sailing and job opportunities were so much better, and then how backwards Hobart was, how far away from everything, and how hard it was to find a restaurant that knows how to cook steak — insinuating, it seemed to Thea, that it was in her power to make Chris move to Sydney, that she was the one who had made him move to Tasmania. She had nodded and smiled and laughed when he laughed and, after twenty long minutes, when the men's meals were put down on the table, had excused herself and headed back to the clinic, hungry. She had known from their time together in Guatemala that Chris didn't get on with his father. After that encounter, she understood why.

'My father likes you,' Chris had said, later that night.

Thea laughed. 'I don't think that can be true.' Chris had already told her how, if he and his brother ever got injured playing sport as teenagers, Bill told them to 'move through the pain'.

'It's true. He said that he'll talk to a physio he knows about opportunities in Sydney.'

'Great.'

'He's been to a physio, once. For a bad back.'

'OK.'

'Complained that they didn't do anything. Came home and said they charged him for the pleasure of looking at him, then told him to do a bunch of exercises on his own.'

'I told you he didn't like me,' Thea said.

'No, now he's saying how miraculous it was. Healed after one visit. He actually mentioned *investing* in you, if you want to move to Sydney and start your own practice.' Chris had smirked and raised his eyebrows. 'Whaddya think? Keen?'

'So keen,' Thea responded dryly.

'I like Hobart,' Chris said.

'I like Hobart too,' Thea had said.

Months later, as the first rays of Christmas were appearing on the year's horizon, Thea had asked Chris what he wanted to do that year — if they should spend the holidays with his family. 'Fuck no,' he'd said, not even looking up from whatever it was that he'd been doing. She hadn't exactly been enthusiastic about the idea of Christmas with them herself but they were his family and, for better or for worse, you should hold on to the family that you have.

'My dad's a jerk, Thee,' he'd bluntly told her when she pushed the idea. 'He's a mean, controlling alcoholic and Mum's never done anything to help. She's always on his side.'

Thea had known not to ask about it — at least, not right then. 'What about your brother? Don't you want to see your nephew?' she asked instead.

'Ant's a carbon copy of my dad. In every way. That kid of his is going to have the exact same childhood that we did. It's painful to watch.'

'Well, we could go to Wellington,' Thea had said, each word a stepping stone towards a suggestion. 'Magda's invited us.'

'Yeah, maybe,' Chris said, wrapping his arms around her from behind. 'But wouldn't it be nice to go somewhere warm?' He put his hand over her mouth before she could respond. 'Like, *actually* warm, Kiwi.' Then he grasped her upper arms and spun her around. 'What about Bali? Or Vanuatu? It's time we got on a plane again, don't you think?'

'You pack the sunscreen, I'll pack the tinsel.' She grinned at him.

'So much sexier than a raincoat and a beanie,' he'd said, his mouth pressed to hers as he walked her backwards into the bedroom.

The following year, they couldn't avoid a couple of days in Sydney over the holidays but the year after that they booked a trip to Noosa. After that, they alternated: Carrington family Christmas one year, a trip away the next. Those Sydney years were never fun, but also not as bad as Thea had first imagined; you just had to stick to the script and know when to slowly walk off stage. In contrast, the trips away are always great — their regular lives are folded away for a week or two and they slip straight back into travel mode, become the truest versions of themselves.

☆ ☆ ☆

Thea and Magda walk along the waterfront to the museum. Its polished floors remind Thea of the house Chris is viewing, with its black stone bench top and copper pots on display. It really is more his style. He will definitely be assessing its suitability for hosting people: his colleagues, not hers. In the lead-up to Christmas, she has the one work function — a picnic or a casual lunch with the rest of the team. Chris has back-to-back events, seemingly the same colleagues and clients drinking in bigger or smaller groups.

He will be considering whether his parents and his brother will be impressed, whether one day they'll agree to spend Christmas with them in Hobart.

Anyway, they won't be hosting anyone this Christmas. This year, they're finally doing the Overland Track, sixty-five kilometres through the wild heart of the island. Thea has camped and walked, in shorter bursts, in various parks across the island but hasn't yet done the iconic walk that brings people to Tasmania. It's a far cry from their usual tropical holidays and they'll definitely be packing raincoats and beanies for this one. It's more Thea's thing than Chris's, so it surprised her when he suggested it earlier in the year.

They'd been in a taxi heading home after dinner with friends.

It was July and raining so hard that the city outside the car had almost disappeared into the white sheets of water. 'Your kind of weather,' Chris had joked. 'I bet you wish we were walking home. Should I ask the driver to pull over?' He leaned forward towards the gap between the front seats.

'No!' Thea put a hand on his shoulder to pull him back. 'I'm wet enough.'

Chris raised his eyebrows, night-time city shadows moving across his face. 'Well then.' He leaned forward again and spoke to the driver. 'Excuse me, could you go a bit faster? We're in a bit of a hurry to get home.'

'No we're not. Ignore him.' She gave Chris an amused warning look but then reached across the gap between them and put her hand on his knee. Through his jeans, she rubbed her fingers around the hard edge of his patella.

'Speaking of things you like to do,' Chris relaxed back into the seat, 'I was thinking we could do the Overland in December. Whaddya think?'

'Really? That'd be great.' She gave his knee a squeeze of excitement. Then she pulled her hand away and pressed both her palms against her own thighs. 'You do realise it's six days, right? Sharing huts with a bunch of random people?' Saying it aloud, she realised even more just how much he'd hate it.

'I thought we could do it in four days,' he said. That made sense to Thea. Hiking in the great outdoors for hours, let alone days, was not his thing; of course he would minimise the time spent walking. If he could do it quicker than the average time, that would be an extra incentive. 'Camping,' Chris added.

'OK,' Thea said. 'If you're sure?'

'Wei did it last summer,' Chris told Thea, referring to his managing partner. 'I've got his trail notes. We might even be able to do it in three days if you're up for it.'

Every time Thea remembers the conversation, she has the same stab of annoyance. *She*'s the one who likes hiking and camping. She's wanted to do the Overland since they moved to Tasmania and, yes Chris is fit, but she's by far the more experienced at long days in the hills. Even if she is a little out of practice, it's in her blood; her muscles have the memory of the mountains in them. Now just because his boss has done it, Chris wants to do it too. And not just that, he wants to do it faster. Of course he does.

When she met up with Chris in Melbourne, it had shocked her to see him exercise. It's not like he'd seemed out of shape in Guatemala — the opposite, in fact — but she never saw him put any effort into it. She assumed he had a fast metabolism, aided by the party drugs that kept him dancing for hours in the night. Seeing his dedication to keeping fit in Australia, she's since wondered if, while she and Sarah were at Spanish school, he was secretly doing push-ups and sit-ups in the room or on the rooftop. It wouldn't surprise her.

She agreed to Chris's plan because she really does want to do the walk, and isn't shy of a challenge, but she's a bit on edge about how it's going to pan out. They go on training hikes together, but Chris has really upped his running too. Not only is he covering longer distances, he's switched from roads to trails. She gets it — if she were a runner, trails would appeal to her so much more than roads. It's not so much the type or amount of running that he's doing. It's more that something about it feels unnecessarily competitive.

She's starting to feel invisible in what is meant to be a trip away together. It's become very much about whatever it is that Chris wants to prove to his boss, or himself, or perhaps his father. Next he'll suggest that they walk the trail in one direction then turn and go straight back to the beginning. 'In three days,' she mimics him in her head.

It's that kind of thing that has brought her here, to this place, this point, this literal and metaphorical sea between them. Thea can see her future if she stays with Chris. Living in a beautiful house, a house that she might agree to buy, but one that he has chosen; their house, but not her home.

It reminds her of what happened with their first flat in Hobart. When they arrived in the city, Chris's work put them up in an apartment in town while they looked for a more permanent place to live. Flat hunting had proved to be a much more frustrating experience than they had imagined. One Friday night while they were out for an after-work drink, Thea had slumped forward with exaggerated exhaustion. 'I can't bear the thought of traipsing around town looking at more places to live.' About half the houses they looked at were much shabbier than the photos depicted or were too far from the city centre; the rest of them were offered to other people — often before they'd even had a chance to look at the place. 'Maybe we should start looking at a shared house,' she suggested, not for the first time.

'Don't stress,' Chris said, grinning at her over his beer. 'We can take the weekend off. It's all sorted.'

'What do you mean?'

'I've found us a place. It's great. You'll love it.'

Thea had straightened up, keen to hear more, but confused. 'Well, when can we look at it? We've got to go this weekend or there'll be no chance of getting it.'

'No, it's *ours*. We've got it.'

'Hold on,' Thea had said, her glass half-raised. 'What are you saying? You've signed us up to a place without even asking me?'

'I had to, Thee. I saw it at lunchtime and it's perfect for us. Like you said, if I didn't snap it up, there'd be no chance of getting it.'

'But you didn't even tell me about it?'

'I'm telling you now. You'd said you were busy all afternoon and I wanted to surprise you.'

'But it's where we're going to be living. We need to make that decision together.' She had been mystified that he would make a decision like that without her and that he didn't even seem to understand why she was annoyed.

'Fuck's sake.' Anger flashed off Chris like a crisp white cloth thrown over the table between them. 'You were just complaining about having to view houses. I've solved the problem and you're still complaining. If you're not going to be happy with anything I do, I'll ring the agent now and cancel it. We'll lose our deposit, but as long as you're happy, that's all that matters.' Chris took a gulp of his beer and glared past her shoulder.

Thea put her glass on the table, her fingertips pressed to the base, as though to hold it in place. The couple at the next table turned their heads towards them. Chris took another, smaller, sip of his beer. Thea breathed deeply then looked at Chris and said, 'Don't get angry with me, Chris. I had a busy afternoon, but I always have time for a quick message. You know that.'

Christ gave a small nod. When he spoke again, his voice was softer. 'Honestly, it's better than anything we've seen so far. In any case, it's a thousand per cent better than the Xaman Ek.' He caught her eye and smiled apologetically. 'No shared bathroom.' He reached his fingertips out to meet hers where they still rested on the wineglass. 'Hot water.' He slid his fingers over hers, trapping the stem of the glass between them. 'No bed bugs.' She tried not to smile back at him, but he must've noticed her struggle and kept listing things until she properly smiled. 'I mean, there's no on-site bar,' he continued, 'but we can walk to plenty.' He had shown her photos of the house and where it was on the map, then said, 'I'll see if you can go and look at it this week. If you don't like it, we don't have to move there.'

She had to admit that the flat was better than all the other places they'd viewed. It was small and a bit noisy but it was clean and they could both walk to work. They'd stayed there for over two years.

Those early days in Tasmania were full of challenges like that. They had to learn new versions of each other, as well as a fresh rendering of the two of them together. Against their new reality of rushing off to work in the rain, bills to pay, and breakfast dishes left on the bench, Thea was haunted by the vision of Chris as a carefree traveller who leaned in to Sarah as though she were the sun. Just as that image would come and go in Thea's mind, so too it seemed like Chris was still flickering in and out of her life. He would forget to tell her if he was working late, or fail to tell her about plans that he had made. But then there was the man who seemed to so desperately need her to hold the pieces of his new life in place until they set, and who designed 'Tassie Bingo' as a way of crossing off all things they'd talked about doing together when they moved to the island.

Now, some eight years later, as she walks around the museum, Thea reflects on how familiar they are to one another. He still has a tendency to do things without telling her, but it's just small things now. If she made a big deal of them, it would seem like she was too demanding, too controlling, and so she's largely come to accept the habit. He wouldn't buy a house without talking to her first. She's sure of it. As she follows Magda into a dim room lit up with the story of how gods and volcanoes shaped her homeland, she recalls the cracks that she thought she saw in Chris when they met in San Pedro. Perhaps the darkness she glimpsed beneath the surface was never as romantic or dramatic as her younger self imagined and was nothing more than this: he's someone who likes to do things his way; what he wants, when he wants. It might still be dangerous, but in such a very ordinary way.

She feels so tired, like all this time she's been swimming over an unseen reef, holding her breath, making herself thinner so she doesn't scrape along the rocks.

She's come here to make a decision. She has to stop avoiding it.

10

The next morning, Thea takes the bus into town with Magda. It's Magda's volunteer shift at the hospice op shop, so Thea's got the day to herself. Hours to let thoughts sweep around her mind, resolving themselves in small increments, like hands around a clock. The insistent tick of 'yes' and 'no', 'here' and 'there' kept her awake until late last night. In the dark room, she couldn't fix her mind on anything, her thoughts flicking from one thing to the other before her feelings could catch up. Even now, her mind can't settle; she's only half in the conversation with Magda.

'What a beautiful spring day,' Magda says as the bus rolls down the hill and the harbour appears glistening in the gap between buildings. 'If I wasn't working, I might even have been tempted to get in the water with you.'

'You should,' Thea says.

Magda laughs. 'Just for a splash around. Nothing like these long swims you do. I'm very impressed.'

Growing up on Auckland's west coast beaches, Thea learned to tumble and glide with pushing, surging white waves. She loved being in the ocean, diving through breaking waves and body-surfing to shore, but in that rough sea, she had never swum any distance. Sometimes just staying upright in knee-deep water was a challenge. Proper ocean swimming, going from point A to B, is new to her. Recently, she and Liz have started training for their first event — a short course, designed for beginners — and Thea's loving it. It still scares her — and she kind of impresses herself with the fact that she's doing it — but mainly it gives her a feeling of true joy to move through the sea as it moves all around her. She loves the way the boundaries of her body dissolve in the water, and then how very much in her body she is afterwards, shrinking back into her tingling skin and tired limbs.

But perhaps most of all, it's made her realise how important it is for her and Chris to have their separate spaces, their own ways to sort through whatever troubles them from time to time. He works his issues through in strides, pushing himself faster and farther to sweat out all the emotion. She lets her concerns ease out in the smooth back and forth of blue laps or lapping waves.

Now as Thea swims out from Freyberg Beach, she's surprised, again, by how clear the inner-city water is. In Hobart, the beaches where she swims are farther removed from downtown. As golden as the sand is on Wellington's city beaches, she expected the water to be slicked with oil from the ferries and cargo ships that do laps across the harbour. Instead, the ocean bed is spread with sea stars, an underwater galaxy. As she gets farther from shore, the stars fade into the depths. The occasional jellyfish pulses past, but far fewer than the day before.

She pauses just out past the first pontoon, assessing the distance to the lighthouse. Or rather, she knows how far it is; she's reassessing whether she's up for it. She woke up feeling exhausted and, as yet, the swim hasn't energised her like she hoped it would. The sea is calm and smooth. It would be a long and tiring swim for her, nonetheless. But she does need wide open space and distance to help her think.

As she treads water, a man swims up beside her. He takes off his goggles, peers at the lenses then swishes them in the sea to clean them. 'Lovely morning for it,' he says, smiling broadly. 'You all good?'

'I was just debating whether to go to the lighthouse,' Thea tells him, glancing towards the point then back at him. 'I haven't done it before. It might be too far for me.'

'That's where I'm going,' he says. 'We can swim together if you want.'

She's tempted. 'I don't want to hold you up. I'll be slow.'

'All good,' he says. 'We'll take it easy and stop as often as you like.'

She does want to push herself, but still, her body has the heaviness of a sea chest sinking to the ocean floor. 'If you're sure?' she asks. If she's honest with herself, she would have said no if he wasn't so good looking. She can practically feel Liz elbow her in the ribs.

'Sure I'm sure,' he says and puts his goggles back on. 'I'm Ashwin.'

Thea introduces herself and they set off, cutting and pulling through the water side by side. She feels so much safer with him next to her. She doesn't worry about deep water or what might be hidden in the depths, she just eases into the rhythm. Every now and then, they stop, Ashwin checking she wants to carry on and telling her about the group that he belongs to.

'Every Wednesday and Friday at seven,' he says. 'All levels. Some people go to the lighthouse, some people just go to the pontoon, but no one swims alone.'

'I'm only visiting,' Thea explains.

'That's a shame.' Ashwin smiles at her.

There are ocean swimming groups in Hobart that she and Liz have been thinking about joining. She'll definitely join one if Liz doesn't stick with it. For just a moment though, she imagines that she lives in Wellington.

Now that Ashwin knows she's not from the city, he pretends to be her tour guide, telling her random facts and personal anecdotes about the city and its sea every time they take a break. She hardly even notices the distance. When they've rounded the lighthouse — the 'highlight of the tour (excuse the pun),' Ashwin states — and are halfway back, he puts on a serious face and says, 'OK, that's enough chit chat. You up for a final push? How are you feeling? Arms OK? Legs OK? Toenails and eyelashes holding up?'

'It's my abs that hurt,' Thea says. 'You've made me laugh too much.'

They put their heads down and aim towards the beach. Thea trails just behind Ashwin. She focuses on the circling of her arms, the roll of her body, the kicking of her legs; the in and out of air in her lungs is a meditation. Thoughts fill her mind and she breathes them out, bubbles dissolving in the ocean. Then there's the sea wall on one side of her and the pontoon on the other. She picks up the pace, drawing even with Ashwin, then edging ahead, but he's up for the race and keeps level with her. The sea stars reappear under her as the ocean shallows out to beach.

They stop a few metres from the water's edge, pulling off their swimming caps and goggles. 'Thank you,' she says. 'That was great.' She can't keep the smile off her face; she's beaming at him, exhausted but exhilarated, stupidly proud of what she's just done. She lies back to float on the surface of the sea and propels herself in slow circles to take in the hills and buildings that wrap around the harbour. 'It really is a beautiful city.'

'You can't beat Wellington on a good day,' Ashwin says. 'But let me know what you think tomorrow. It's forecast to be gale-force winds.'

Thea closes her eyes. In a different life, every day here could have a tomorrow. Her stomach flutters. So slightly she might have imagined it. It's as light as a single mote of dust settling to earth. A mote of stardust with a million glittering possibilities of life.

And this is the other part of the truth that she hasn't told Magda. Or Chris. Or even really let herself acknowledge until now. She's pregnant. The test last night confirmed what she had suspected for the past few days.

Of course Thea's imagined having a baby with Chris. It's a thought that's crossed her mind over the past couple of years like a migrating bird back and forth across the ocean. So she doesn't quite know why she's avoiding the reality of it now, why she came so close to accepting Ashwin's invitation for a drink.

She opens her eyes and stares up into a blue sky wisped with clouds. That's not true. She has a good idea why she's letting her thoughts glide away from her. For all his faults, Chris could be a great father; he's got so much energy and loves to joke about. He just needs to decide it's what he wants to do. So far, it's not a choice that he's wanted to make. He knows one shape of childhood and sees it repeating and repeating like a spirograph into the future.

'You've met my father, Thee,' he said to her the first time it came up. 'And you've seen what Ant's like with his kids.'

'That doesn't mean you'd be the same,' she'd said, running a hand down the side of his arm in gentle reassurance. 'You *wouldn't* be the same.'

He shrugged, and she didn't know if he was shaking off her touch or just dismissing the idea that he could be a different kind of parent. Then, after a beat, he'd looked at her and said, 'And what about your family, Thea?'

She jolted back, involuntarily putting space between them. 'My family? What's wrong with my family?'

'Longevity doesn't exactly run in the genes, does it?' Thea felt a physical change in the air between them. Chris must've felt it, too, or at least seen the look that crossed her face. He reached for her hand and pulled her into him. 'Babe, I'm sorry, that was a stupid thing to say.' He kissed the side of her head as he held her to him. 'It's just that your mum was really young when she died. And breast cancer can be hereditary, right?'

'That's not actually that common,' she said, her words muffled against his chest. *And*, she thought but didn't say aloud, *it's not like having a baby would make it any more likely.*

'I can't even imagine losing you, Thea.' He squeezed her tighter. 'And then to have our child grow up with just me for a parent.'

'That's so unlikely to happen,' Thea said, moving away from Chris and sitting upright. She'd thought all this through before, but for some reason it made her uncomfortable knowing Chris had imagined a world in which she was dead. 'Mum was a really rare case. Besides, treatments have got so much better since then.'

'Let's not talk about this anymore,' Chris said, kissing her head again. 'I can't. It's too awful.' The next day, as they were heading out to dinner and a gig with friends, he'd laughed and said, 'Wouldn't be doing this if we had kids.'

That was a few years ago now. Things have changed. They don't go out quite so much. People they know have started families. It could be the right time. But, still, this wasn't planned. Until she suspected she was pregnant, she was on the pill. There was just that one time she forgot. She didn't forget to take it: she was very aware that she hadn't taken it. She just literally forgot to take it with her on a camping trip. She can still picture the packet, sitting on the vanity, ready to pack but lost in the distraction of loading other things into the car. She'd told Chris when they were lying in the tent on the second night of the trip and he rolled towards her.

'You never forget,' he said. 'I'm sure your system's built up a barrier from all the other days or however it works.'

She laughed, pretty sure he was joking. 'Like immunity? Or micro-dosing? I'm not a doctor, but I don't think it works like that.'

'You can take two when you get back,' he said, shifting his whole body to close the gap between them. 'And then change to something else before we do the Overland so this doesn't happen again.'

'We really shouldn't,' she'd said as she responded to his kisses, her body arching forward to meet his.

'The whole point of this trip,' he'd murmured as his hands moved across her body, 'is to try out our camping gear. So we really do need to give these air mattresses a proper test.'

Chris knew the risk. It would be unfair of him to blame her.

That's the thing that's making her so reluctant to let her thoughts come in to land. She knows that what has always worked with her and Chris is this: she lets him decide for himself what he wants to do. Sometimes she sees the bright ghost of Sarah, shimmering with all her energy and enthusiasm. The more she pushed to get a younger Chris to join her in her plans, the more he hardened like clay baking in the sun. Back in San Pedro, Thea used to get so annoyed at him on Sarah's behalf, and exasperated, too, that Sarah kept putting up with Chris.

But, look at her now. Of course there are times when she nudges him in a certain direction, a gentle tap to send him the way she wants to go. It's just that she never *tells* him what he should do. It doesn't stop her from doing the things she wants to do, but she never makes him do them if she knows it's not his thing. She could just deal with the pregnancy without telling Chris. Or tell him after. She could imagine being flippant about it — him picking her up from the airport and asking about her trip and her responding, 'It was great. So lovely to see Magda. Good to get an abortion. You know, pretty standard stuff.'

But, no, she could never say that. It makes her turn cold just to think of it. And, with each hour that passes, she's more certain that she could never terminate this pregnancy. Afloat on the water, she imagines their child growing inside her. The slow and rapid coming together of molecules to form something so unfathomably beautiful. The whole universe moves inside her, like the turn of the Milky Way across the night sky. Chris can make his own decision. She's made hers: if she has to do it all on her own, she will.

☆ ☆ ☆

That afternoon, hair rinsed clean of sand and seawater, Thea waits for Chris to speak. She takes in the familiar details of the living room of their flat on the screen behind his face while the silence spreads into their conversation. She looks at the rainbow stripes of the book spines on the shelves behind Chris's left shoulder and tries to breathe steadily. She forces herself to keep quiet, to not fill the silence with explanations and apologies. Her eyes flick to his face then back to the bookshelves. It's as much his baby as hers. He needs to say something.

'That's amazing!' Chris's face breaks into a broad grin. 'It's a fucking massive shock, but it's an awesome shock.' Thea lets out her breath and she can't help it but she knows she's going to cry. She presses her hands against her face. Chris hasn't stopped talking. 'When are you coming home? I wish you were here right now. I just want to give you — both of you — the biggest hug.'

Thea realises that she probably should have waited a day or two and told him in person. She's cheated him — and herself — out of this moment of joy together. If she'd known he was going to be this happy, she'd have waited to be in the same room, to jump up and down together, to fall in towards each other and hold on tight.

'Magda must be ecstatic,' Chris says.

'I haven't told her,' Thea says. 'I wasn't going to tell anyone before I told you. And it's early days — I don't think you're meant to tell anyone until after a certain point, are you?'

'Rules schmules. We can tell Magda, right? Is she there? Let's tell her now, together. We can wait to tell my parents and everyone else.'

Magda won't be home for an hour or so. When Thea realised she had the house to herself, she took the opportunity to make the call to Chris. She wishes Magda were here; now she's told Chris, she wants to tell everyone.

'Why are you crying, Thee? I know it's not what we planned, but aren't you happy about it?'

Thea laughs through her tears and nods her head until she can get the words out. 'I'm happy,' she says.

They're both quiet for a moment, Thea's words sitting in the space between them. After a beat, Chris breaks the silence. 'Wow, just think: all those tiny atoms inside you, coming together to form a whole new life.' Thea silently berates herself for ever doubting him. Sometimes she thinks back to how they got together and the same sense of shame washes through her as it did all those years ago; sometimes she feels she's just waiting for him to realise that it was the wrong thing to do and to end things between them. Then there are moments like this when she is overwhelmed with love for him and everything feels right. He pauses then speaks again, his voice quieter than before. 'I'm all in, Thea. I'm going to be a good dad. I really am.'

'I know.' The words rush out before she's had the chance to think. 'I know you are.'

They talk for a while longer, repeating themselves as they process the way things are about to change. She's floating, happy; but like an icy current under the surface of the springtime sea, something cold slides around her middle. He's saying all the right things and she believes that he believes it. She's not convinced, though, that he understands just how much will have to change. 'We definitely need to buy that house now,' Chris says just before they end the call.

As Thea sits there, lost in thought, the screen goes black; smooth and shiny like polished granite.

☆ ☆ ☆

'What's wrong?' Magda asks as soon as she sees Thea sitting on the sofa. 'You've been crying. Are you OK?'

'It's good,' Thea reassures her.

Before she's even finished telling her, Magda is hugging her. 'Darling, that's wonderful. You're going to be a fantastic mother.' And then, 'I'm going to be a grandmother!' And that makes Thea cry again, to know that their child is already loved, that it doesn't matter to Magda that they're not related by blood.

In one shape or another, it's all they really talk about for the rest of the evening. 'Do you think I can still do the trek?' Thea asks at the dinner table, voicing something that she's already been wondering to herself. She's see-sawed between yes and no. She's fit. Plenty of women do high-intensity exercise while pregnant. She's far from being an elite athlete, but she intends to keep active throughout her term. She wants this baby to breathe in mountain and sea air right from the start, to know the sensation of tree-dappled light and shadow, to hear the cries of birds in flight and roosting at day's end. And yet, it's one thing to stay fit and active, and another to take a gamble with life. 'It's not the walking,' Thea continues before Magda has said anything. 'I'm not sure I'll want to sleep in a tent or carry a pack for days.' Magda says nothing, just murmurs to show she's listening. 'And then there's the weather. It's so changeable. It can snow in December.' Thea's voice trails off.

After a time, Magda pats her on the knee. 'Just enjoy getting to know the little one,' she says. 'You don't need to make any decisions today.'

'I really wanted to do it,' Thea says. 'Chris will be so disappointed.' They hadn't talked about the trek when they spoke.

'He'll understand,' Magda says, and stands to take their empty plates through to the kitchen. 'Besides,' she calls through from the other room, 'the mountains aren't going anywhere.'

'That's true,' Thea says. In years to come, the mountains will still be there. Perhaps one day this child of hers and Chris's will tackle their grandfather's goal of climbing the island's highest peaks, a goal that she has never tried to make her own. Neither Thea nor Magda know how many mountains Andy did climb, nor which ones. Andy was an experienced and energetic mountaineer and rock climber, but Thea's come to learn how rugged the landscape can be, and how isolated some of those peaks are. Perhaps he was only one mountain away from victory. Or perhaps becoming a solo dad made the goal just a dream.

When Thea had asked Magda about it a couple of years before on a trip to Melbourne, she was surprised to see a look of sudden sadness on Magda's face. 'I don't know, sorry, darling,' Magda said. 'I wish I'd paid more attention to his stories. Committed them to memory.'

'Me too,' Thea said, suddenly understanding Magda's sorrow. All those adventures lost.

'A lot of his books and journals are in the roof space,' Magda told Thea. 'Do you want me to get them down when I get home? I can send them over to you.' Magda reached out and put her hand over Thea's. 'I have a box of your things up there too.'

'Thanks, but it's OK,' Thea had said. 'Wait until I come over.'

Now, Thea glances up, as though the box is sitting right above her head and at any minute the ceiling might collapse, an avalanche of plaster burying her. She knows she should deal with it. But she's not getting up on a ladder, crawling around in the dust, and hefting a carton back down at the moment, nor is she going to ask Magda to do it. When the baby is born, she and Chris will make a trip over. With Chris's help, she'll deal with her old stuff to make room for this new life.

She's exhausted. Neither the boxes nor the mountains are going anywhere. But the weight of both press down on her as she says goodnight to Magda and makes her way to bed.

☆ ☆ ☆

The ping of her phone jolts Thea awake. She has her phone set to 'do not disturb' from ten o'clock each night, but it's not that late. She's fallen asleep with the light on, phone on the bed beside her. The message is from Chris, a big grinning smiley face. Not long after, another message comes through. *I'm buzzing. Can't stop smiling.* Thea smiles and is about to respond when her phone pings again. *Thought you might like this better. What do you think?*

She clicks on the link that Chris sends through. A photo of a house nestled in the trees opens on her screen. She clicks through the rest of the pictures. It's gorgeous. Instead of the dark granite surfaces of the other house, this place gleams with polished wood. Like the other one, it has large windows that let in the light, but the views are of brown-green treetops instead of rooftops.

I love it, she messages Chris.

Thought you might. His response is quick and she can see him sitting on the sofa, pleased with himself. *I'll arrange a viewing for when you're back.*

Thea swipes back through the photos. They would be happy there, the leafy sea outside the windows, wind and birds in the sky above. It looks like a home.

11

Lake St Clair National Park,
Tasmania, Australia, 2015

'Not a single snake,' Chris declares as they stand beside the sign for Shadow Lake on Christmas Eve. 'The ranger doesn't know what he's talking about.'

Thea laughs. 'Thank goodness. Still, we're only halfway.'

Chris takes the drink bottle out of his pack and hands it to her. 'How're you doing?'

'Good. Definitely looking forward to washing off in the lake when we get back though.' It's a scorcher and she's been noticing the uphill but is otherwise feeling fine. She's so happy to be out on the trails. It might not be what they planned, but it's a great alternative. In fact, it's better.

When Thea got back from New Zealand, they'd sat down together and talked through whether or not to do the Overland. 'You could still do it,' Thea had said to Chris. 'I know how much you want to.'

'Are you kidding?' Chris had laughed. 'I'm not going without you.' He shook his head affectionately. 'I do really want to do the track but I want to do it with you.' Then he'd pulled her onto his lap and put his hand on her stomach. 'We'll buy a bigger tent. We'll take a few years to train up little Atom here and the three of us will go together.'

She kissed him. 'Thank you. In any case, we might have a new house to spend Christmas in.'

'Fingers crossed.'

When she'd walked into the house behind Chris and the real estate agent, Thea knew it was the one for them. The property listing dubbed it 'The Treehouse' but it reminded her of a tall ship, sailing over the treetops. It seemed to hover at the crest of a wave, a sense of open space and possibility around it. Standing in the patch of sun stretched across the lounge, she didn't see ghosts, just the bright present and a future. She was ready to put an offer in without looking through the other rooms. She caught Chris's eye while the agent was talking about the proximity to public transport and schools, and nodded.

Two days later, their offer was accepted and they celebrated with a glass of sparkling apple juice. They clinked their glasses, had a sip and grimaced at the sweetness. 'Sorry,' Chris said. 'It was meant to be a nice idea.'

'It was very thoughtful.' Thea poured the rest of their glasses and the bottle down the sink while Chris got himself a beer from the fridge.

A few days after that, Chris came home from work, excitement zinging off him. 'Tell me if you don't like this idea,' he said, 'but I was thinking we could hire a campervan and drive up to Cradle Mountain-Lake St Clair for a few nights over the break. We could do day walks or chill at the campsite, whatever you feel up to. It's not the Overland, but it's something?'

'That's a great idea.'

'Would you rather have our first Christmas in the new house though?'

'I think we might want a break from boxes by then. And it might be our last adventure for a while. It's a great idea. I really love it.'

'Do you really love me?'

'I really, really love you.' Thea laughed at their cheesiness, but it had never felt more true. She could hardly believe her own emotions yet there was freedom in abandoning herself to them.

'I'll book it now,' he said. She had leaned into his back and looked over his shoulder when he sat to open his laptop. 'Leave it to me.' He playfully shooed her away. 'Don't you worry about a thing.'

And suddenly life was busy with planning for the baby and planning for the move and planning for the holiday. Chris was in his element, thriving on big ideas and spontaneity, a sense of change. This time Thea felt that she wasn't just being carried along by Chris's momentum; she was an equal part of it, as though they were holding hands and spinning wildly in circles, creating the whirlwind together.

Thea had been truly touched by Chris's campervan idea. Part of her had expected him to go trekking without her, perhaps leaving on Boxing Day as a concession and using the delayed departure and her absence as more incentive to do the Overland as fast as he could. She spent a couple of days waiting for him to announce a new plan, but he'd embraced the Cradle Mountain-Lake St Clair trip. He's really making an effort.

The morning they were due to leave, she had stayed at home, trying to do some more unpacking of boxes and packing of holiday gear, while he collected the camper from the rental depot. She laughed when she saw it coming along the street because it was much bigger than anything she thought Chris would go for. She assumed they'd get a regular-sized van in which they would be forever constructing and deconstructing the table and the bed, folding up one to make room for the other.

As he turned into the driveway, she had a sudden glimpse of him in her mind, thirty years older, leaning forward over the wheel to navigate unknown roads. Then he leapt out of the vehicle and he was back to his familiar self. 'Ta da!' He spread his arms. 'It's all they had left when I booked,' he explained, 'but it's a pretty sweet ride. Good excuse for a touch of luxury.' He flung open the side door of the van and ushered Thea inside. Chris had strung tinsel around the van, Blu-Tacked a miniature tree to the bench top in the back and hung three small stockings underneath it.

'Chris, this is so cool,' Thea exclaimed. 'I can't believe you did this.'

'Do you think I've finally made it onto Santa's "Nice" list? Maybe he'll give me a trophy for being the world's best partner.'

'If Santa doesn't, I will.' A small, cynical voice in the back of her mind muttered "Most improved", but she quickly dismissed it. Now when he makes plans without telling her, it's *because* he's thinking of her. She's really enjoying this version of him, of them.

Now, as they finish the walk and head past the visitor centre to the carpark, Thea's glad to have the extra room and comfort. She doesn't want this to be the model for all her future camping trips, but it definitely works for this one. Even small things like being able to stand upright to strip off her walking clothes and put on togs makes a difference. And then, once they've freshened up in the cold, clear lake, she can lie on something close enough to a proper mattress to read her book and doze off.

When Thea wakes from her nap she sees that Chris has set up the picnic table outside the van, spread a tablecloth over it and placed a candle in the middle. He instructs her to take a seat while he brings out an assortment of nibbles. He gets himself a beer from the fridge and offers her some sparkling water.

'So peaceful,' she says, as the light slips to the periphery of the earth and the sky above darkens. 'I can't even imagine how different next year's going to be.'

'Next year's meant to be a Sydney year,' Chris says. Thea doesn't respond; the words flicker in the night air like bugs. Chris takes a sip of his beer then speaks again. 'I think next year we should stay at home. They can come to us if they really want to.'

Thea murmurs in agreement and reaches over to take Chris's hand.

In bed later on, Chris turns off the main light then reaches down beside the mattress.

A second later, the ceiling twinkles with a web of golden fairy lights. On the lapping edges of the national park, it's not hard to pretend they're lying under the stars. They point out constellations to one another, the way children find shapes in clouds.

☆ ☆ ☆

The next morning, Thea snuggles into Chris. 'Good morning,' she says and kisses his unshaven cheek. 'Merry Christmas.'

'Merry Christmas,' he says, adjusting his body to fit her better.

'Do you know what I want?' She props herself up so she can look into his face. 'What I really, really, really want —' she pauses, moving a hand down his bare chest — 'is to know what that bulge . . . in that stocking is.' She inclines her head in the direction of the Christmas stockings that now have the weight of presents in them. 'Looks like Santa came last night,' she says.

'He sure did,' Chris says. Then, just as she knows he will, he adds, 'Now it's my turn.'

A while later, Thea picks up the conversation. 'But seriously, I'm very curious.' She's so often heard people say how having children makes Christmas extra special. Already, she's more excited about Christmas Day, remembering her own childhood and thinking about traditions to pick up again. When she was a child, she woke at dawn and dragged her stocking from the foot of her bed into her parents' room. As she sat between their blanketed feet, her mum and dad were just as excited as she was to see the bright-coloured paper piling up. Then they'd all stumble into the lounge where Thea would find a present for each of them under the tree. They opened them, one at a time, all of them delighting in seeing what the others got. Even after her mother died, and there were gaping holes under the tree and in their lives, her father kept the shape and rhythm of the day intact.

'I'm going to make a cup of tea,' Thea says to Chris. 'Should I make you a coffee? Then presents?'

'Sounds great,' Chris says. Then, 'No, actually, let's do Santa's presents first.'

Chris has told Thea how, as kids, he and Ant were expected to stay in their rooms until Bill and Cath were up. They were then allowed to open presents from Santa, which were left under the Christmas tree in the lounge. All other gifts waited until late afternoon, when the extended family were gathered under one roof.

Thea collects the three stockings and brings them back to bed. Each one has a cardboard tag attached to it with ribbon: Thea, Chris, Atom. She hands Chris his. 'Doesn't look like Santa gave you as much, but there's a bit of heft to it.' Grand romantic gestures aren't unusual for Chris, but the small, sweet things he's done on this trip have taken her by surprise. She was touched when he decorated the van but had assumed the stockings were merely for show. She can't believe he's filled them all.

They both unwrap their presents. Thea's stocking contains several gifts: a tube of hand cream, chocolate-coated ginger, a book of puzzles and, nestled into the foot of the sock, a set of graphite pencils in a tin. 'Santa knows me well.' She smiles at Chris.

'Santa probably thought that if you were too tired or sick to walk, you might want to sit and sketch while your annoying boyfriend left you in peace for a few hours.'

'Santa's so thoughtful. Thank you, Santa. What did he get you?'

He shakes his head. 'Santa obviously doesn't know me very well or he'd know how much I hate novelty mugs.' He hands Thea the small pottery espresso cup that he's unwrapped. 'At least it looks good, and it's the perfect size.'

Thea cradles the mug in the palm of her hand. Small letters are etched into the deep purple glaze: 'World's best dad'. She turns the mug and on the other side it says, 'But first, coffee'.

'That's so sweet, Chris,' she says, then presses her lips together because she has to actively stop herself from gushing and Chris is being strangely shy.

He shrugs. 'Figured every dad has to have one. *One*. So don't let that child of ours ever buy me a single other novelty mug. Ever.' He leans towards her stomach. 'Did you hear that?' He sits back up. 'That's one thing I actually agree with my father on.' He starts to get out of bed. 'And now, coffee.'

'Hold on, we've still got Atom's presents to open. Or aren't we allowed to open them yet?'

'You open them,' Chris says.

'There's two,' Thea says, pulling them from the stocking and putting them on the bed. 'One each.' Chris sits back down, takes one of the presents to unwrap and hands the other to Thea. Thea laughs as soon as she sees the bright yellow beak cracking through the paper. 'I never realised Santa was so cute,' she says, holding up the stuffed kiwi. She laughs again when Chris shows her the Tasmanian tiger toy that he's unwrapped. She's seen the exact same tiger toys in the visitor centre a couple of hundred metres from where they're parked. She suspects it was a last-minute purchase. But the kiwi, that must've taken a bit of effort.

They spend the day loose and relaxed. There's a friendly, festive vibe among the other campers and walkers. They swim, they stroll under tall trees, they eat. Thea treats herself to half a glass of wine and sketches Chris as he sips his second and third glasses. At the end of the day, they fall asleep with another year behind them and their own private universe twinkling overhead.

☆ ☆ ☆

On Boxing Day and the day after, they drive to different parts of the park to do longer walks. The following day, Chris asks Thea what she feels like doing. 'I'd just like to take it easy: sketch, read, snooze,' she tells him. 'My back's a bit sore and I'm feeling tired.' He massages her shoulders. 'You should still go for a hike,' she says over her shoulder. 'Or a run.'

He gives her shoulder a squeeze. 'If you don't mind?'

'Of course not,' she murmurs as he nuzzles into her neck. 'I don't want you pacing around the campsite all day. Go burn off some energy.'

That morning there's been a spot of blood. Just a tiny fleck. It's nothing; she's heard it's not unusual. She doesn't want to keep Chris here, tethered to her side, for something that's probably nothing.

She'll give it an hour. If anything changes, she'll find a doctor.

Chris tells her that he's going to run alongside the lake. 'Out and back. No more than two and a half hours.'

☆ ☆ ☆

The cramps start about fifty minutes after Chris leaves. Thea's at the café in the visitor centre. She puts the glass bottle of juice on the table for fear that she might squeeze it so tightly that it breaks — although she'd welcome a sharp slicing open of her hand rather than the pain that grips her around the middle. She exhales, a conscious slow release. She inhales. She needs to get back to the van.

As soon as she gets back, she wonders if she should have stayed at the visitor centre where there were people who could help her. There's no way she'll make it back there now. She staggers through the vehicle, holding on to the edge of the table, the cupboard, the bench for support. In bed she curls tightly in on herself, as though she can protect her baby from her own body.

Chris doesn't answer when she rings. She leaves a message even though he never checks his voicemail and even though she doesn't think that what she said will make any sense. She types a message. *You need to come back. Please. Hurry.*

He calls back a moment later, talking before she's said a word. 'Thea, Thee, what's happening? I'm on my way.' He stays on the phone the whole way back, running as fast as he can, sometimes talking to her but often saying nothing. Underneath the ragged tide of his breath, she can hear his footfalls on the trail like a heartbeat.

☆ ☆ ☆

Later, in the hospital, the doctor tells them statistics about just how many pregnancies end in miscarriage and that the reason is often never known. 'The one thing I can tell you,' the doctor says, leaning forward and looking Thea in the eye, 'is that it's nothing that you did.'

Thea nods, but it's just for show. She must've done something. It's her body. The doctor's still looking at her, but she turns away to stare at the framed print on the wall. Sunshine filters through tall straight trees. The ground is thick with pine needles. She imagines walking through that forest, the whoosh of the wind through the treetops and the silence underfoot.

☆ ☆ ☆

Days pass, weeks pass. The span of a whole lifetime that ended before it began passes. Magda comes to stay for a week. Kirra and Liz come to visit. Thea knows that Chris must have called them. They come with kind words and small touches, light fingertips on a forearm, a wrist, a shoulder. Outside, the breeze breathes a lullaby through the treetops.

Mostly she feels nothing. She moves through days like snow falling softly through conifers. But some days she feels a raw and visceral anger towards Chris for not being there when it happened. And then the knowledge grips her round the middle that it was her that sent him off that day. She let him leave even though her body was sending out small signals of distress.

☆ ☆ ☆

One day after Magda has gone back to New Zealand and the house has a new depth of emptiness, Chris walks through the lounge where she's sitting and into the kitchen. As he passes through, he lets her know he's going for a run. A lightning strike of panic courses through her. 'How long are you going to be?' she asks him.

'An hour,' he says. 'Maybe a little longer.' He comes back into the lounge, paying more attention to her than before. 'I need to get out for a bit, Thee. I'm—' He stops, takes a deep breath and starts again. 'I just need to.'

'Are you taking your phone?'

'I wasn't going to,' he says, hesitation in his words.

'Can you take your phone?' she asks. 'In case something happens.'

Chris sits beside her, perched on the edge of the couch, poised to get back up. 'You remember what the doctor said, don't you? There was nothing anyone could have done.' He's quiet for a moment then his words tiptoe up to her. 'It was already too late.'

'Maybe it wasn't,' she says, not looking at him. 'I should have known. I should have done something sooner.'

Chris looks at her, surprised. 'The doctor was really clear, Thea. Sometimes these things just happen.'

'Maybe I was careless,' she says.

'You did nothing wrong.' He runs a hand through her hair.

'Maybe we didn't deserve a baby, Chris.'

His hand snaps back from her. 'I was trying, Thee. I was really trying my best.' She doesn't respond. After a while he speaks again. 'It's fucking devastating but it's no one's fault. It's not my fault. It's not your fault.'

Her anger shifts in shape; it focuses on the way he can accept something so easily that she can't accept at all. 'Just go, Chris.' He stands up and looks down at her, as though deciding whether to say something else. 'Enjoy your run,' she says and turns away from him. He lets out a breath and walks away.

When Chris has left, Thea distracts herself with small domestic chores. She puts on a load of washing and folds the basket of clothes that has sat beside their bed for days. She wipes the kitchen benches and takes the recycling and rubbish bins to empty into the bigger bins outside.

On the path beside the bins, the light reflecting off something catches Thea's eye. It's a shard of deep-purple stone, shining dimly like a remnant of a now-dead star. She bends to pick it up. She rubs her fingertip over the smooth surface; her breath catches as the pad of her finger passes over the letters etched in the glaze. She lifts the lid of the bin and looks inside; pieces of curved purple aspiration sit smashed and discarded. Thea presses the point of the piece of pottery that she's holding into the fleshy heel of her hand to stop herself from sobbing. Back inside, she separates the two halves of the ceramic kina that Magda sent her and which she keeps her earrings in. She places the curved piece of pottery against the inside sweep of the bowl.

Chris goes straight to the shower when he gets back from his run. Thea waits for him to come into the bedroom to get changed. She puts her arms around him from behind, leaning into his naked back. 'I'm sorry,' she says. 'I'm sorry I got angry. I'm sorry I said those things.'

'You don't need to apologise,' he says, laying his arms over hers. 'You definitely don't ever have to apologise.'

They lie down side by side, facing each other.

☆ ☆ ☆

The next day, Thea gets back from a walk to see Chris coming out of the carport, a hammer swinging from his hand. He has a look of determination on his face. 'Is everything OK?' she asks.

'Come with me,' he says and goes into the house.

She follows him into the hallway. A series of framed

photographs are lined up on the floor down the hallway, resting against the wall at regular intervals. Chris picks up the first one and hands it to her. It's her, Kirra and Liz with the Bruny Island lighthouse behind them, taken on their first weekend away together. While she's looking at it, he bends down to get the second one. It's the three of them again, this time with the white wingspan of Wineglass Bay stretching out of shot. 'What's this?' she says, still holding onto the first picture and taking slow steps down the hall.

'Kirra and Liz dropped them off. A couple of weeks ago.' He watches her as she crouches and stands, crouches and stands, making her way along the wall. 'They were meant to be a house-warming present.' He pauses. 'They still wanted you to have them, but we didn't know . . .' His words trail off into the darkness at the end of the hall.

There are eight of them, each taken in the last weekend of March, a year apart. Their annual girls' weekend has become one of her favourite times of the year. It's always a fun weekend, and a chance to explore somewhere new: their destinations get less touristic as the years go by, stretching into the farthest corners of Tasmania — but what she likes most about their trips is how they anchor her to the island. She needs to get in touch with Liz and Kirra. To say thank you, but also to make a plan. She's been letting days go by like the ocean slipping through her fingers. Now it's March and for the first time since they all met, they haven't organised a trip away. That's because of her; she's been so distant, so reluctant to engage with the world. She needs to get away; she needs them. Even if the only place available is a few kilometres down the road, she'll make it happen.

'We're going to fill this house with good memories, Thea,' Chris says, standing beside her and looking at the photo over her shoulder. 'It might not be the photos we thought we'd put up here, but there are still a lot of good times to remember. And more to come.' He shrugs. 'It's something.'

'It's . . .' She doesn't know what word comes next. She puts her palm against the bare white wall and stands in silence for a moment. It doesn't fill the empty space inside but, yes, it's something. 'It's a great idea. Thank you.' She looks at the photo she's holding in her other hand and gives a soft laugh. 'We were so young. I can't believe it.'

'Still are, babe.' He kisses her and takes the photo from her. 'Now, give that back. I don't want the order to get mixed up.'

She laughs again. 'I can tell you the order.' She closes her eyes briefly and recites the places in her head, an incantation to conjure up happiness.

'Yeah, I guess I could work it out from how you're ageing in each picture.'

She turns sharply to look at him. He's trying not to smile. She tries to look offended, tries not to smile back.

He puts an arm around her shoulder. 'We've got through tragedy before, Thee. We'll get through this.'

She leans into him, grateful for his words. Even if she doesn't believe them.

PART 3

12

Hobart, Tasmania, Australia, 2021

Thea walks along the quay towards the restaurant. The sky is a heavy purple gloom above her, the threat of another night of rain, but she feels light. Weekends have a different pace when Chris is away. It's not like she does anything very different, but everything she does somehow feels more like her own. She misses him, she does, but it's nice to have two nights and almost two whole days to feel the shape of herself in the space they share, for her own silence to fill the rooms. Chris will be back late tomorrow with his loud laughter and wide arms, those parts of him she still loves so much. By the time he gets back, she'll be impatient to feel his arms around her, to be enveloped in his presence, but for now her time is hers to weave to suit herself.

She spots Kirra at a table on the far side of the restaurant. The two women hug and are already talking before Thea sits down. 'Where are they this weekend?' Kirra asks her while they wait for Liz.

'Mount Field,' Thea says, ordering a gin and tonic from the waiter. So many things have been cancelled or put on hold over this past year or two, but throughout the pandemic Chris has kept up training for his ultramarathons and often heads away with Liz's husband, Joe, for training weekends or events. They have a race in the Blue Mountains lined up in May next year; one hundred kilometres, starting early and running into the dark. This weekend there's a night run on their training programme so, even though Mount Field's an easy drive from Hobart, they've made a weekend of it. 'Overachievers decided to do a run this morning, then the night run tonight,' she continues. 'I think Joe really just likes the excuse to have a weekend away from the kids.'

'Fair enough,' Kirra says. 'Don't ever tell Liz I said it, but those kids are hard work. Hard. Work.'

'You think all kids are hard work.' Thea laughs. Then the two women lapse into silence. Thea watches the bubbles rise up in her glass and disappear on the surface.

A moment later, Liz arrives, full of hugs and kisses, smiles and apologies, trying to catch the waiter's eye as she sits down. 'Sorry I'm late. Joe had to take a work call and it went on forever, way longer than it was meant to, so I got stuck making the kids dinner.'

'Joe?' Kirra asks before Thea can. 'I thought he was away with Chris.'

'He was meant to be, but something urgent came up with this deal he's working on. He's going to be at it most of the weekend. His work is an absolute nightmare at the moment. Chris still went, right?' Liz looks to Thea for confirmation. 'Joe wanted to reschedule, but . . .' Liz shrugs her shoulders and leaves the sentence unfinished. 'Anyway, it's worked out for the best.'

Thea nods absentmindedly as Liz talks. She's trying to remember if Chris had mentioned that Joe had cancelled. Chris can be so single-minded when it comes to training; he probably didn't even consider rescheduling. Besides, he needs this weekend away. Running is still his release, his way to expel the frustrations of the day, to balance out the long and stressful hours that he works. She remembers the storm-cloud crackle in the air around him as he was packing the car the night before, the prickle and snap of the office sparking off him as he told her that his boss had asked him to go to Launceston the following week to pitch to a potential new client. Thea had congratulated him, remarking what a great opportunity it was. 'It's a great fucking load of work, that's what it is,' he'd said, slamming the car boot, 'and fucking short notice.' She's not surprised that he's gone away without Joe, but she is surprised he didn't tell her.

'What do you mean it's worked out for the best?' Kirra asks Liz.

'There's no babysitter that I have to get home to relieve.' Liz takes a big sip of her wine and reaches across the table to clink her glass against Thea's and then Kirra's. 'And no potential lawsuit or medical bills to pay as a result of leaving someone with those two demons for an evening. Seriously though, Mount

Field wouldn't be a nice place to be at the moment. Is Chris going to come back tonight?'

'What do you mean?' Thea asks, glancing at Kirra, who shakes her head to signal she's in the dark too. 'The plan was to stay until Sunday. I think he'll still try to get two runs in.' Thea supposes that Chris could come back earlier if Joe isn't with him; it's now just a training weekend, not a boys' weekend, but she doesn't want him driving home in the middle of the night after a long run, especially on his own. He's much more likely to want to go straight to sleep anyway.

'It was on the news when I was making the kids dinner,' Liz says. 'Absolutely tragic. They've found some poor girl's body up there.'

'At Mount Field? That's awful,' Kirra says. 'What happened?'

'They didn't say much, just that some bushwalkers found the body of a girl — a woman. They reckon she's in her twenties but they haven't given any other details. A hiking accident, I guess. It's so sad. I really hate hearing about things like that.' Thea and Kirra murmur in agreement, but no one says anything for a while, each of them thinking their own thoughts and trying not to fix an image in their mind of a body lying broken across a pile of rocks or in a stream. 'I wish people wouldn't go bushwalking on their own,' Liz continues after a while.

Thea knows the comment is directed at her. Liz, who was always the party girl of the group, has a cautious side that still surprises Thea. It's a well-travelled conversation between the three of them: Liz cautioning Thea about walking on trails or home alone; Kirra arguing that women should be able to walk wherever they want; Liz agreeing that yes, women should be able to walk alone, but that's not the world they're living in. And in any case, it's not just murderers and rapists, there are snakes and spiders and, well, everything in nature. She worries just as much about Joe when he runs on his own. Thea sees her point, she really does, but she also knows that things can happen whether you're by yourself or not; being in a group is no guarantee of safety or survival. Sometimes she just needs space and movement that is hers and no one else's.

After a moment, Kirra looks across to Thea. 'Has Chris said anything?' she asks.

Thea shakes her head. 'No, nothing,' she says. When Chris is around, he's so present: he's the one telling jokes and filling glasses, just like he's always been; he still takes the time to talk — to listen — to everyone. After years of building a life together, she now trusts that he thinks about her when they're not together, that he factors her in to his decisions — and yet, when he's away his messages are functional more than conversational: *I've arrived. Heading out for a run now, back in a couple of hours. I'm back at camp.* He tends to focus solely on the thing he's doing, be it work or running or time away with mates. He'd mention something like this, though, she's sure he would. The chances are he's run or slept his whole way through it. 'I'll text him,' Thea murmurs, but leaves her phone in her bag.

The waiter comes over to see if they're ready to order. They're not, but it's the change of direction that they need. The conversation moves away from the tragedy onto the menu, another round of drinks, and then onto finalising details for their next girls' weekend. After all this time, and all of life's demands and commitments, celebrations and heartbreaks, they haven't missed a year. It's still months away, but they like to book it well in advance to ensure the rest of life doesn't push it to the side. In fact, it's the push and pull of life — and death — that has made it so important.

Even when most of the rest of the world was in some state of lockdown the year before, the three of them sat, sipping wine and watching the sun set off Maria Island, talking about how lucky they were just to be out of the house, out of the city, together, under a roofless sky.

The hours pass and they eat and drink and laugh, slipping and sliding between old jokes and new adventures, wrapped in the warmth of their own world in the way of people who have loved each other for years. But Thea sees her there, that unnamed girl, sitting quietly but insistently in the fourth chair at the table throughout the evening. She's younger than the rest of them, frozen in time, a ghost from across the sea, from across the years. And, even though Thea's flanked by her two closest friends, the air around them ripe and rich with laughter, she feels suddenly and profoundly sad. There's no better word to capture the depth and simplicity of the feeling. And, yes, it's the unnamed hiker she feels sad about. And, yes, it's Sarah she's sad about. But it's also herself. How did she get here, so far from the life she thought she was going to have? It's not a bad life. She can't complain. But how has she lived so much of it? Look at her now, almost forty, and she doesn't know how it happened.

☆ ☆ ☆

Thea steps off the brightly lit night bus into the pool of orange street light. Beyond its reach, the reserve spills darkly down the slope, away from the road. During the day, she enjoys walking along the boardwalk through the browns and muted greens and sometimes sits on one of the wooden viewing platforms to sketch. The sway and hush of treetops is calming. But tonight the reserve is a heavy presence beside her, a dark lake rising and falling against the edge of the road. The two-pitch call of a boobook slides out of the darkness. The sound pulls at something deep inside Thea — the feeling of being in her childhood bed listening to the soft call of a ruru from the stand of rimu, tawa and kahikatea at the end of the road where she grew up. Her body reverberates with the vibrations of home.

Thea lets herself into the house, takes off her shoes, hangs up her jacket, and walks through to the lounge, all without turning on the light. It's the meditative familiarity of the house. Of home. She can navigate her way from one end to the other without thinking, like walking a labyrinth to its inevitable centre. She lies on the couch and opens her messages to contact Chris. He's out there running through the dark, nothing but a foggy moon and his head torch to guide him. He could slip, or trip; he could fall off the trail, another broken body for someone to find.

She's distracted by a chat from the girls. *Thea, did you get home safe? Let me know or I'll call the police. Or fall asleep and forget.* She laughs to herself as she reads the message. To Liz, the reserve is not a beautiful space of calm; it's filled with black-gloved hands that could reach out and pull Thea into the trees. And yet, with two energetic young children, sleep trumps everything.

Yep, home safe. Didn't get murdered. Thea thinks about deleting the second sentence, but leaves it. She lies in the dark, grateful for her friends and the plans they have and the life she has, but conscious, too, of a lapping sorrow, small ripples of something not quite right. Tonight she'd felt like cutting loose, not just drinking too much, but sitting on a beach somewhere, a driftwood fire burning, music playing, smell of sweet skunky smoke in the air, people stumbling into dunes and out of waves. Sometimes she wants to say fuck it to the security and routine of her life. To have just one night of madness. Some days she wants to pack a bag and head off to distant lands for months on end.

They'd stayed for another drink after dinner, but neither Liz nor Kirra had been up for a late night. There's always something with kids, or partners, or tiredness from work, some kind of event or commitment. Life getting in the way of living. Thea had swallowed down her frustration and walked to the bus stop. Besides, she doesn't really want to wake up, head hangover-heavy as though filled with wet sand, doesn't want to give up everything she has, this good life of hers. And go crazy all she wants, she can't travel back in time.

She opens the last message Chris sent. Even if he's sure-footed and safe, he must've heard about the woman. It must've shaken him, like it's shaken her. They talk about Sarah less and less as the years go by. When they do, her name jumps through the conversation like a stone skipping across the surface of the lake: brief mentions that quickly sink into a deep silence. But Chris must think about her, like Thea thinks about her. Whenever there's news about the death of a young woman, or when she sees a flash of a long orange skirt, Thea is tumbled back through the golden suns and silver moons of fourteen years. Because they talk so rarely about Sarah, the words don't come to Thea now. She types out something quickly. *Thinking of you. How are you? xx.* She hopes she hasn't woken him.

Drinking gin was a mistake, she thinks, trying to dismiss her melancholy as she cleans her teeth and washes her face. In bed she reaches to switch off the lamp beside her, but picks up her phone instead. She brings up the news. 'Woman's body found at Mt Field' is there on the homepage, a photo of an ambulance parked in the campground, doors open, a paramedic looking inside. There isn't much more than what Liz has already told them: the body of a young woman was found by bushwalkers earlier that day, less than two kilometres from the campsite — the same one Chris is staying at — and four metres off the trail. Her name won't be released until her family has been notified.

Thea wonders how long she lay there, among brown leaves and curls of bark, small stones pressing into her flesh, and when exactly she breathed her last breath. She wonders how many people walked past before she was spotted. She can visualise the scene so vividly: snakes nearby, waking up after the winter, slithering from under rocks and out of hollow logs, tiny insects scuttling through the leaves. She can imagine all the minute details, is tormented by the scene. But the one thing she cannot bring herself to picture is the woman's face. She lies unnamed, her face unseen.

Thea closes the news site. She shouldn't be reading this. She's not even sure if this is the kind of thing that should be on the news, some poor person's death a fascination for thousands. Her phone pings. It's Chris: *Sleeping. Talk tomorrow.* She woke him; she should've waited until morning. A few seconds later, another message comes through: *xx*. Thea releases tension she didn't realise she was holding, loosening the grip on her phone. He's not annoyed.

She turns off the lamp and closes her eyes, letting the weight of the darkness and the day push her towards oblivion. From the reserve, the boobook calls through the trees to its mate. As black-gloved hands pull Thea into an inky black sleep, the answering call comes back.

13

Outside the bedroom window, trees cascade down the hill, a blanket of dull green joining the earth and the morning sky. Thea hasn't been able to sleep in, but she's determined to lie in, determined not to waste the time she has to herself. She startles as a group of black cockatoos breaks through the canopy, squabbles in the air, then settles down again among the trees. When she first moved to Tasmania, she heard that black cockatoos signal rain, that they come down from the mountains when wild weather is on the way. Some time after she had been living in Hobart she'd asked a client if he'd packed his wet-weather gear, as the black cockatoos had been sitting in the trees outside her house that morning. He'd laughed at first, as though she'd made a joke, then looked at her and said, 'You know that's a myth, right?'

Whatever secret knowledge the cockatoos may or may not have, they had settled in the eucalyptus the afternoon before, and hours later, in the night, furious gusts of wind began to race across the treetops. She'd woken at one point to fistfuls of rain hitting the windows, as if the weather were trying to get her attention. She'd fallen back asleep, but for the remaining hours of darkness had tossed and turned as though twisting her body to avoid the needling rain.

She hears the sound of a car pull up and, moments later, the front door opens. 'Chris?' she calls down the hall.

'Hey,' he responds from somewhere by the entranceway. Tracking his movements through the small house, she can hear him carrying things inside, putting them down in the kitchen, the laundry, the hallway cupboard. She starts to get up, but he's at the bedroom door, leaning against the jamb and smiling at her. 'Is this what you do when I'm away? Just lie around in bed all day?'

'It's only like eight-thirty or something,' she says with a laugh. Then she puts her book down and says, seriously, 'You're back early. I heard about what happened. Are you OK?'

She can't see his expression as he peels his t-shirt over his head and says, 'Yeah, of course.' He looks at her as he steps out of his jeans. 'Mind if I join you?' He's already lifting up the covers. Thea automatically moves over to make room for him, but looks at him with mild disbelief. He catches her expression and says, 'What? It's not like I'm the one who died or anything.'

'Chris!' The sheets are cold underneath Thea as she moves away from him. 'I can't believe you said that.'

He looks sheepish. 'I know, I'm sorry. I didn't mean it. I just—'

He pauses and sighs. 'It's been a tough weekend. I don't really feel like talking about it.'

Thea feels like talking about it. If she can speak about it, maybe she'll stop thinking about it. 'It'd be good to talk,' she says, a palm pressed to Chris's chest to hold him back. 'Don't you think?'

'No,' he says, leaning in to kiss her shoulder. 'No thinking. No talking. I've done enough talking about it.' He kisses his way up her neck.

She lies back, her body stiff, but she can't help tilting her chin up as he kisses the space behind her earlobe. She allows herself a breath before twisting her head away. 'To who?' she asks.

'Last night,' he says, sharply. 'They wanted to talk to everyone who was there. You know, standard stuff. I didn't expect to come back here and be grilled.'

Thea's not sure who 'they' are or where exactly 'there' is. Surely he means Mount Field in general? Surely he wasn't actually right there when it happened? She's got so many questions. 'Were you—'

'It's my turn to ask questions.' He cuts her off, his face so close to hers she can't focus on it. 'Like, why have you got all these clothes on?' He plucks at the neckline of her tank top, then kisses her on the mouth as he presses his weight down on her. He lifts her arms above her head, gripping her wrists with one hand as he slips the other one up under her top.

Afterwards, they lie side by side but not touching. 'Liz said Joe couldn't make it,' Thea says, looking for a different way into the conversation.

'Yeah, he messaged me at lunchtime on Friday. He had to work all weekend. Apparently.'

'What, you don't believe him?' she asks. 'Why would he make that up?'

'I believe that he had to do *some* work. But nothing that couldn't wait until this afternoon. I think Liz just forgot to book a babysitter and bullied him into staying so she could have her night out.'

'That's not true,' Thea says, propping herself up to look at him. 'It's not exactly like we had anything special planned. Just dinner. And Liz is the one who called the night to an end so she could get home.'

'Well after the kids had gone to bed, I bet.'

It's no secret that Liz and Chris have never liked each other, although neither of them seems to care how the other feels about them or what they say. Thea thinks she's the only one who gets cut by the barbed comments they make, and sometimes she wonders if that's the intent — perhaps each of them hopes that if they prick and stab enough, she'll cut the other one loose.

'Couldn't you have postponed? Gone with Joe another time?' Chris had work to do this weekend, too, but she won't point that out to him.

Chris lets out a quiet huff of breath, turning to look at her. 'I could've, but then he just would've cancelled the next trip. And the next. If Joe wants to run a hundred K on the back of patchy training, that's his call, but I'd prefer not to die on the finish line.' Thea's going to say something, but just sighs and lies back onto the bed. Now Chris pushes himself up and looks at her. 'Look, I really do think he had to work. I don't think Liz is exactly thrilled about how much time his training takes up though, and I think she might have "suggested" that he do one or the other this weekend. Poor bastard, I think he could've done with the break.'

For Liz and Joe, with small children and busy jobs, life is a hectic juggling game. But Thea's never heard Liz seriously complain about the amount of time Joe spends running. A six-year-old shadow darkens the conversation, at least where Thea is. Sometimes she feels as though she's standing in the shade, waiting for something, for someone, while Chris strolls onward through the sunlight.

They had talked, months after, about whether they could ever try for another baby. 'Could you go through that again?' Chris had asked, stroking the side of her face and pushing her hair back, as they lay in bed facing each other. 'I mean, could you even take the risk?'

'It doesn't mean it would happen again.'

'I know, I know. But if it did?'

'I don't know.' She had no idea if she would survive such loss again, or if *they* would survive it.

A few weeks later, she had brought it up again. Chris walked over to her, held her upper arms and put his forehead against hers. 'We made a decision,' he said. 'We can't keep revisiting it. It'll destroy us.'

'A decision?' Thea asked. 'We didn't—'

He tightened his hold on her. 'I can't do it again. I can't—' He swallowed and raised his head from hers to look across the room. 'I can't see you blame yourself like that again. I need *you*.'

She remembers the miasma of those months, but maybe she doesn't remember all the details, doesn't understand what it was like for Chris.

She still talked about the loss to Liz and Kirra and to Magda, but every time she raised it with Chris, he looked so stricken that she stopped. Life is what life is and she has made one that works for her. Most days are good, but those times when she thinks about their unborn baby, she feels so hollow. She suspects that Chris feels weightless.

She rolls back over to face him. She opens her mouth to speak, but his eyes are closed. She prods him gently but there's no response. He's sound asleep.

☆ ☆ ☆

'I might as well get a start on that fucking presentation for the Launceston pitch this afternoon,' Chris says, screwing the stovetop coffee pot together as though wringing someone's neck.

Thea makes sympathetic noises as she slices tomatoes for their brunch and Chris rants about his colleagues. She almost suggests that he forget about work for the rest of the weekend and they do something fun instead, but she's already mentally mapped out the hours she'd expected to have to herself. She's reluctant to give them up to hear him complain about site visits, meetings and presentations.

'You should find a new job,' she says. 'That place works you way too hard. It's not worth it. Can you tell them you're not willing to get on a plane at the moment? Tell them that I'm annoyed about you taking the risk, if you want.' She thought it was the supportive thing to say, a nice thing to offer. Besides, it's true: she doesn't want to get Covid just because Chris's firm wants to increase its profits.

'That's not how it works, Thea. My clients don't just walk in the door. Or limp, or whatever.' They've had this conversation before. It's not worth her explaining, again, that she might not have fancy functions and catered meetings to attend, but she works hard for referrals and reviews. Chris's words get louder as he talks. 'It's not exactly a good time to pack it in now, is it? Anyway, this is a great opportunity.' He repeats her words from earlier in the weekend. He breathes in deeply then expels the air — the noise that always reminds Thea of a sweat-slicked horse, ears pinned back, hoof poised to kick.

Thea picks up the plates to take them to the table while Chris pours the coffee. A fork slides off and clatters to the floor. 'Sorry,' she says, wincing at the noise. She puts the plates back on the bench and crouches to pick it up.

'No, I'm sorry. I'm not pissed with you. It's just been a fucker of a week,' Chris says. He pulls her in to him, wrapping his arms around her from behind as she stands at the sink. 'You'll be pleased to have me out of your hair for a few days while I'm out of town.' Thea murmurs something non-committal in response while Chris continues talking. 'And today I'll just sit quietly. You won't even notice I'm here.'

'It's OK,' she says, standing still within his embrace. 'I'm heading out. The house is all yours for the afternoon.' She breaks through the circle of his arms as she reaches out to turn on the tap and fill up a glass of water. She waits until he moves away before lifting it to her mouth. She takes small sips between slow breaths, and imagines immersing herself in the meditative blue depth of the pool, being cocooned in the underwater calm, the outside world muffled and out of reach.

☆ ☆ ☆

The days roll through the week. Thea has a late-night clinic one evening, drinks with former colleagues the next. Chris works late, coming home stressed and short-tempered. But everyone is stretched tight these days. The grind of the pandemic, of cancelled holidays, of families separated, of job uncertainty, is slowly wearing people down; the threat of Delta at the borders, of getting sick, of vulnerable loved ones dying, is steadily taking its toll. A traveller from Melbourne has been discovered to have breached quarantine, spending the better part of the day a loaded gun on the streets of Hobart. Every client that Thea sees talks about the quarantine breach, the threat of Delta, and Melbourne's never-ending lockdowns. And the rain. Every day it seems to pour down. They're near the midpoint of October and are set for record-breaking levels.

On Thursday morning, the alarm pierces Thea's sleep earlier than usual. Just a single stab of sound before Chris silences it and pushes himself from the bed. He leans over her in the dark, kisses her and tells her to keep sleeping. Through half-closed eyes, she watches him lift the coat hanger with his suit and shirt off the hook on the back of the door, as though he's carrying his own shadow out into the hall. She hears him close the bathroom door, the shower mixing with the sound of the rain on the roof, and briefly considers getting up too. Instead, she waits until she hears Chris's airport taxi pull up outside and the front door close.

She texts him during the day, between appointments with her clients. *I hope it's going well. I'm sure you'll impress them.* She's about to hit send, then adds *Wear a mask!*, deletes it, then writes it again and adds an *x* and sends it. There's no response. She imagines him reading her message and flipping the phone face-down.

She thinks about calling him after work but she's meeting Liz for a swim, and he's said he plans to squeeze in a run before heading to a function. She sends a message instead.

I hope the hotel's nice. Rest up and good luck for tomorrow. Let me know how it goes xx.

Thanks. Sleep well. Talk tomorrow x.

Friday is overcast but dry. Thea works almost without a break until mid-afternoon, when she follows her client out to reception. One of the other physiotherapists, Iluka, is standing at the reception desk, talking to the receptionist, Marlene.

'Lockdown,' Marlene says, looking between Thea and her client.

'What?' Thea asks.

'The Premier has just announced it. Three-day lockdown starting at six this evening.'

Three days, thinks Thea. *That's not so bad*. That's not nearly as bad as other places. That's just a weekend at home and a day of online consultations, or cancelled consultations. The worst part will be the rest of the week, when they try to squeeze those appointments into other days.

'Is it all of Tassie?' Thea asks.

'No.' Marlene angles her computer monitor towards Thea. 'Just the south.'

The area is marked on a map of Tasmania on Marlene's screen, a red zone spreading through the southeast ventricle of the island like a blood clot.

Chris is landing just before six, flying in from the north to the south, from the blue on the map into the red, flying from an unrestricted area into lockdown. Three days, that's not so bad, that's nothing really. She hopes Chris's presentation went well.

At home, Thea listens to the news while chopping up vegetables for dinner. There's nothing new: it's all about who's in lockdown, who is not; what can be done, what can't. The newsreader lists the places where the man went, they stress the need to get vaccinated, then talk about the hours-long queues at testing stations. If Thea hadn't started chopping up the chicken breast, her fingertips tainted and slimy, she'd turn it off.

And then, after all the Covid news and before the sport and weather: *The woman whose body was discovered at Mount Field almost a week ago has been named as twenty-six-year-old German citizen Gretel Fischer. Ms Fischer has been living in Hobart since August 2020, settling in Tasmania after spending several months travelling around the rest of the country.*

Thea's ashamed to realise she'd forgotten all about the girl.

It's been a busy week, but still. And although it shouldn't make a difference, she feels worse knowing now that the woman was a foreigner. She'd lain there, alone, so far from home. With the international border closed, her parents can't even come to accompany her back to Germany. Some government or medical official will put her on a plane, then turn around and drive away before the plane has taken off.

By the time Thea had arrived in Australia, she and Chris had already poured out their feelings in emails, trying to process what had happened with Sarah and how it had affected them. By then they were both just growing new skin over the shock and grief and it was too painful to open up those wounds. They got to know each other in a new way — healing, not through words, but through the absence of them. After they'd settled into their new life together and found each other's rhythm, they faced it again, staggering through the things they'd said before and stumbling into new territory. Chris had told Thea how he'd said goodbye to Sarah's father and brother in the hotel lobby, watching from the doorway as their taxi drove away. He could've left when they did, taking the same flight to LA before they parted ways and flew to different corners of Australia. Instead, he had begged his parents to book him on a flight leaving a couple of days later. 'I couldn't do it, Thee.' He'd looked at her, shaking his head slowly as though he was afraid any more vigorous action would send tears spilling down his cheeks. 'I couldn't spend another day with them, all that time on a plane and in transit or whatever. I felt so bad about not being there for Sarah at the time, and it was awful saying goodbye, knowing I was never going to see her again, but

I just needed to be on my own.' She'd felt a surge of love for him then, like she desperately wanted to take care of him and make everything all right. 'I'm pretty sure they didn't want to spend any more time with me anyway,' he had continued. 'You know, after they told me to fuck off and go to hell, that I had quote-unquote blood on my hands.' It was a while before either of them mentioned Sarah again.

Thea never did go to Margaret River. She thought she'd have plenty of time once she was living in Hobart, but there was always something to stop her going, or just enough to give her the excuse to put it out of her mind: her new job, drinks to get to know her new workmates, the tiring search for a place to live. And, when they did secure a flat, renting on their own was expensive, and so were flights across the country. But, really, it was more than that. How could she explain to Sarah's parents who she was and why she was living in Australia? How could she reveal to them that the person they held responsible for their daughter's death had moved on so quickly? And with Sarah's friend, no less? Even if she slipped into Western Australia without visiting them, how could she sit beside Sarah's grave and explain all of that to her? To herself?

Then, just as the scar tissue had thickened enough to withstand prodding and flexing, there was the miscarriage, tearing every old grief and all the guilt back to the surface. The more time that passed, the more she was able to convince herself that it didn't matter — that you don't need to sit by a person's grave to remember them or to feel their loss, that Chris was right all those years ago back in Melbourne when he said that it wouldn't make her feel any better. Except, she never really did convince herself. There's a dark honeycomb of holes inside her: places, if she were to shine a torch there, she'd see the dead still occupied.

☆ ☆ ☆

It's after eight when Chris walks in the door. 'Fuck me, what a day,' he says, heading straight for the kitchen. 'They're a bunch of fuckers, all of them. Every single last fucking one of them.'

'It didn't go well?' Thea asks, standing behind him as he grazes directly from the fridge. 'I can cook up a stir fry?' Even though he has his back to her, she gestures to the cut-up vegetables on the kitchen bench.

'That'd be great,' he says, turning around to give her a kiss. 'No, the presentation went fine. Great, in fact. They're just a bunch of fuckers. Do you need any help?' He picks up the wine bottle sitting on the bench and pours himself a glass. 'Started without me, I see.' He tops up her glass and holds the wine bottle up to the light.

'Thanks. Dinner's almost done. You relax.'

'I thought everyone was meant to be at home, but every single person in Hobart is out there driving around. Traffic was a fucking nightmare.'

Thea knows. She's been waiting in queues for half the afternoon, making sure they had enough food for the weekend. It's not like she's been at home all afternoon, feet up, drinking wine. She just needed that one glass to take the edge off everything.

'It's great that the presentation went so well. That'll be a huge help to get a promotion, right?'

Chris pauses with the wine glass halfway to his lips. 'It would be. If they hadn't just put the promotion round on hold.'

'Again?' Thea says. *Again*, she thinks to herself. She's heard all this before, but she's starting to wonder whether all promotions are on hold, or just Chris's chances.

'Yep, again. I had to listen to Geoff justifying it the whole flight back. Apparently in the "current environment" they can't afford to promote anyone or give any pay increases.' Thea opens her mouth to say something but, anticipating what she's going to say, Chris adds, 'It's just an excuse. They can definitely afford to pay everyone more. Honestly, I wouldn't actually be all that worried about the pay, but the real kicker is they expect us all to do more. My reward for pulling off the preso today is that I now have to do everything that Geoff would normally do — which is a "great development opportunity", by the way. Oh, and the best part is, Geoff promised that "we" would meet with them again on Monday to answer this fucking long list of questions that they have.' Thea can hear the inverted commas dripping like acid rain through the air.

She doesn't know why he stays in that job, except when it's good, it's good — or so he says. She knows better not to suggest, once more, that he leave.

Chris drains his glass and pours another. 'What?' he asks when he notices her looking at his glass of wine. 'I'm catching up.'

She won't mention Gretel, not tonight. She murmurs something sympathetic instead. As she speaks, she imagines running her hand over the black velvet neck of a horse; long, calming strokes. Outside, the rain continues to fall.

14

Sunday is wet and grey. Beyond the rain-streaked windows, the eucalyptus and tea-tree crackle and clatter as the wind turns their leaves inside out. Thea's always loved the view from the house, the birdlife and the breeze, the light and shadow splashing across the treetops. But today her thoughts keep falling through the canopy to the shady spaces between the trunks. They've crept past the halfway point of the lockdown. It's nowhere near as bad as other places, she reminds herself. Melbourne has been in lockdown — again — since August; so has Auckland. It's only three days. But there's something stifling about being told you can't free-roam the city. It brings the threat of those other places where days have stretched to weeks and months, the fear that life might be a five-kilometre radius for an unknown time. A two-person bubble. While the rain comes down outside, inside the air hums with cooped-up tension.

She thinks of the polar bears they had at Auckland Zoo when she was a kid. Yellow-tinged, pacing from one end of the high-sided pit to the other and back again, swaying and going mad on a slab of concrete ice that would never freeze and never melt. She knows her own meandering pace from the kitchen bench to the window, down the hall, to the bedroom, the bathroom and back again is getting on Chris's nerves as he types loudly on his work laptop. There's a dull, unstretched feeling in her limbs, a heaviness that craves the sea, the pull and kick through a gentle swell out around the buoy and back. She sits down at the other end of the table from Chris and picks up yesterday's newspaper, left in their letterbox that morning by their neighbour so that she can do the cryptic crossword and other puzzles.

There she is again, on the inside edge of page two, past the headline news of Covid queues and quarantines. Gretel Fischer. There's a close-up of Gretel's face inset against a bigger photo of the campsite, and four short columns of text below. It's a human-interest piece, a story that's obviously caught other people's attention, too, as is so often the case when a young, attractive woman dies. *But there's something more than that*, Thea thinks. It evokes something of the zeitgeist, this story of the girl who chose to stay half a world away from home when the world went into lockdown. She had made the decision, the article said, relaying what Gretel's housemates had said, that if she was going to have her freedom restricted, it'd be somewhere new. She chose to stay away from home, but she never thought it would be for the rest of her life. It's a Covid death, but not a death from Covid.

Gretel loved Tasmania, the article quoted one of the housemates as saying. She loved camping and bushwalking, often taking off at the last minute for a night away. She enjoyed her job working in an art gallery. She'd recently started seeing someone. 'We thought she was going away with him,' the housemate had said.

'This is so sad,' Thea says aloud, looking over at Chris, who is frowning at his computer. He doesn't respond. After a minute or so of silence, she takes a deep breath and speaks again. 'Did you talk to her?'

'What's that?' he asks. She tries to catch his eye, but his gaze flicks from his laptop to his phone.

'The woman who died at Mount Field last weekend. It's so sad. Just awful.'

Now he looks at her and draws in a breath as though preparing himself to explain something that he's explained a hundred times already. 'I didn't even see her,' he says. 'Maybe just, like, across the campground or something.'

'It can't have been very busy? It's been so wet lately.' Chris used to tease her for walking in the rain, but he would run through a monsoon if that's what the training programme said.

'It didn't rain much last weekend.' He picks up his phone again, zooms in on something, then looks back at his laptop. 'This lockdown better not go on long. If it's still in place on Tuesday, I'm going into the office to pick up a monitor.' Then he looks up at her, as though he's just thought of something.

'The trails weren't in great shape though. Muddy and slippery. It's probably why she fell.'

Thea looks down at the paper, at the picture of Gretel. There's something about her that reminds her of Sarah. Maybe it's the long feather earrings, or maybe it's just that she's young, healthy and happy, with a shiny face, hair and smile. As she stares at the ink and newsprint, another memory surfaces. There was a time, shortly after they moved to Hobart, when a group of them had gone to a music festival and she and Liz had headed over to another stage to watch a local band. When they'd gone back to meet up with the others at the international stage, they'd seen Chris at the side of the crowd in the shadow of the speaker stack, dancing behind a girl. Thea hadn't seen her face, just the tattoo of stars falling down her arm as she raised her hands up to catch the music, the tumbling shine of her bracelets and the hair cascading down her back. He'd leant down to say something in her ear, his hand briefly resting on her hip. Thea's gut reaction was to pull back into the space behind, back into the current of people walking between food trucks. But without saying anything, Liz had danced her way up to Chris and when she was beside him, she raised her arms up, moving her whole body to the music, then bumped her hip into his, knocking him off balance. Still swaying her hips from side to side and smiling broadly, Liz had turned to him and said something. Standing a few metres back, Thea couldn't hear the words. She'd just seen Chris nod and Liz, without losing the rhythm of the music, turn back to look for Thea, pulling her into the crowd with a sweeping wave of her arm.

'Is that what happened?' Thea asks. 'She fell?'

'Yeah, I guess go,' Chris says. Thea looks down at the paper, staring at the photo of the campsite as though she might be able to see Chris's tent there, or the flash of his blue running jacket in the background. When she looks up, he's focused on her, his mouth a firm straight line, his dark limbal rings emphasising the pale browny-orange of his irises. 'I was asleep when they found her. I woke up to all the drama.' *He can sleep like the dead*, Thea thinks to herself, then realises what a terrible expression that is. 'They talked to everyone who was there,' he continues. 'They didn't give us many details, but it sounded like she fell. Why, what does it say in the paper?'

'No, nothing, I don't know. It doesn't say anything.' She looks down at the paper as though she's scanning for information, as though she hasn't already read each word. 'It sounds intense. It must've been awful.'

'Yes. It was.'

She opens her mouth to say something, without knowing exactly what she wants to say or how to say it. 'I just—' *I just want you to talk about it*, she thinks. *I just want us to talk.* 'I just,' she starts again, 'don't think I realised how full-on it was for you.' It's not what she wanted to say. *You were there*, she wants to say. *Talk to me!* she wants to scream at him.

Neither of them says anything for a while. A cold tension steps silently into the room. Two polar bears on a concrete iceberg. 'Did it make you think . . .? Thea trails off, hoping Chris will pick up where she left off. He's watching her closely, but doesn't say anything, waiting. '. . . of Sarah?' she finishes, her voice sounding thin and weak against the backdrop of wind and rain.

'What do you think?'

He sees ghosts, like she sees ghosts; he surely must. 'We never talk about Sarah,' Thea says, her voice quiet. *There's so much we never talk about*, she thinks but doesn't say.

A hairline crack runs through the hush. Chris speaks. 'No, we never talk about Sarah.'

Their silences have built on each other, two tectonic plates slowly colliding to form a mountain range. For a long time Thea thought that it was Chris who didn't want to talk about what happened. She thought she was doing him a kindness, not wanting him to relive the blame Sarah's father and brother had thrown on him. She knows what it's like to carry the burden of someone else's death, whether or not you're at fault. But she's the one who, from time to time, alone at home, has checked the cost of tickets to Margaret River, then shut the browser and cleared her search history. Maybe it's suited her not to remind Chris of lovely, vibrant Sarah.

She had come home one night that first year on the island and had told Chris about the trip she and Liz and Kirra had spontaneously booked over drinks that evening. 'Our grand plan is to go to every national park in Tasmania. Over the years.' She'd been so happy, not just to have made such good friends in a short space of time, but to have a vision of that friendship stretching into the future. 'We've already booked it but it's not until March. There's an arts festival that Kirra knows about. We might go away before then too. Girls only, sorry.' The words had gushed out of her into a still, grey silence.

She'd expected Chris to join in with her enthusiasm, maybe pretend to be offended that he wasn't invited and perhaps be disappointed that it wasn't something the two of them were doing together, but to acknowledge what a great idea it was and to be excited for her nonetheless. Instead, he said nothing at all. After she pushed and prodded, asking him what was wrong, he said, 'Do you have absolutely no idea what the date is?' Confused, she waited for him to go on and, after a short while, his words slid into the room like ice. 'It's been a year.' Even then, it had taken her a moment to catch up. Before she could gather the right words together, Chris had said, 'I'm glad everything's working out so well for you, Thea. Good for you.' He'd walked out of the room.

Later that evening, she had apologised and tried to explain to him that there was a whole calendar of dates she kept in her head of days that shaped and changed her life. The only reason Sarah's hadn't stuck was that she hadn't heard the news until a couple of days after her death. She tried to describe those black-hole days following the call with Michael when she drifted from place to place, only half-engaged in the world around her. On a high shelf in the hallway cupboard, there's a sketchbook filled with grey lines and smudges, mapping out her journey down to Panama. But even if she were to turn slowly through it, page by page, she'd struggle to separate one day from another in her memory. Chris had only looked at her and said coolly, 'Well, it doesn't matter now, does it? You've got a boyfriend, a job, new friends, a great new life. You didn't spend days in that shithole city being accused of all sorts of things. You didn't give up everything and come home. I should be in London now, with a great new life of my own.' The truth in his words had stung like lemon juice squeezed over paper cuts. Not just how well things were going for her, but his admission that he'd rather be somewhere else, living a different life.

That night Chris went out, not returning until late, bringing the smell of a crowded bar into their bed. Thea had lain awake for hours, chest tight, while Chris breathed deeply beside her.

The next morning, between clients, Thea had looked at flights back to New Zealand: to Auckland as well as to Wellington. Expensive, but her savings were building back up now that she was working. Walking to lunch, she saw a poster advertising the arts festival that Kirra had mentioned. She thought of her swim squad and her drawing class, and then her elderly client who would need months of physiotherapy to recover from hip-replacement surgery. She didn't want to leave, not with all that she had and all that there was to look forward to. She didn't want to start all over again. Between her afternoon appointments, she looked at rooms to rent. Just to see what her options were.

In the evening, the atmosphere in the house was heavy like the dark underbelly of a storm cloud about to break. As they were cleaning up after dinner, Thea turned to Chris. 'Should I move out?'

He turned the tap on, a fury of cold water hitting the plate he was holding. 'What?'

'We could talk about the timing. If you want to go overseas, we could give notice now and I'll move—'

'What the fuck, Thea,' he cut her off.

'I could leave—'

'Of course you could. That's what you do, isn't it? Leave? Run away as soon as things get hard.'

She drew in a sharp breath, felt a plunging drop in air pressure. 'That's not true,' she said quietly. He turned the tap off and turned to look at her, holding the plate between his fingers, water dripping onto the kitchen floor. It was true, though, she knew that. But if it was true of her, it was just as true of him.

'Go if you want to,' he said. 'Do what you want. You always do.'

'I don't want to go,' she said. 'You do. I thought you wanted to go to London.'

'That was ages ago. I can't do that now, can I?' Thea didn't know why not, but didn't want to ask. 'If you want to leave me, I can't stop you,' Chris continued. 'I've never been good enough for you, have I?'

'That's not true,' she said again. She felt the cold rush of loneliness inside her and took a step towards him. 'I'm sorry if that's how I've made you feel. I love you, Chris.'

'Do you though?'

'Yes.'

The gap between them was narrow enough that, if she chose to, she could reach up and put her arms around his neck. Instead, she stood, arms by her sides, afraid to move. For a moment they stood in silence, then Chris spoke. 'Don't leave me, Thea.' She took a tiny step towards him, so that there was only a slither of space separating them. Enough room for their body heat and breath to mingle. He threaded his free arm around her waist, pulling her tight into him. She took the plate out of his other hand and reached around to put it on the kitchen bench. Then her arms were clasped around his neck and his hand was on the back of her head, damp fingers entwined in her hair. They fell in towards each other, the gravitational pull of shards of glass in a kaleidoscope.

It's not Gretel's death that's troubling her so much, she realises now. Of course it upsets her — it's tragic beyond words — but there's something else, buried deep below. 'I can't believe it's been so long,' she says. Fourteen years, in fact. 'What happened? With Sarah?' she asks quietly. 'I never really understood.'

'I don't know what happened,' Chris says, eyes fixed on her, his voice the low growl of gravel under tyres. 'It's not like I was there, watching.'

'That's not what I meant.' Thea suddenly realises that she shouldn't have started this conversation. She's kept her questions quiet for years. This isn't the time to ask them.

'What the fuck *did* you mean?'

'Nothing,' she says. 'It's just that I feel bad that I don't actually know what happened.' An explanation, a reason, a bright red thread to lead her through the storm to safety: she just needs something to help her understand everything that happened. 'It seems wrong. But it's not important.'

'It's not important?'

'That's not what I meant,' she says for the second time in a short space of words. She wants to leave the room but feels trapped at the table, like she's not going to be able to go anywhere until whatever she's started is over.

Chris sighs heavily. 'Do you really want to know? Do you really want to go there, Thea?'

'I do.' The words come out before Thea has a chance to really think about them.

'Sarah had started spending a lot of time in the village.' Chris's voice is steady. Tyres on the open road. 'She wanted to check out that weaving place in the village. You always talked about it, so she really wanted to go. She got to know the woman who ran it — Maria. She was there a lot.'

What's Chris saying? Thea wonders. That it's her fault because she told Sarah about the weaving co-op? What's that got to do with anything? She never even went there herself. She wanted to, ever since Chris told her about it, but she never did. It was Chris who told her about it. Chris.

Chris is still speaking. 'It was right next door to Alice's restaurant. It was probably some guys from Guatemala City, doing a delivery to Alice, or something like that.'

Thea reaches back for the echo of words from years ago. Michael from the Xaman Ek used to laugh about how everything got blamed on Guatemala City. It was just a bitter joke, albeit not entirely unfounded, given the series of kidnappings and violence in the 1980s instigated in the capital city. Every time they had a small drama at the hostel, Michael would dryly say that it was thanks to some guys from Guatemala City: 'Sorry, we're out of ice — some guys from Guatemala City took the last cube.' 'No electricity, folks — some guy from Guatemala City tripped over the cable and pulled out the plug.'

Thinking back, she can remember meeting only two people from Guatemala City in San Pedro, and they were tourists just like her. A couple about her age, down for the weekend because they found the highlands, resplendent with volcanic beauty and alive with colour and tradition, just as worth seeing as she did.

Thea thinks the word Michael used was *desconocido*. Unknown. Outsider.

She knows Chris well enough to sense that there's something he's not telling her.

'Sarah changed,' he says as he shuts his laptop. 'She was different in those last few weeks.'

Thea thinks back to the emails she got from Sarah in that brief period of time after she left San Pedro and before Sarah was found trapped in the reeds, the shallow lake water lapping over her. Brave Sarah. Independent Sarah. Sarah who wasn't just sitting around waiting for Chris anymore, but who was exploring San Pedro and discovering herself in the process. 'She sounded like she was enjoying herself,' she says.

'Oh yeah, she was enjoying herself.'

'What do you mean?' she asks.

He sniffs and rubs a finger under his nose, looking at her meaningfully. 'You remember how *bumpy* the roads around San Pedro were, don't you, babe? How do you think Sarah suddenly became brave enough to stroll around town on her own? A little bump before she set off, another in the plaza or wherever she went each day.'

It doesn't sound like Sarah. She was no prude. She got stoned from time to time. But Thea never saw her touch any other kind of drug. Sarah had seen the addiction in San Pedro: in the Americans who crossed the border, escaping whatever they thought they needed to escape. They travelled south until they found their slice of false reality by the lake. What started as easy and recreational became too easy and habitual, addictive. And then there were the backpackers — like them — who found the good times and stayed too long, and the longer they stayed, the harder it was to leave, the more normal they thought it was to get high each day and ignore the world around them.

'I don't want to be like them,' Sarah had said to Thea on more than one occasion, and Thea had agreed, but never thought there was a risk of it with Sarah. After all, Sarah wasn't trying to escape anything. 'But if I stay . . .' Sarah had said, leaving the sentence unfinished.

'You won't stay,' Thea had said. 'Not forever. Probably not much longer. Here for a good time — here for way too long a time. But definitely not here forever.'

Sarah stayed.

Still, it doesn't sound like her. There's something Chris isn't telling Thea, she's sure of it. 'Even if that's true,' Thea says to him now, 'where did she get it from, Chris?' She thinks of Chris, a strobe-light figure in and out of the shadows of San Pedro. Behind the bar at Xibalba, or in the crowd, always talking to someone, heads close and low, parting with a shake of the hand. Up and down the road to Alice's restaurant, circling round the tables at the Xaman Ek, everybody's friend.

'You know where,' he says, rubbing at a spot on the table. Then he suddenly looks up at her and, speaking quickly, adds, 'But who knows what else she was getting from Alice, or Maria, or whoever.'

Something's off. She can't quite work out what. It's like

watching a movie and not being able to work out if it's badly scripted or badly edited. 'She always had a thing against coke. What changed?'

Chris looks back down, then off to the side — anywhere but at Thea. Finally, he says, 'She asked if you had ever tried it.'

Thea stares at him across the table. She doesn't move, but feels a hot tremble under her skin. 'So, what? You're saying she became a coke addict because of me? And then what? Became mixed up with Alice's restaurant somehow?' She can't remember the words of Sarah's emails but can remember the feeling of them — so much excitement to be out exploring, a hint of pride for finding the courage, and a growing frustration at the insular gringo community of San Pedro. In those emails, it felt as though Sarah was becoming more herself, was — whether consciously or not — preparing to leave San Pedro, even if that meant leaving Chris behind. There was no sense of Sarah changing so completely in the way that Chris is suggesting. 'I still don't really understand,' she says. And then, because she doesn't know what else to say, or how to say it, she asks directly: 'How did she die?'

Chris looks at her, his face washed in sadness. 'I really don't know. The Guatemalan police were useless. They didn't want to get involved in the death of a foreigner. It all happened around Independence Day and I think there was a bit of anti-gringo sentiment. I could've pushed harder, but I honestly don't think it would've made a difference.'

'And then they could've found out about the drugs,' Thea says. *Your* drugs, she thinks.

'Yeah. That too. Then Sarah's dad and brother tried to ask

questions, but it was too hard and too late, and they just wanted to take her home.' Thea can understand that, but she can't help wondering if, later, they were angry at themselves for not asking more, for not insisting on a full investigation. Or maybe they did get told more, but just didn't tell Chris about it.

Or maybe he's just not telling her. 'Why did they blame you though?' she asks him.

Chris looks up at her, a flash of confusion passing over his face. 'It was my fault,' he says, as though it's a simple statement of fact. 'She was there because of me.'

'What? By the lake?' Thea asks, and it feels like she's been given a glimpse at some kind of truth, like a strip of wallpaper starting to peel back at the edge.

'No, in San Pedro. She would never have been there in the first place if I hadn't been there. And she wanted to leave when you left.'

Well, there's no secret there. Thea can understand Sarah's family's rage towards Chris for that. It's true, Sarah died because she was in San Pedro, and she wouldn't have been in San Pedro if not for Chris. 'What *was* she doing by the lake?' she asks.

'I don't know,' he says, pushing his chair back and resting his elbows on his knees. 'I don't know. I just know that it's my fault.' He hides his face in his hands.

And yet, it feels like there *is* more.

She looks at him, slouched over, head in his hands, as though he's posing for a painting, the perfect portrait of sorrow.

She can't reconcile this version of Sarah with the girl she knew. She doesn't believe that Sarah would have developed such a serious drug habit at all, let alone in such a short time; so serious that she was, what, buying directly from the local dealers? Something worse? But she can believe that sometimes things go wrong. Sometimes things turn out so much worse than you ever imagined they could when you started your day. She's angry at Chris, but she's angry at herself, too. She's never really pushed to hear the truth of how Sarah died. Was the coke cut with something toxic? Did he give her too much? Cold dread runs through her. Did he lose his temper, impatient with being told, once too often, that they should leave San Pedro? Thea's always known there was something Chris wasn't telling her, but instead of digging through his words, she's let a thick silence fall down, a blanket over the truth. She's had her reasons for that, a trail of footprints in snow.

She and Chris fitted together when they both had empty spaces to fill; his lake-deep shadows and her ice-blue guilt sliding together the way a glacier can be dirty with morainal rubble. In their cracks and silences, they've helped each other carry secrets over all these years. And their secrets have been slowly crushing them.

There has to be some way to climb out. All this, it can't have been for nothing.

She doesn't believe what he's told her, but senses there's a streak of truth in it. And although she's not sure that she wants to know the truth, she can't go any longer without it. He'll never be honest with her, if she's not honest first. So for the first time in the longest time, she's honest with herself.

She tells him everything.

PART 4

15

Ruapehu maunga, New Zealand, 2006

Marcus stands on the doorstep of the hut, the door closed behind him to keep in the warmth. The sky is starting to ignite from black to red. There are only a few clouds on the horizon, catching and holding the colour of the rising sun. It's early, but not as early as it should be.

As the sun lifts in the sky, the first rays hit the mountain's eastern slopes, a glowing streak of orange across the white. Ruapehu lets a new day wash over her. She isn't waiting for anything. She doesn't keep a tally of all those who climb up, and all those who come back down.

Tāne Whakapiripiri, the red-roofed hut, sits in a hollow. It's in the lee of the prevailing wind, positioned to look up towards the summit in communion with the mountain. When people approach from the bottom, it seems as though the hut has its back turned to them, shunning them; but for those who return back down the mountain, Tāne Whakapiripiri sits open-armed, drawing them in. Marcus walks a couple of metres out into the snow and looks up the slope towards the sky. Last night's forecast said that bad weather was on the way, but it's looking good for now. He needs to wake the others.

When he gets back inside, Richard is putting a pot of coffee on the stove. 'Bonjour,' Richard says over his shoulder. 'How's it looking out there?'

'Good,' Marcus replies. 'Anyone else up yet?'

'Not yet. More coffee for us, mate.' While the coffee is on the stove, Richard starts to make himself a bowl of porridge. He's quietly efficient, like a slow-flowing river, always making progress but in a way you hardly notice. 'Let's give them five more minutes.'

They'd planned for a 5.30 wake up, aiming to be out the door by about quarter past 6, 6.30 at the latest. Marcus checks his watch. 6.13. The late arrival at the hut has thrown them out. Even with the sleep-in, they haven't had a proper rest. He's only had about four hours himself — he'd been hovering just below the edges of sleep when the last of the group arrived sometime around 2 a.m., their rustling quiet but enough to rouse him. He'd fallen back asleep, but it had taken a while. He thinks of it like a set of scales: on the one side, there's the need to have enough rest, enough energy for the day ahead; on the other side, there's the need to make the most of daylight and clear weather, enough time for the task at hand. He mentally calculates, finding the balance point. If they leave at 7 — or, say, 7.30 — they'll be back by 3, 3.30 at the latest. If that bad weather does roll in as forecast, they'll be back at the hut, sipping tea, then wine or whisky, by the time it hits.

'Cheers, mate.' Marcus takes the mug of coffee that Richard hands him. It's good. Strong enough to keep him going all day.

There are ten of them altogether on this trip, a mixed group of ages, skills and experience from the Auckland and Wellington branches of the Mountain Sports Club. Marcus and Richard initiated the trip, advertising the weekend in the club newsletter, booking the hut and organising the carpool. It's just a social weekend, not an instruction weekend — an excuse to get out of the city, to spend some time together doing what they love. Since they met in their first year at Auckland University more than ten years ago, they've been climbing partners, flatmates, best friends, and now godparents to each other's children, even though neither of them is religious. Evenly matched in fitness, skill and experience, they've built a deep trust and understanding over the years, agreeing with each other's plans and decisions before they've been made. Despite now living in different cities, they still know who will buy the pasta, who will write their trip plans in the DOC intentions book. They know who will bring the rope, who will carry it.

The others start to stumble in from the bunk rooms downstairs. Marcus looks up from where he's kneeling beside his pack when Thea walks in. 'Mōrena, you sleep all right?'

She yawns then stretches. 'Not bad, just not enough.' She

nods at the coffee cup sitting on the ground beside his pack. 'I'll just get me one or two of those.'

'It helps,' he agrees, and imagines the caffeine running through his veins to balance out the lack of sleep.

Marcus continues getting himself ready, sorting his gear and making lunch, in between fielding questions about the day ahead and helping some of the less experienced club members with their packing. As more pots of coffee are made, and more bowls of porridge are eaten, the group becomes more lively. Extra layers are rolled and folded into waterproof bags, sandwiches and chocolate bars are stashed in packs.

'How're you feeling?' Marcus asks Richard, as he rinses out his coffee mug.

'I think I've shaken off the worst of it, but I'm still not one hundred per cent.' Richard had been going to climb the south-east ridge of Te Heuheu with Marcus, but had pulled out the day before, opting to join the group doing the less challenging climb up the Whangaehu Glacier. He'd texted Marcus about his change of plan on the drive up from Wellington. 'Bloody flu. I got the vaccination too.'

'Yeah, bad luck, mate. Glad you could come on the trip, though. And it's still a nice walk up the glacier.'

'You've roped in Thea instead?'

'Yeah, mate, replaced you, just like that.' He snaps his fingers.

Richard laughs, 'Gee, that's the end of our climbing partnership, is it? If I'd known we were never going to climb together again, I would've had a speech prepared.'

'Nah, of course not. Just this once. You're irreplaceable.'

Marcus claps his hand down on Richard's shoulder, grinning. 'OK, we'd better get this lot moving.'

'Righto, let's get going. Any word on that storm?'

'They said it'd be later this afternoon, actually more like evening. It's bluebird out there now. If we get going soon, we'll have perfect weather, then be back for the show.' He nods towards the large window, which is like a cinema screen. He imagines sitting back in the comfort of the hut after a long day climbing, watching the storm play out.

☆ ☆ ☆

Back outside, Marcus looks up at the mountain once more, standing still but feeling the need to get moving building inside him. It's almost 7.30. He feels a tap on his shoulder and turns to see Thea. 'Photo time,' she says. Marcus puts his gloved hand on Thea's shoulder while Penny takes a photo. Then they take a step apart and point up towards the summit, laughing as they look back at the camera.

'Very nice,' Penny says, taking another photo. 'That's one for the club newsletter.'

Marcus turns to Thea. 'You all sorted?'

'I hope so,' she says. 'How'd you describe it? Gnarly? You might be carrying me down.'

Marcus checks his watch again. It's 7.32. Here, all gathered in front of the hut, phones fully charged, they have access to the 3G network. No one checks the forecast one last time. Marcus has been watching the sky — blue in all directions with just a few puffs and wisps of cloud around the edges. 'Let's go!' he shouts.

The mountaineers head away from Tāne Whakapiripiri, walking in single file like a pack of wolves until the route diverges. There, they gather into their climbing groups, standing opposite each other for a moment, a stretch of white space between them.

'Whoever gets back first can start dinner.' Marcus steps forward and puts a hand on Richard's shoulder, knowing that the trip up the glacier and back will take a lot less time. 'I'll have the steak, *monsieur*, medium rare. And don't forget to open my top-quality mountain wine to let it breathe.'

'Don't worry, mate. I'll definitely have the wine open.' Richard grins at Marcus. 'Have fun.' Richard turns to the five others in his group. 'All right, let's do this! Onwards and upwards and back downwards.'

The remaining four — Marcus, Thea, Jim and Penny — turn to traverse the flank of the mountain. Jim strides out ahead. Marcus doesn't think Jim will be able to keep the pace up for long, but knows he's realistic about that. He's been stretching and has told Marcus he doesn't want to let his knee get cold, but expects to drop to the back later on; he's just chuffed to be on the mountain again after his operation several months ago. Penny traverses the mountain by herself, as she always does at the start of the day, taking the time to properly wake up before she talks to anyone.

Marcus and Thea walk together. They've stopped so that Thea can take a photo, looking back across at where they've come, Tāne Whakapiripiri cloaked in white, the tussock-tasselled brown plateau feathering out beyond. 'Last photo,' Marcus says. 'We should catch up to the others.'

'I think Penny prefers to walk alone.'

'But still, we need to get moving.'

Marcus has known Thea since she was a teenager, through his friendship with her father, Andy, and recently she's babysat his daughter, Sally, once or twice. She's fit. She's done athletics since she was a kid, running and hurdling and leaping. Of course, she's tramped a lot, too, with Andy; but mountaineering is new to her, despite her father's efforts over the years. The slow, weighted trudge uphill, the technicality of ropes and tools, and the inescapable cold are all things she's learning now, without her father. Marcus misses Andy, but can't imagine what it must be like for Thea. He thinks of Sally, turning three in a couple of weeks, still so new to her feet, stumbling around and crashing into things as though she's made of rubber. As soon as she's a bit more steady, he's going to get her on the mountain.

Thea sometimes reminds Marcus so much of Andy, it's uncanny. There's something in her quiet manner, her way of taking everything in without making a big deal about it that makes him feel like Andy's there — or, perhaps, it's more that the similarities between father and daughter make climbing with Thea feel more familiar than it actually should. Today, though, Thea's talking more than usual, asking questions about the route, the terrain, the time it will take, whether he thinks they'll need to use ropes. She'd spent an hour or so in the car debating whether to join them on the harder route, oscillating between enthusiasm and self-doubt. He knew it would be a challenge for her, but nothing that she couldn't do. He knew how proud she'd feel when it was done. So he encouraged her until the scales tipped over to enthusiasm. He hopes now that he hasn't talked her into something she didn't really want to do.

Marcus and Thea catch up to Jim and Penny, who have stopped to rest before the mountain sharply rises. 'Cracking pace, Jim,' Marcus says. 'How's the knee?'

Jim laughs and leans down to give the side of his knee a rub. 'Bloody warmed up, that's for sure.'

'All right, let's get moving,' Marcus says.

Snow-streaked bluffs stand watch as the four move out of the broad white basin onto the steepening slope. The sun glints off distant ice, a Morse-code mirror signal.

16

The great expanse of snow in front of Thea is intoxicating. A swoop of white flying under the vast blue sky, yellow-tipped in the early morning sunlight. She keeps taking photos to show her father. She wants to hand little glossy rectangles to him to say, 'Look Dad, I'm here, I'm doing it.' Then she remembers that he'll never see them. Excitement fades to sorrow. Just as quickly, the reality of the day ahead rushes in and her sadness blurs into apprehension.

She tries to stay in the here and now, footsteps and metres, seconds and minutes. She tries not to look beyond the wide stretch of snow to where the bluffs stand casting shadows and snakes of ice lie in crevices. That's where the real climbing begins, where the ice tools become more than an accessory for the photos.

They pause just outside a pocket of shadow. Ahead, Te Heuheu Ridge climbs into the gathering clouds. 'Reckon we'll be OK without the rope?' Jim asks, tearing a muesli bar open with his teeth. They have their harnesses on already, prepared to rope up if need be.

'Yeah, should be all good,' Marcus responds.

As they speak, the cloud starts to drift down the mountain: a light brush of shading over paper. In the distance, Taranaki juts his head out, then disappears again behind the thickening grey. Thea looks behind her, the slope seeming steeper than it did on the way up, but still a lot less daunting than the way ahead. She could turn around and head back to Tāne Whakapiripiri, hidden in a dip in the mountain's contours, unseen but awaiting their return. But if she did that, the others would urge her up and on. Marcus would tell her about the time he climbed this route with her father, scattering Andy's words of wisdom behind him like breadcrumbs for her to follow to the summit. And if she really insisted, if she stubbornly refused to carry on, he'd only turn back too, going with her to make sure she got back safely. She doesn't want to ruin his day out, and besides, she wants this too, she really does.

☆ ☆ ☆

The steady thwack of axes into ice marks time as the climbers make their way up the slope. There are still streamers of sun across the sky, but the clouds have lead bases. The steep incline keeps them facing forwards, looking up the mountain but not into the sky. Penny leading, they follow the path of least resistance, skirting patches of shiny ice, crunching through the granular tufts of crispy snow. The rime increases the higher they get, evidence of more exposure.

The wind has icy fingers. It prods them to keep moving. Just a jab, now and then. They cross a stretch of sastrugi, white waves of snow formed by the wind, pointing them onwards. When Thea glances up, the world is swaddled in a fine gauze.

As she climbs, the air wraps tighter around her, like bandages binding broken ribs, compressing her breath. She should've turned back. She's not good enough for this. The air feels thick, like something she could pick up and shape with her hands, like something she has to push her body through. She's moving painstakingly slowly. The only reason she keeps moving at all is because she wants to get off this steep face. Her teeth are gritted, as though that will keep her on the mountain, clenched-jaw resistance against the polished-slip of ice beneath her boots. Her hands tightly grip her ice tools, bracing herself for the claws of wind that sideswipe her out of nowhere. They reach out of the white, then disappear into stillness, then lunge again. She shouldn't be here.

Her steps are tiny. She's taking longer than she should to kick each boot into the snow, not trusting it to hold. But each step takes her closer to the top and that's what matters, that's all she needs to do. Head down, she doesn't see Jim and Penny ahead of her reach the ledge and slam down, belly-flat, into the snow. She doesn't see them crawl towards the shelter of a crop of rocks. It's only when her head gets level with the top that she feels the full force of the wind ripping across the mountain. She drops down onto her hands and knees, a life-preserving instinct, her body knowing before her mind that she needs to get low, out of the wind, away from the edge. Like bass thumping out of speakers at maximum volume, the wind comes in waves and gusts, so loud it's almost silent. It's like her ear drums have exploded and all that's left of her hearing is the rushing loss of it. Marcus comes up beside her, pressed horizontal into the snow. 'Fuck me,' is all he says. They lie there for a moment, side by side, watching the mass of black clouds churning towards the mountain, tossing and rearing up, tumbling against each other. They're 2410 metres above sea level.

She's hypnotised. It's like nothing she's ever seen before, as though the sky is much closer than it should be: a charcoal-grey lahar slow-flowing down onto the mountain. Marcus taps her sharply on the shoulder and gestures towards Penny and Jim, crouched below a stack of snow-covered rock. As they crawl towards them, the wind buffets Thea from the side. She can barely see through the swirling white dust. Her hands and knees soak up the cold.

'We need to head back down,' Marcus says, yelling above the noise of the wind and making an exaggerated gesture with his arm. The others nod. Thea's enormously relieved. They're so close to the top here, she's sure the others would want to push on, up through the rolling mass of black to the summit. Then she thinks of what they just climbed up. She can't go back that way.

As though reading Thea's thoughts, Penny shouts, 'Going down's going to be a nightmare.'

'To be honest,' Jim says, 'I'm not sure that my knee can handle that. It's not doing as well as I'd hoped. I think the downhill will be worse.' He pauses, then continues, 'Might've bitten off a bit more than I can chew.'

That's exactly the phrase that's been going through Thea's head. She chose the challenge, but she hadn't shaken off the doubts niggling at the back of her mind. Her uncertainty has been building with every step.

'So we traverse along the leeward side of the tops, across the plateau, then down?' Marcus suggests, waving his arm and pointing to get his message across. 'It's longer but easier, and we should avoid the worst of this weather.'

Penny and Jim nod. Thoughtful nodding, not yet quite nods of agreement, of a decision made.

'So we go up and over?' Penny asks. 'Up to go down?'

Thea notices Marcus looking at her. 'It'll be tough going for a bit,' he says to her before addressing all of them, 'but better in the long run.' He nods, a decision made.

They turn and look upwards. Thea feels it as a collective movement, a deep drawing of breath. Then Jim starts climbing, and Penny follows, and she and Marcus fall into step behind. And up they go.

17

Thea sits with her chin on her forearms, which are resting on her tucked-up knees. The last bit of uphill — the wind coming straight at them like wild horses charging across the snow, her body taut with concentration and fear — has left her completely drained and frozen. She watches as Penny loosens the strap on the side of her pack and passes a snow stake to Jim. She lets go too early, or Jim's too slow to grab it, and it drops into the snow at his feet. Marcus is paying out the rope, ensuring it's free of kinks and knots. Jim drives the snow stake into the slope. Thea watches him attach a sling and carabiners, carefully building an anchor from which they can abseil onto the plateau.

She feels distant from it all, like she's watching a movie. The idea sticks in her head and the more she thinks of it, the more convinced she is that the other three can't see her. While they busy themselves securing the rope to the mountain, she's safe on the other side of a fogged-up silver screen.

She snaps back to herself. She *is* here. She's part of this. But it's OK. They've made it up. The hard part is done. She needs to stay focused and get on with things. They're heading down. She takes a deep breath of icy air.

Anchor built, Jim attaches himself to the rope, gives the other three a salute, and slides out of sight. Marcus asks Thea if she's all right to go next. She gives the thumbs up with her fat-gloved hands, then nods, then adds a 'yes' for good measure, hoping one of those things will be understood in the swirling, whipping white. She secures herself to the line and lowers herself backwards, a few cautious steps down the slope, then over the lip into the white nothing.

As she abseils down, Thea focuses on the rope moving through her belay device. Without it, there's no sense of movement, no sense of space or time, just cold infinity. She's suspended in air. For a moment it feels like she's sliding into some kind of state of non-existence, where it's just her, all alone. This is pure peace. This is absolute loneliness. And then she feels the ground, and she can see the snowy stretch of the plateau, a space of visibility under the layer of cloud. She detaches from the rope, but stays holding the ends, keeping them from lashing up as Penny descends, then Marcus.

Once they're all down, Thea is about to start pulling the rope down, but she's hit by a wave of exhaustion. It's all she can do to keep standing. She can't imagine hauling at the ice-laden rope now, a tug of war against the wind. Her stomach growls and, seeing the others all eating, she pushes her pack to rest on the ends of the rope and rummages inside for something to eat. She'll have more energy after food. Her cheese, salami and chutney sandwich is flattened but not frozen. When she takes her first bite, it seems as though she's never tasted anything so good.

As soon as she finishes, she feels hungrier — ravenous — and wonders what the time actually is. The darkening sky makes it feel like evening, closer to dinner. Back at the lodge, there's a pack of ravioli, fresh tomato sauce, broccoli and chorizo for her and Penny to share. She's about to delve back into her pack to find more food when Marcus breaks through her thoughts.

'Let's keep moving,' he says, reaching for his pack.

'Good idea,' Jim says. 'If I sit here any longer, I think my bloody knee is going to seize up.'

'You right there, mate?' Marcus reaches out a hand to Jim to help him up.

Thea starts pulling at one end of the rope, tugging hand over hand to bring it up through the anchor some twenty metres above her. As she does so, she looks over her shoulder to check on Jim. She's got a small first aid kit in her pack, with a bandage and some tape. She's already offered to strap his knee. He'd said he was OK, but that was hours ago. She opens her mouth to offer again, but Penny's voice cuts loudly over hers.

'The rope!'

Thea looks up at the loose end of the rope whipping around high above their heads. It's a viper slashing through the cloud, long bright pink body and tiny knotted head. Knotted. Thea's stomach plunges. She'd forgotten to untie the knots at each end of the rope — the knots that climbers always tie as a backup safety measure to prevent abseiling off the end and off a cliff. Those same knots will stop a rope from going through the anchor and falling back down to ground.

Thea wants to cry. She can't believe she's made such a stupid, basic mistake. The loose end of the rope is too high up for Thea to reach it now. Penny grabs hold of the half of the rope leading from the anchor through Thea's grip and to the snowy ground. She puts her gloved hands in the spaces between Thea's and together they pull. Thea knows it's useless, just as Penny must, but keeps tugging anyway. They don't have another rope.

Their combined effort pulls the rope out of the sky and towards the anchor, but no amount of desperation or determination will defy physics. No matter how much they haul down on the rope, the knot will not pass through the carabiner.

'Leave it,' Marcus says. He kicks snow over the spaghetti pile of rope on the ground to weigh it down so it doesn't whip back up in their faces.

'I'm so sorry,' Thea says, still trying to keep the tears away. 'I can't believe I did that. I'm so, so sorry.'

'It's OK, we're all tired,' Jim says. 'Any one of us could've made the same mistake. I wasn't being much use, was I?'

'We'll manage,' Marcus says. 'There's just one short scramble, then it's a cruise. We probably weren't going to use the rope anyway. Come on, we need to get going.'

They set off without saying anything more. As they cross the plateau, they're sheltered from the wind by the reptilian line of the summit ridge above. Its spines are softened and rounded with the snow. The stillness gives the air a different kind of chill. It seems as though cold and silence were one and the same, an emptiness so complete that it becomes a part of Thea. The flatter terrain makes it feel like there's more sky above them than before, the pencil-grey underside of a lake rolling and rippling in all directions. It darkens with every step, with every breath.

Thea silently berates herself. She wants to keep apologising, but also doesn't want to annoy the others with useless words or for them to waste energy trying to make her feel better. She just wants to be back at the hut. Forget dinner, she's going straight to bed as soon as they get back. She pictures herself walking in the door, taking off her pack, bending down to unlace her boots, pulling off her waterproof pants, and hanging up her jacket in the entrance room. She sees herself sliding into her sleeping bag, which is rolled out and waiting on the bottom bunk.

They're walking in the gloom of evening now, headlamps on, casting spots of bright light onto the snow, flashing off the bright blues and reds of jackets and packs. As they walk, the mountain starts to slope downwards and they lose the shelter of the ridge above them. Suddenly they're in the full force of the weather again. Thea can't tell if the storm has got more ferocious or if it's just that she had forgotten how bad it was. It's like the wind wants them off the mountain. *Calm down!* she wants to shout at it. *We want off, too.* She tries to ignore the wind tearing at them from all directions. She knows it's stupid, but now it's dark, the wind seems more sinister — like something that's been stalking them, waiting to really have its fun, and now it's time. She takes a breath as though about to dive under water. She pictures herself gliding down to a place of calm, skimming across the surface of the mountain, beneath the wind, as though swimming along the sandy bottom of a tropical sea, scooping up handfuls of soft sand. Breathe. Dive. Skim. Scoop. It becomes a mantra. A word for every step.

Then they're at the last technical part of the downhill, a rocky drop of shadow. It's steep, but not far. Marcus goes first, climbing backwards, face-in to the mountain. She watches him placing his ice axes and crampons with rhythmic deliberateness. When he gets to the bottom, Penny starts down the short face. While she waits, Thea looks up into the sky, remembering the awesome beauty of last night. There are no stars tonight. Instead, the sky is weighted and alive with fury: gusts of sleet and hail in place of quiet constellations. She turns around and lowers herself down the icy rocks. She keeps her eyes focused on her axes as they glint silver in the beam of her head torch. She wills each placement to hold. Snow falls on her shoulders, slides down behind her pack. Breathe. Dive. Skim. Scoop. Breathe. Dive. Skim. Scoop.

Suddenly there's nothing under her foot. The solid rock beneath her boot falls away, her foot kicks backwards, and her body drops. The points of her ice axes slide slightly then catch, holding her to the wall like fingernails scratching into skin. Breathe. Skim. Dive. Breathe. Breathe. Breathe. She tries to calm her thoughts. The front points of one crampon grip the ice. Her calf muscle starts to cramp. She kicks her other boot into the icy wall. Breathe. She's not far from the bottom. There's no need to panic. It's not like she would fall far. She'd only drop half a metre. It's more that she can see herself peeling off the wall, falling backwards, and snowballing down the slope behind her, bouncing down the ridge and into oblivion. She keeps her focus on her tools and boots, watching the metal points jab the ice, left and right, left and right. And then she's down, and she can breathe.

Marcus is standing not far off, his arm outstretched as though reaching across a dark and deserted ballroom, inviting someone to dance. There's no one there. There's no one there, Thea realises. Penny's gone. She looks beyond the tips of Marcus's gloved hand, into the black below. The bright tail of a comet races through the darkness, the blue-white of a head-torch flying, rolling, bumping, sliding down an icy slope. Penny's gone.

18

Marcus sees it happen. He doesn't think Thea realises what she's done. She's facing inwards, fiercely concentrating as she climbs down the outcrop. She kicks her right leg, blindly searching for a foothold. A football-sized piece of icy rock dislodges and Thea jams her boot into the space left behind. Marcus sees the rock, illuminated in the beam of his head torch, fly off the mountain and whack into Penny's shoulder. Penny, standing with her back to the mountain. She had been staring out into the night, lost in space. And then the rock hit her, and she careened into the darkness, an untethered astronaut tumbling into the void. Marcus's crampons grip the ice with Rottweiler jaws, but he lunges his top half forward, an arm outstretched in a futile attempt to grab her.

He wills Penny to twist herself around, like a falling cat, to flip herself so she can throw her ice axe into the mountain and stop the sliding fall. In this freezing wind, the snow is as hard as diamonds. Even the most experienced climbers would struggle to self-arrest. He wills the point of Penny's axe to claw through the glittering, glassy crust and find a hold.

He watches Penny's head torch bounce through the darkness. It's a meteor through the night sky, a sliding streak of light vanishing into nothing. He watches until it dies away. He hopes that, against the odds, Penny has slid to a stop in time. Somewhere down there, the steep walls of a ravine wait like cupped hands to catch broken climbers.

He calls her name but the wind carries it behind him and into the sky. His lips start to freeze so he pulls his merino scarf up again. He listens for her cries from the slopes below, but it's the mountain that's screaming at him.

'Penny.' Thea's voice is an undercurrent of breath behind him, a whisper under the wind. She starts making a groaning noise, like a tree before it falls. Then Jim is beside him, shouting Penny's name into the night. Marcus pulls his scarf down and calls out again, but even with their voices clinging together, they can't be heard above the storm.

'What happened?' Jim asks Marcus, standing close.

'Something hit her. A chunk of ice. A rock.' He holds his hands up to show Jim the size of it, but he feels like he's holding them over a crystal ball, trying to find an answer from nothing.

'Was it my fault?'

Marcus and Jim turn to look at Thea, the light from their head torches flashing over her. Her face is completely covered against the stinging ice. Her body sags, weighed down by hours on the mountain, a coating of ice, and now this.

'No,' the two men say at the same time.

'She wasn't looking,' Jim says. He turns to Marcus. 'We need to go after her. We need to hurry.'

'No,' Marcus says. 'We can't.'

'She might be hurt.'

Marcus is silent. She's probably worse than hurt, but it will do no good to say those words aloud. He doesn't even want to think them. He sees it again, Penny with her back to the climbers, staring out into the darkness, no time to brace against the impact of the falling rock.

'We have to check,' Jim shouts through the noise of the storm.

'If we go down there, we could all . . .' Marcus leaves the word unsaid, letting the scream of wind and sleet finish his sentence. The storm is coming at them with teeth and claws, a hundred spiny tails whipping through the air. The snow and ice are building up on them, even as they stand there. He can feel it forming an icy exoskeleton over his limbs and torso, adding weight to his already fatigued body. It's like the mountain and the storm are working together to claim them. They have no place being here. They need to get down. But it's also right to try to find Penny, to help her if there's any possibility that they can.

'We're heading down anyway,' Jim says, as though reading his thoughts.

Marcus moves his hand through the air, like he's spreading a layer of mortar over bricks, cutting off the way in front of them. 'Not that way.' The two men are still looking in the direction that

Penny fell: the wrong side of the ridge. 'We need to go that way.' Marcus turns and points in the opposite direction, the gesture exaggerated in his need to be understood.

'I'll head down. Find her. Traverse across to meet you.' Jim shouts close to Marcus's ear, breaking his sentences into chunks that can be heard in the noise of the storm.

As Jim's talking, Marcus looks down. Jim is tentatively bending his knee. At first it looks like he's eager to get going, a runner at the starter block, but Marcus has been watching Jim lean down to rub his knee every time they've stopped.

'We need to stick together. We get down then get help,' Marcus says. He knows he's right. Yet, to leave a fellow climber lying there tears at him, a deep twist of wrong in his gut. He mentally unfolds a map of the mountain in his head. He tries to picture where the contour lines break into rocks and bluffs; the steepness of the drop off the ridge, and the climb back up and over. He pictures the dotted line marking the track down the mountain. He sees black circles in the snow, like footprints, leading them back to Tāne Whakapiripiri. He feels a cup of hot tea in his hands, the taste of a gingernut.

He looks across to Thea and Jim, standing face to face, Jim's hands on Thea's shoulders. The snow is piling up on top of their packs; their arms and legs are thick with icy snow. If they stand here much longer, they'll be frozen in place, part of the mountain until they're chipped away by a rescue team or thawed by the spring sun. They have to get down, back to the hut. Marcus nods to himself. It's like that thing about fitting your own oxygen mask before you help others. He knows that's what they have to do, and yet it makes him breathe a little harder, his lungs cold and heavy.

They trudge down the ridge, bracing themselves against the sideways wind. He walks slowly, but every time he turns around, the space between him and the other two is growing. He stops, gesturing for them to pass him, then drops into position at the back. Now in front, Jim keeps a steady pace, but Marcus can see his limp getting more pronounced. He starts wincing with every step Jim takes, imagining his pain. It reminds him of an ad that was on TV when he was a kid, showing a bone being smashed into broken glass. He thinks it was an ad for arthritis. Or rheumatism. What's the difference? He's never known, never had to know.

He and his brother, Stefan, had laughed at that ad when they were kids, back when they were bendy-boned boys with healthy, young parents. They used to crawl in front of the TV when it came on, yelling out 'My bones! My bones!' He wonders what Stef's up to right now. It will be morning in Amsterdam. Marcus hopes that whatever he's doing, the sun is warm and soft on his face.

They walk on, a few more metres down the mountain. Jim limping, Thea stumbling. Slow, but progress nonetheless. He couldn't stop Penny from falling but they can still get her help. He'll get himself safely back to the hut. He'll get them all back. They'll do it together, the three of them, then someone will go get Penny.

They're walking into the wind now and he can hear Jim's voice carried back to him. He tries to make sense of what Jim's saying, but the words slither past and slip away, a jumble of nonsense. For a moment, Marcus is back on city streets, walking past the unkempt man who strides from the bottom of Queen Street to the top then down again, always shouting, arguing with someone no one else can see. He shrugs off Jim's shouting as some kind of argument against the storm or perhaps himself, the words a way of propelling him forward. Then he realises that Jim's singing, if yelling words into the cold dark air counts as singing. Marcus pieces the song together from the snippets dashing past him in the wind. It's 'Across the Universe', and that makes Marcus profoundly sad because he's grown up with The Beatles — their albums forced on him and Stef by their father, who claims there's a Beatles song for every occasion. The song feels like exactly the right choice, in exactly the wrong way.

Marcus has never been into the mystic stuff. He likes tramping and climbing precisely because it's as down to earth as you can get; he loves the simplicity of leaving all the usual comforts behind and just walking. But as Jim belts out words into the endless space, Marcus sees them all floating in the cosmos, three tiny stars in a vast night sky. And it makes him feel so little. So very, very small. Then as the words spin past him, he understands why Jim is singing in this awful moment, and suddenly, somehow, it feels like everything will be all right. All they need to worry about is themselves; everything else will come when it comes. Just take one step at a time. That's all they can do. Break it down into the smallest possible action. Every single step, each black dot on the map, takes them closer to Tāne Whakapiripiri.

Then Thea falls to her knees. There's a moment when she

seems suspended, held up by the force of the wind, before she topples forward, hands planted into the snow, as though someone's shoved her in the back.

19

The trench is narrow and shallow. It barely gets them out of the wind, even with their packs stacked behind them. It feels like they're hunkered down behind a sea wall, white wind-whipped sea foam scudding overhead, dropping down in clumps. Marcus berates himself for being so disorganised. They only had one snow shovel between the three of them. One rope. One shovel. Why hadn't he checked? It wasn't meant to be that kind of trip. Wasn't meant to go like this. He wasn't meant to be in charge. At least they all have emergency bags. They're huddled inside them now, three silver cocoons on the side of a mountain. They're genius, those things, so light to carry, the weight of them belies their power. His is doing the trick — he's roasting now. He pushes the foil bag down to his waist.

He was already hot from chopping out the trench. They'd

walked in circles, feeling for somewhere that was slightly less like concręte than everywhere else. Suddenly in the freezing storm, he was sweating, rivulets running down his skin inside his clothes. It had been bloody hard work, the rock-hard snow, the small shovel, the ferocious wind. He and Jim had taken turns while Thea sat, the packs heaped up around her.

After Thea had fallen, she'd managed to push herself back up onto her knees, then stand with help from Jim and Marcus. Then Thea fell again, and then again, and it was clear to Marcus that they needed to stop. The next time she fell, she might slide and roll, and be gone forever somewhere off the side of the mountain. He can't let that happen. She could bowl into Jim and take him with her. Marcus can't walk back into the hut alone. He's going to get them all back down.

He's lined their burrow with the thick plastic bag from inside his pack. He's sliced it lengthwise, so it runs the length of the trench. Hunched over, they're like those three monkeys who see, hear and speak no evil. There needs to be a fourth one, Marcus thinks — a monkey clutching its head in a declaration to think no evil. There's no evil here, Marcus knows, staring up at the night sky. There's only nature. He remembers Andy telling him, 'There's no such thing as bad weather, just bad decisions.' There's no such thing as evil, just unhelpful thoughts. They can't let their unhelpful thoughts overtake them. He knows that Thea isn't stumbling from exhaustion and the cold — well, there's that too, but it's guilt that's knocking her to the ground. 'She's gone because of me,' Thea's been saying from time to time, her words dropping dangerously, like icicles from the eaves above a door.

He's tried to talk her out of her guilt, tried to be the think-no-evil monkey.

Marcus leans back into the icy wall behind him. On his left-hand side, a growing snowdrift weighs him down. 'Foam,' he hears Jim yelling and Marcus grins to know that Jim's there on the beach with him, dirty dry sea scudding across the sand in front of them. Then he shakes himself. Phone. It's why they've stopped. Walking wasn't going to work. They need to let people know where they are.

Reception's patchy this far up the mountain, but it's there blown in gusts towards and away from them. Jim doesn't have a phone with him. 'Jesus, mate, I'm sorry,' he said when they'd first stopped to dig and Marcus had no reception. 'I didn't bring it with me. I never do.' Marcus knows Jim's not alone in that — there are plenty of people who get out in nature to escape technology, to be unreachable for a day; he used to be one of them, until he became a parent. His own phone is running low on battery, the cold having sucked it out throughout the day. Thea's is already dead.

Send help, he messages Richard from his phone. *Above Wh glacier. 3 stopped no Penny. accident. V cold. Low batt.* He presses send and imagines the blue-square message, drifting luminous down the mountain towards the hut.

Richard is already worried. His concern is there in the missed calls and messages on Marcus's phone. Now Marcus pictures his friend, camped out by the window, looking into the storm and darkness, counting each minute that they're overdue. Or maybe he's walking up towards them, step by step against the storm. Maybe rescue is already on the way.

His phone lights up, the pinprick of a glow-worm in his bare, cupped hands. *Hang tight mate. Help is coming. Preserve batt.*

Marcus slumps back, a warm vein of relief running through him. It's in Richard's hands now. Marcus doesn't have to be the one to save them all.

☆ ☆ ☆

Hours pass. The snow builds up on Marcus. He's on the windward side, sheltering the others with his body. Richard texts. *Rescue underway. Weather causing issues but hold on. Help is coming.*

Jim sings. Thea talks. Time passes. The snow banks up. Richard texts again. *Sit tight. Rescue coming.*

Marcus texts. *Tell my family I love them.*

Richard texts back. *Tell them yourself. Keep warm.*

He thinks of Sally. He thinks of the way she climbs into his lap and puts her little hands on his shoulders, leans her face right up close to his and says, 'Stand up, Daddy! I want to go on a snail hunt with you.' He wants to tell her to keep going on adventures, to lift up stones, to crawl under bushes, to climb hills and mountains. Will Krissy still take her camping, climbing, kayaking? Or will she keep her close to home, adventures confined to the safety of the backyard and playground from now on?

Jim's singing slips into humming. The endless push of the wind piles the night up on them, heavy heaps of endless darkness. At some point Marcus thinks he hears voices, sees lights, but no help emerges from the storm. They've set up Jim's head torch to flash a signal down the slope. *Here we are. Here we are.* A three-beat call for help, repeating into the night.

Earlier Jim spoke of getting up again and carrying on. Marcus argued against it. Jim said he'd set off alone, direct rescue to where they are. Marcus talked him out of it, but now he thinks that maybe Jim should go. Thea said both he and Jim should go. Marcus isn't doing that. It's bad enough they had to leave Penny, but the chances of her surviving that fall were slim to none and they had to focus on keeping themselves safe. It was the right decision in the circumstances. He's not leaving Thea to sit on the side of a mountain, the life freezing out of her. She's only here because of him, because he talked her into doing something that she wasn't ready for, hadn't planned to do, wouldn't have done if not for him. He's ashamed of himself, of what Andy would think if he were still alive. He learned so much from Andy; Andy, who'd stepped into a role his own father had no interest in — not from want of love, just from it being beyond the football fields and beaches that were his world. Andy had taught Marcus most of what he knew about the mountains. He'd wanted to repay that, to pass on to Thea all the things that Andy couldn't teach her now. But instead he'd led her here.

Marcus's thoughts return to his own daughter. He watches her skipping across the snow, whirling under the falling flakes, face upturned, laughing into the sky. They'd wanted her to be a big sister, had started trying for another baby. He thinks of Krissy, his wonderful Krissy, having to tell Sally that her father isn't coming home. Maybe having to say it over and over again, explaining why he wasn't ever coming home. Not just tonight. Not ever.

Marcus texts Richard. *Keep an eye on Krissy. Give Sally cuddle. Promise?*

The search and rescue team have told them to preserve the phone battery for the rescue effort, to use the phone only to communicate with the rescue team. Marcus hadn't wanted to worry Krissy anyway. He'd planned to call her when they were back at the hut. Later, they'd sit together on the couch at home, Krissy's legs over his, and he'd tell her everything. But now he wants nothing more than to call them. He wants to talk to them and to hear their voices rushing up to meet his. He texts her now. *I love you Krissy. Always x.*

Marcus's phone dies. He watches a monkey lurching across the snow, its hands clasped to its head. It looks back over its shoulder at Marcus. Its hands drop from its head, long arms dragging through the snow as it walks away.

20

Time expands and contracts. The only constant is the mountain.

The cold settles on Thea like a cloud of sandflies — a presence so insistent and all-consuming.

Then it's gone.

Her body so cold that it starts to feel warm.

They wait through the night.

The endless, slow-spinning, star-exploding night.

Thea thinks she hears voices in the dark, sees the fuzz of lights through the storm. But nothing emerges from the blizzard. No one comes. Jim's phone is sitting on his bed in the hut and hers and Marcus's are dead.

They throw words to each other, Thea catching Jim's words as they blow past, gathering them up and passing them down the line to Marcus, then bundling Marcus's words up and tossing them towards Jim.

Hours pass.

Lips numb. Fingers freeze.

Silences stretch.

The mountain sits at the centre of time, the pivot for the slow-shrinking universe.

Jim's head torch still flashes out its call for help.

We're still here.

We're still here.

It's a night of frozen statues. What was bone and ligament, tendon and muscle, is now rock and snow. Three beautiful figures sculpted out of ice, sitting in a winter garden. Overgrown and lost to time, like a spellbound kingdom.

Someone has to break the spell. That's how fairytales work.

They sit and wait.

The sun rises. Thea imagines the creep of light along the eastern side of the mountain, washing over spurs and ridges until it reaches them, slipping into their shallow trench. Hot water filling up a bath. But daybreak just brings a different kind of shapelessness. A thick, featureless white that the sun can't pierce.

The wind begins to drop.

She hears voices.

Not Jim's.

Not Marcus's.

Not her own.

Figures kneel in front of them. There are three men, dressed all in red, with their bulging packs and crackling radios, their words as solid as hot pies in paper bags.

'How are you doing there?' one of the men asks, looking from Jim to Thea.

'I'm dying for a cup of tea,' Jim says.

The man laughs, a soft and gentle sound. 'I can help you out with that.' He pulls a thermos from his pack. 'Easy,' he says to Jim, holding the cup up to his lips. 'Easy now.'

He turns towards Thea, one hand on her shoulder, the other tilting the cup towards her.

And if the taste of heaven is a cup of tea, the sound of heaven is a chopper's blades cutting through the sky.

☆ ☆ ☆

Thea doesn't realise her hand is resting on Jim until someone picks it up and tucks it in beside her body as she's strapped onto the litter. As the man finishes tightening the straps around her, he looks over his shoulder and shouts to Jim, 'Your turn next.'

Thea strains to hear Jim's response, but only hears the rescuer's answer back to him. 'No, you next.'

Jim must say something else, or maybe it's Thea who's spoken, because the man looks at her, then back at Jim, then her again. She's not sure if she's heard him properly, or maybe she's only hearing words inside her head, but she thinks he says, 'Don't worry, he won't be on his own. Someone will stay with your friend.'

The mountain falls away below her. Thea tries to look back, but her body's packed tight onto the stretcher. She can only look upward, towards the metal underbelly of rescue. She doesn't get a single backward glance at Ruapehu, or Jim. She doesn't get one last look at Marcus.

21

Auckland, New Zealand, 2006

Thea stands on the deck of the house overlooking the sea — 'Magda's house,' she's getting used to saying — no longer 'Dad's place.' She's been staying there since Ruapehu. Magda had been waiting at the hospital and didn't discuss it with Thea, she'd just scooped her arm around Thea's waist, led her to the car, and driven her to her flat in Mount Eden. Thea thought that was it, a ride home, but Magda had waited while she packed some things, then had driven them both out of the city, through the green sprawl and on to Muriwai.

Thea has barely left Muriwai since she arrived. Magda tries to get her to join her on errand runs and made-up outings, but she stays between the beach and bush and house, the trees and sky and sea, only leaving when she has to for a medical appointment or to pick up a prescription. She walks along the sweep of black sand and up the hill to the cliffs spread with tākapu like a pilled blanket. Every day it seems like more birds arrive, navigating the winds from Australia. For days they glide the currents from rocks and islands off the coast of Victoria and Tasmania. Suddenly, after all that open sea and sky, they're hovering over land, flapping madly against the winds that brought them here. They drop onto a tiny patch of clifftop, home until the sun starts to slip away again towards autumn.

Jim has called and texted her. Darling Jim, who she will love forever, but never wants to see again. She'll always be grateful for his presence on the mountain. The three of them had sat there, trapped inside a snow globe, fixed in place while the storm shook all around them and they slowly ran out of oxygen. Every once in a while, Jim would throw lyrics out into the wind, nudging her to draw her attention to the shimmering burst of song in the night sky. But mainly he talked to her, his words providing comfort through the dark hours. There on the mountain, Thea was caught with the urgent feeling that it was words that would keep them alive; that she could save them all if she could just find the right thing to say. But as the spaces between their speech stretched out, she hadn't been able to shake the memory of a story she was told in primary school when they played the game 'Broken Telephone': after weeks spent in a muddy trench, troops received the uplifting message 'Send three and fourpence, we're going to a dance' only to be plunged into despair when it was repeated, loudly, slowly, decisively, as 'Send reinforcements, we're going to advance'.

She had watched slow-moving half-sentences and syllables traversing the space in front of them, a luminescent universe of plankton, and even though they hovered there, right within reach, she couldn't seem to focus long enough to put the right pieces together or lift her hands to grasp the necessary sounds. They slurred and blurred and broke apart, dissolving in the wind, scattering into space. She can't remember her last words to Marcus, but whatever they were, they didn't save him.

For the past few days, she's read Jim's messages and decoded what he really meant.

It wasn't your fault.

It was your fault.

She fell.

You made her fall.

She wasn't looking.

You weren't looking.

He had kept sending them, even though she had only responded to his first two texts. All week she's wanted to send him another to say that she's not going to be able to make it to Marcus's funeral, but she can't come up with a good excuse. When she told Magda that she wasn't going to go, Magda had pressed her fingertips gently into the back of Thea's wrist and said that she didn't need to decide right then. Thea hates herself for thinking it, but there's a part of her that wishes she was more physically damaged by Ruapehu, that she was still hospitalised so that she would have a reason not to go and face everyone. Of course she doesn't really want that, but the thought of walking into the chapel sends a wave of exhaustion over her so large and heavy that she wants to sink right down, wherever she is, and lie on the ground until time stops.

Now the day has come and she knows that, if she doesn't head back to the house to get ready, Magda will come looking for her. And, anyway, she knows she has to go. She owes that much to Marcus. She asked him to take her up to the summit when she wasn't ready for it. She should've known her limits. Without her, they would have been up and down, and back at Tāne Whakapiripiri to watch the storm from couches and through windows. She slowed him down, and then she brought him to a complete stop. If she hadn't made Penny fall, the four of them would have come in after dark, their bones starting to freeze together, but able still to warm up under blankets and with hot cups of tea. If she hadn't been so useless, if she hadn't been so completely useless after Penny fell, all of them would have made it home.

She doesn't want Krissy to have to look at her, not ever, but especially not today. Krissy, who must feel the absence of Marcus like a phantom limb. How will Krissy feel when she's sitting there, the loss of her husband a dense shadow-gap beside her, and in walks Thea, still occupying space in the world? She doesn't have the words to say to Krissy how sorry she is, and even if she did, what good would that do? But it would be worse not to be there, to look as though she didn't care, to seem as though she didn't so desperately wish that there was something she could do to change it all.

She's afraid of seeing Penny, holding herself together, her

arms wrapped around her broken ribs, her shoulder slung and splinted awaiting surgery, two half-fingers lost to frostbite. When Thea had seen her in the hospital, tentatively standing at the door to the ward, Penny had smiled at her — a wide and open smile, just the same as if they were meeting up at a café. Thea had felt a rush of relief and love, like morphine flooding her veins. She had held Penny's hand, wanting to squeeze it as tightly as she could, wanting to feel the realness of Penny in the room, but then she remembered how much pain she'd caused her friend. She had hunched in on herself and told Penny how sorry, sorry, sorry she was. Penny had smiled at Thea and had made a joke about not going clubbing for a while and was about to say something else when the nurse came in and ushered Thea out. It feels like they only had half a conversation and there must be more to come. When Penny's physical pain subsides, will she throw an ice storm of words at Thea, describing step by step how she dragged herself off the mountain, climbing out of a white grave several hundred metres deep and into the earth-dark night? It's what Thea imagines night after night when she tries to sleep.

And then there's everyone else. She knows what they're all thinking. She doesn't want to hear their polite kindnesses, asking her how she is, all the while weighing up her actions and their consequences, weighing her absence of a family against all the love surrounding Marcus, sizing up the small gap she'd leave compared to the black universe of space left by him. She doesn't want to hear it, but she wouldn't blame anyone for it.

22

Thea stays close to Magda as they walk across the carpark towards the funeral home. She wants to physically cling to her, the way a child clings to a parent in strange surroundings, but she makes herself leave space between them. This is her penance, not Magda's. She looks around at the groups of people standing outside. Everyone has puffer jackets and beanies on against the cold as though they're standing at a climbing crag.

There are a lot of people she knows, and others she doesn't but whose faces are familiar. Many of them were at her father's funeral, and Magda nods her greetings as they get close, small smiles and half-raised hands passing acknowledgements between them. Thea finds herself nodding too, her lips pressed together tightly. 'Let's head inside and find Krissy,' Magda says as she loops her arm through Thea's and pulls her close, steering her past people and into the building.

Krissy has dark smudges under her eyes and seems to have shrunk in on herself. She stands, one hand resting on her stomach, the other entwined with the arm of a woman who looks like her, but has dyed red hair. Her eyes are scanning the room as though there's something else she might need to do, somewhere else she might need to be.

Thea tries to listen to the low words that Magda says to Krissy as she leans in for a hug, like they could teach her what to say, but she knows she has to find her own way through. The only words she can find are plain, but not simple. 'I'm so sorry.' It's the same thing that everyone else is saying to Krissy, but she doesn't know how else to say all the things she needs to say. She repeats the words, then, after a pause goes to say something more, but Krissy speaks before she can get anything else out.

'Thank you.' Krissy's voice is soft and quiet like clouds over the sea on an overcast day. And then, 'How are you, Thea? Are you OK?'

Thea stands, mouth open, no words. The kindness of Krissy's question is like a sinker pulling her to the sea floor. 'How are *you*?' Thea asks Krissy, and can't believe she hasn't asked until now. It seems like the most obvious, and the most ridiculous, thing to ask.

Krissy shrugs, a tiny movement, like there's a truth she knows but doesn't want to accept. Amid the low buzz of background conversation, the two women are silent. After a while, Krissy wipes her cheek and speaks again. 'I wanted to thank you — for being there with Marcus.' Something gets sucked out of Thea. She wants to say something, but can't find air to breathe, let alone words.

'I keep having dreams,' Krissy continues. 'Of Marcus, all alone. He's not on Ruapehu — he's in the oddest places . . .' Those dreams are written in the fine lines and sagging skin around Krissy's eyes. Thea wants to reach out to Krissy and enclose her in a hug, but she knows that kindness can sometimes be what breaks a person. She hesitates, and then Krissy's speaking again, and Thea stays silent to let her say what she needs to say. 'I wake up and it's awful, so awful, but then there's this enormous sense of relief that he wasn't alone. It doesn't change anything or make it better. But those dreams when he's all alone, it's just the worst feeling, I can't describe it, and I'm so grateful to you and Jim that he *wasn't* alone.'

Thea steps towards Krissy, tentatively pulling her into a hug. 'Don't thank me,' she manages to stutter. 'I didn't do anything. I didn't help him. I couldn't help him.' *He wouldn't have even been there if it wasn't for me.* How does she say that she wishes Marcus and Jim had kept walking; that, if anyone, it's her who should have died in the snow that day?

After a long moment, Krissy pulls back from the hug. She keeps her hand on Thea's upper arm. 'You stayed with him.'

Stay. Thea hears it again, the word that's been whispering through her head since she woke up in hospital. She's not sure she said it aloud that night on Ruapehu or if it thumped inside her like a heartbeat. She has a marrow-deep memory of thinking it, of willing it with every exhausted ligament and sinew as she sat hunched up on the dark mountainside. *Please don't leave me here.* She remembers the frozen ground beneath her and a visceral desperation to keep the others close to her. *Stay. Please stay. Stay with me. Don't leave me here.* The words are stitched through her dreams and her waking thoughts like lead weights.

Thea shakes her head, 'Please, Krissy,' she says. 'Don't thank me. I'm so sorry. About everything.' How desperately she wishes she'd told Marcus and Jim to go.

There's a hovering queue of people waiting to offer their condolences to Krissy. Thea moves away. A new seam of guilt opens up in Thea that here, at her husband's funeral, Krissy was concerned about her. She didn't know what she expected from the conversation, but that wasn't it.

She sits, listening to the words of Marcus's father, his brother, his friends. The photos of his life roll by: Marcus standing next to Krissy on their wedding day; holding Sally as a newborn; on a mountain top with Richard and Andy. She's glad that these are the memories that Krissy has, these vivid squares of happiness, and hopes that Krissy doesn't ever try to picture in her head what those last hours on the mountain were like for Marcus. Those hours where Thea sat beside him; not Krissy, not Sally, not Stefan, Richard or anyone else. Those hours when he sat, not in an armchair, an old man with a life behind him, but in an ice-cold trench, slowly freezing.

☆ ☆ ☆

Outside, close family and friends wait by the hearse, which will drive the short distance to the cemetery for a private burial. Richard is talking to Marcus's brother, Stefan, but excuses himself when he sees Thea. She doesn't know Richard all that well, but he hugs her before asking her how she is. 'I know it's kind of a stupid thing to ask,' he sighs, 'in the circumstances.' He's clean shaven and dressed in a suit, but looks exhausted, like he's been walking uphill into the wind for hours.

'I feel awful,' she says. 'How are you?'

He looks briefly at her, then over her shoulder out across the green lawn. 'I can't stop going over things in my head. I can't stop thinking about it all.'

'Me too,' Thea murmurs, although as she says it, she's not sure if it's true. She doesn't know whether to trust the things she remembers, or the order in which they happened; and then there are wide, dark spaces in her memory: the lost time. But most of all, she's trying hard not to think about any of it.

'I'm so angry,' Richard says suddenly, his eyes flashing back to her face. Cold meltwater rushes through Thea. She waits for him to say more. He glances around to see if anyone is listening, but they're on their own. 'I'm so angry at him,' he says. 'I know I shouldn't say that, but I'm so damn angry at him.' Thea's shocked to hear the words. It's not what she expected but maybe, just maybe, it's more than that. She feels the smallest glimmer of recognition in his words. Richard closes his eyes briefly, then continues talking. 'And I'm so damn angry at myself.' Thea has heard how Richard and two others set out to find them while they awaited the search and rescue team, but how the storm turned them back within three hundred metres of the hut. 'We made such fucking stupid mistakes,' he says.

She's about to tell Richard that he's not to blame, but she's cut off by a piercing cry and tear-stained screams. They both turn to see Krissy kneeling beside the hearse, wrapping her arms around Sally's flailing limbs, her cheek pressed to the top of her daughter's head.

'I'm sorry. I shouldn't have dumped all that on you. I'm sorry,' Richard says, his words tumbling out. He looks like he's going to say something else, but the funeral director is approaching them. The other pallbearers are standing together by the hearse. 'I'd better go,' he says, already turning away from her. 'Take care, Thea.' He touches her briefly on the elbow as he walks away.

After a short while, the crowd of mourners gather into a tighter group, standing together to watch as the hearse pulls away, a small number of cars slotting in behind. Thea finds herself standing between a couple of club members on one side and some people she doesn't know on the other side. So many people grieving Marcus. They all stand in silence as the convoy drives around the back of the building and off towards the waiting grave. Somebody in the back of the crowd starts sobbing. After the procession dips out of sight, the mourners start to disperse and Thea walks back towards the car, away from everyone, to wait for Magda.

All the things that Krissy said and Richard said, all the things that Thea didn't say, swoop and dive in the air around her. The spoken and the unspoken twist together, spiralling up into the sky. Whatever was said or not said, whatever other people did or didn't do, Thea's here and Marcus isn't. Krissy and Sally are here and Marcus isn't. With a sudden plunge, the words jab at her: *It should've been you.*

23

Six weeks later, Thea joins Magda in the kitchen, sorting through the cupboards. Day by day the two of them have been tackling a different part of the house, boxing up things to keep and things to let go. Magda first mentioned that she was thinking of moving to Wellington months ago. Her sister has been urging her to move there since Andy died. In her unassuming way, Magda let the idea sit, like a saucer of milk left outside for a stray cat. Putting the plan out there, but not demanding any kind of reaction. A while later, she mentioned it again, a more definite thing, but still didn't fix a date. A few weeks after that, she started talking about being in Wellington for Christmas, but didn't start packing. Then the Ruapehu tragedy happened, Thea moved in, and nothing more was said until the week before when, kneeling in front of the bookcase, Magda had turned to look at Thea and said, 'You could move to Wellington with me. You like Wellington.'

Thea does like Wellington, and agrees the move is right for Magda, but she's never thought of moving there herself. Magda's suggestion surprised her. After her father's stroke, she was overwhelmed by loss, and within that heartache, there was an intense sense of loneliness. Aloneness. Yes, she had friends and they were wonderful, but all her family were gone now, or too distant to be anything more than names on a Christmas card. Thea thought that, without her father, Magda would drift out of her life. And perhaps she would have if things had been different. But Ruapehu had happened, and without being asked, Magda had picked Thea up from the hospital and driven her to Muriwai.

Thea had continued to pay rent on her room in Mount Eden for a while, but at some point had given notice and had emptied out all her things. This past week, she's started looking online for rooms in flats, just a quick scan through the listings every now and then, getting a sense of what's out there, where she could go. She has to go somewhere. She knows Magda won't go to Wellington to be with her own family until Thea's settled somewhere. Even though it's not the house Thea grew up in, she knows Magda's giving her time to be OK with everything being packed up and sold. Thea's not ready to live in a house with other people, to go back to work, act normal, but she's not going to make Magda stay for her.

'That's enough for today,' Magda says, kneading her lower back with one hand while pushing a cardboard box towards the hall with her foot. 'Let's have something to eat and then I'm going to pop out to the library and shops if you want to come along.'

'Thanks, but I think I'll go for a swim,' Thea says. 'Lunch sounds good, though. I'll make sandwiches.'

It's cold but the sun is shining, so they sit outside, enjoying the fresh air. After they've eaten, Magda picks up their plates and heads inside. 'Right, if you're sure you don't want to come, I'll head off now.' At the ranch slider she turns back to Thea, pauses for a moment as though weighing her words, but all she says is, 'Enjoy your swim. I'll see you in a couple of hours.'

Thea sits for a bit, finishing her cup of peppermint tea, then goes to get changed into her togs. There, lying on the bed is a brown envelope, bright in the patch of sunlight stretched across the duvet, the crossed axes of the Mountain Sports Club in the top left corner. Thea imagines Magda easing open the bedroom door, taking four or five steps across the room to place the envelope gently on the bed, ready for Thea to open in private. A few weeks before, as they were sitting together watching TV, Magda had mentioned that the club had completed an internal investigation. Magda had paused, and it seemed to Thea that she had more to say, but Thea had pretended not to hear and made an inane comment about the ad playing at the time.

She picks up the envelope and holds it between her fingertips for a moment. Then she slips it under the flap of one of the boxes in the room, pushing it in as far as it will go. Perhaps one day she'll open it, but she doesn't need to read it now. She knows that, stamped in black and white and folded up inside the envelope, will be the words that no one has yet said to her face: inexperienced, ill-equipped, unprepared.

She grabs a towel and heads down to the sea.

☆ ☆ ☆

The sound of the gannets from the clifftop is unceasing, like the roll of pebbles under crashing waves, an endless churning over and over on top of each other. On the beach below, the sand stretches out like the dark shadow of a dream. The water rushes up in wide, white, overlapping fans and a rhythmic whisper. *Stay. Stay.*

The beach rises and falls beneath Thea's feet as she wades out. The dumping waves and west coast winds stir the sea floor into holes and ridges. One moment she's standing in water up to her knees, the next she's dropped into a waist-deep pocket. She doesn't go out far. It's enough to feel the salty waves crash against her, to scoop the water up in handfuls and throw it against her face. She's grown up on this coast and is well aware of the dangers in the rips and undertow. Mid-week and early in the season, she's almost alone. There are just two surfers much farther down the beach and a walker, disappearing ghostlike into the sea-spray haze. The surf lifesaving tower sits empty. If she were to get pulled under, carried out to sea, no help would come.

Thea turns to face the horizon, looking at the line where the sea and the sky connect, but picturing the stretch of black sand underwater. Here it is soft and fine, but it will be rougher and rockier farther down the coast — past the mouth of the Waikato river and back to the maunga where the sand began life as volcanic rock. Under her feet is the slow tumble of stones down a mountain, the rolling-skipping wash down the river and the journey north on longshore currents, the gradual grind of rock to sand. All around her, the world is slowly moving. The slow flap of a wing, the drift of sand. She doesn't have to stay here.

She can't stay here. She can't be a constant presence in Krissy and Sally's life, a reminder that she made it off the mountain and Marcus didn't. She can't go to Wellington, where she might run into Richard or one of the others from the trip. The release of the club's accident investigation report will bring the trauma back: for Krissy, for Penny, for Richard, for Jim, for the search and rescue team who lifted Marcus off the mountain, for all his family and countless others who have been affected; it will bring back the heaviness of grief, the hot rage, the confusion of loss. Thea knows the tangle of those sensations — not just in the way you know the names of knots in a book, the illustrated loops of rope you have traced with your finger; she feels the grip of them across her body, tying and tightening until they bind her permanently to her guilt.

'Go,' she says quietly, the word skipping across the water and out to sea.

☆ ☆ ☆

Thea does her round of goodbyes. She ends her extended sick leave and resigns from work. She meets Penny for coffee in town, then sits in her car and weeps. She loves her friend but she can't bear to see her again. She walks through the white picket fence of Helensville Cemetery to sit beside her parents' grave, with its plaque in two pieces: the top half with her mother's name, a pīwakawaka engraved in one corner, a tūī in the other; the bottom half, slotted in sixteen years later, with her father's name and a border of mountains etched along the bottom. She runs her fingers across the grass tips and doesn't say anything, just lets the years of her childhood run through her. Before standing, she presses her palm flat into the grass, about where their hearts would have been, and says, 'I love you. I miss you.'

She leaves the cemetery and drives past the vineyards and over the bridge spanning the far reach of the harbour to the rolling green of North Shore Memorial Park. She sits by Marcus once again and places words on the fresh dirt, hoping they will sink down through the earth and somehow reach him. 'I'm sorry. I'm so sorry.'

She spends hours watching the tākapu nesting and fishing, the birds either huddled low to the white rock or circling high in the grey sky. The layered chattering of the gannets continues as she turns away and climbs the path in the direction of Te Henga. She drops onto the Hillary Trail, dipping in and out between bush and beach, walking for hours. When she returns to the start of the road up to Magda's house, the sea is a slow-moving orange smudge and the sky a blaze of setting sun, a reminder that there are other places, far from there.

☆ ☆ ☆

She hugs Magda goodbye as she walks through the departure gate at Auckland airport, passport and round-the-world ticket in her hand, off to Thailand, and then to the next warm place, and the next, wherever the currents take her. For the first time in months, she feels the possibility of a future, the lightness of air bubbles rising up through water to the surface.

PART 5

24

Hobart, Tasmania, Australia, 2021

All night it rained. Water falling through the leaves outside. Words falling through the darkness inside. Enough words to flood a room. In the fifteen years since she left New Zealand, she's never told anyone what happened on the mountain. Last night, as she and Chris sat at opposite ends of the table, she told him everything.

She started steadily, one word at a time, slow steps back into memory. A red-roofed hut emerged from the dark. A crisp blue morning. A wisp of wind.

She told him of the excitement and anticipation, the sense that her world was changing; that, although she was still grieving for her father, she was stepping into a new self, a life that fitted, years of adventure in front of her.

She spoke of the undertow of doubt that tugged at her as she climbed, of the times she turned to look down the mountain but said nothing and turned up again towards the summit. All the ways she could have changed the outcome. Clouds rolled in. The wind picked up.

Words came more quickly as she found her way back in time. Memories and dark spaces flashed past like train carriages across a viaduct at night: fear, cold creeping panic, a sudden sense of inevitability, and finally the settling weight of acceptance.

As she spoke, thoughts she didn't even realise she had came to her. Hidden things still exist. She remembered Penny confiding how she'd had hardly any sleep before the trip: as well as the late night out with Thea on the Wednesday, she'd spent Thursday night with a girl she'd met in a bar. She had the ghost of a memory of Marcus rushing them out the door before they'd done one last equipment check, and of Jim choosing to do the summit trip even though his knee was still recovering from surgery. A chill wind rushes up from deep in the past, bringing with it a confusion of blame and sorrow.

Finally, saying the words more for herself than to Chris, she spoke of waking up in hospital with the cold dread of being alive. The guilt of not feeling any relief at all in being saved.

Hours later, a landslip of words around them, Chris turned off the light and they walked through the dark house to bed.

'It wasn't your fault,' he had said and pulled her in towards him. 'A lot of things went wrong, some of it just bad luck.' Pressed against his chest, his arms around her, she started shivering, and shivering, and couldn't stop. 'It wasn't your fault that he died.'

Thea's starting to realise that there's some truth to those words. In a box in Magda's roof space, there's a brown envelope, which, if opened, would tell her just how much truth: a black-ink account of bad decisions, but not hers alone; an updated weather forecast that was never checked; and the futile rescue efforts made by members of the club who turned back rather than succumb to the snow themselves. It would tell of weather too wild for the helicopter to fly until hours had passed; and of the storm-felled tōwai blocking access up the mountain road, the critical delay as it was chainsawed and hauled clear. But none of those facts matter now. Thea knows that it wasn't all her fault, but she was part of it. Nothing will ever change that.

Unable to stop shaking, Thea had got out of bed. She stood under the shower, turning the tap farther and farther around, hotter and hotter until she finally stopped shivering. By the time she finished, the bathroom was thick with white steam. The bedroom was filled with the heavy in and out of Chris's breath.

Now it's morning, thin and grey as though the sunlight can barely stretch to cover the night. Thea feels adrift, floating like pumice, a brittle collection of holes on the surface of her past.

Chris wasn't awake when she got up. She has no idea how he's digested her admission in his sleep. Her back is turned when he comes into the kitchen and for a while they move around each other in the small space, opening cupboards and drawers, getting breakfast ingredients from the fridge, barely saying a word to each other. Then, putting his hands on her upper arms, he steers her in the direction of the table where she sits while he makes breakfast. She watches him, trying to gauge his mood. He takes the coffee pot off the stove and pours it into two cups.

'That wasn't true, was it?' she says at last. 'About Sarah?' There's no accusation in her words. All she wants to know now is the truth, and it doesn't feel like there's much to lose in asking.

He puts the plates down on the table, then goes back for the coffee. He doesn't seem surprised by the question and is matter-of-fact in his answer. 'It's true enough.' She's about to ask what that means, but he sees her open her mouth and speaks before she can say anything. 'It's what I told my parents,' he says, 'and whoever asked.'

'Why?'

'I had to tell them something,' he says. 'My parents made me see a psychologist. "Don't let this ruin your life",' he says, in imitation of his father.

'But why not tell the truth?' she asks. *Whatever the truth is*, she thinks.

'I don't know what the truth is,' he says, plainly. Thea can feel herself growing frustrated, but doesn't want to show it. She doesn't breathe in too deeply or out too loudly. She keeps her grip relaxed on the coffee cup, but beneath the table her toes are tightly curled, tensely waiting to see if he'll say more. 'Everyone *needed* to know what happened. They just wanted to hear me say that I blamed myself, that I felt awful, I'm a terrible person, et cetera, et cetera, so they could talk me through it, give me some "coping tools", and cross a problem off their list. Give themselves a gold star for a job well done.' Thea's not sure if Chris means the psychologist or his parents. Probably both.

'So you made up a story? Let them think Sarah was an out-of-control addict?' She tries to keep the absolute disbelief out of her voice.

'Not a full-on addict, just . . . Anyway, it's not like they knew her.' He cuts through his omelette, parcels up the mushrooms, spinach and melted cheese on his fork. 'And it's what they imagined anyway — they thought all backpackers were basically dirty vagabonds. Still do. I only told them what they expected to hear, and I only said it because they wouldn't stop harassing me.'

'Except, in that version, *you* didn't give her any drugs.' It could be a question, but it's not.

He makes a sound like laughter, but without any humour in it. 'Anyway, you should be pleased. They were so thrilled when they met you. They would've imagined you as some kind of strung-out backpacker junkie, then Dad met you and all was well with the world. His son was not quite the massive failure that he thought.'

The terrible thing, Thea thinks to herself, is that what Chris is saying kind of makes sense — or rather, now that he's telling her, on some level it doesn't really surprise her that it's what he did. As unbelievable as it is. She doesn't want to make him angry, but she can't let this go. Not now.

'If you don't know what the truth is,' she says, carefully, like taking steps across a frozen lake, 'what *do* you know?' *Just tell me!* she wants to shout at him. *I've told you everything. Just tell me what happened. Tell me what you did.* She stays silent, listening for cracks.

'I've told you,' he says, grit in his voice, 'I don't know.'

'Chris.' Her sharp tone catches his attention. She can't quite name the look that passes across his face, but it's like he's thinking about something, making a decision. 'Why was Sarah down by the lake?' she asks. What she really wants to ask is if he was there.

Chris hunches in on himself, elbows on knees, head in his hands. 'I really don't know. I think she was just walking. I wasn't there. I wasn't with her.' Thea stays silent. For a while there's just the sound of the rain hitting the windows. He glances up at her, as though to check whether what he's said is enough. Thea says nothing and waits.

'We were at Xibalba,' he continues after a while. 'I was working. Sarah was just hanging out, dancing, drinking, you know. I didn't see her most of the night. It was a crazy night. Really busy.' He's staring at the ground, almost rocking, not crying but a look of misery on his face. 'Then she wanted to go back to the hostel.' He sighs and pauses. Thea waits. 'She wanted me to go with her.'

You could've done that, Thea thinks. The hostel was only a couple of minutes from the bar. Even if he was working, he could've taken a ten-minute break.

'The night was wrapping up and a couple of us from the bar were going to hang around and have a few drinks. Unwind.' Chris's eyes flick towards Thea and away again, as though he's realised he's made a mistake. She pictures Sarah, dancing for hours, passing time until closing, waiting patiently until Chris was done, ready to go to bed. *But you stayed*, she silently accuses him.

'So . . .' Thea prompts, leaning forward to try to catch his eye.

'So I stayed. Sarah went back to the Xaman Ek.' He straightens up, leans back in his chair, as though the worst part is over. 'Or I thought she did.'

She can feel the buzz of anger through her veins, electric pulses of rage. 'But what about when you got back to the hostel? She wasn't there, was she?'

'I know. I know.' He rubs his face with his hands. 'I was going to go out and look for her, but I just lay down for a while.'

'You fell asleep,' she says, her words a jagged crack, cold dark water seeping through. *You fucking idiot*, she thinks, looking across at him. *You fucking, fucking selfish prick.*

He doesn't respond, but she doesn't need him to. It wasn't a question. She wonders how long it took him to click that she wasn't there. Was her body discovered before he even realised that she was missing? She imagines some poor person on their way to work coming across Sarah, at first unsure what they were seeing and then having the horrifying realisation. A group of people pulling Sarah onto land. Trying to work out who she was. Who to tell. All while Chris slept.

There are so many things she wants to say to him. Erratic, overlapping thoughts. In the end, she lands on the simplest and yet most complicated question. 'Why did you lie? Why did you tell that bullshit story? To me, last night?'

He waves his hand in the air, gesturing towards her. 'Because of this,' he says angrily. 'Because people expect me to feel guilty. I didn't do anything to her. Why is it my fucking fault?' In the space that follows, Thea realises it's stopped raining. There's just his breathing, loud in the room, and her heartbeat, loud in her ears. 'It's not my fucking fault she was so afraid of walking home alone. *You've* always been fine with walking on your own. It's not my fucking fault that the one time — the *one time* — I didn't walk her home something happened.'

The one time? She wonders if he even knows he's lying. She thinks of him, the night before, telling her that Marcus's death wasn't her fault. She thought they were words of comfort. In daylight she can see them for what they really were — thin threads of a spider web, words designed to bind them with a shared ambivalence, sticky words of absolution. If she accepted that she wasn't at fault, she had to accept that he wasn't either. And if they weren't at fault, why should they care?

Thea thinks of a rock flying off a mountain, tumbling and snowballing its way down the slope, a catapult of rock and ice followed by a whirl of arms and legs.

She feels a sharp clutching at her stomach, the ache of a star collapsing in on itself.

For Thea, there's no sharp division between fault and blamelessness. It's a wavering high-line strung between two mountaintops. When you topple into the void below, it doesn't matter if you're at fault or not, the guilt still rushes past like a cold wind. You don't have to be responsible for a tragedy to care about the consequences.

Time is slow and wide, and deep enough to hold memories and secrets out of sight for years. She remembers a story her father told her once about a plane that crashed on Mangatoetoenui glacier and was swallowed up in the blue-white crawl and not released from the ice until years later. She never had the chance to ask more about it. Who was on the plane, and did they get out? Did it emerge from the glacier in broken bits — a wing, a tail, a curving side? Or was it, somehow, miraculously whole?

25

Thea had always thought of people as a collection of the places they'd come from, the places they'd been. Places built up in layers to form a person over years or generations, with all the silt and rubble of the in-between places filling the cracks to hold them together. Beaches and mountains, lakes and cities, sand and ice stacked to make a person.

She realises now that the opposite is true. People leave pieces of themselves in the places they go: a small chip that crumbles into nothing; great blocks sheared off and too heavy to carry away. More and more pieces are left behind so that all that remains are the holes in the honeycomb, the empty spaces between the photographs. Sarah is forever part of Lago de Atitlán, washing in and out among the reeds. Gretel is now in the soil, the leaves and the strips of bark littering Tasmania. And Thea? A part of her is still on Ruapehu, sitting beside Marcus in a snow-filled trench. A part of her returned to stardust before it ever shone.

☆ ☆ ☆

Thea stands in the living room, feeling the quiet. Chris has gone out for a run, winding back and forth through the reserve, racking up distance all without going more than five kilometres from home. She'd like to be out there, too. Out of the house, feeling the cool calm of the earth beneath her feet, the clean peace of the trees above. Instead, she opens all the windows in the living room and kitchen to let the rain-fresh air sweep through the house.

She listens to the radio while she washes the dishes. The news is all the same these days, whether it's online or on TV or radio: a climbing tally of Covid cases, Covid deaths; cancellations, vaccinations. The words are just background noise, something to fill the room, exfoliate the air, then be blown out on the breeze.

Then, something catches her attention: confirmation that the snap lockdown will end as planned at six o'clock that evening. It's only been three days, but something collapses inside Thea. She wants to weep with relief. She leans against the kitchen bench and draws deep, steadying breaths.

The newsreader keeps talking: *Despite being infectious in the community, the quarantine escapee did not transmit the Delta virus to any Taswegians.*

And then: *With the lockdown lifting, friends and colleagues of*

German citizen Gretel Fischer will be going ahead with a planned vigil in her memory on Wednesday morning at the gallery where she worked. It has been confirmed that Ms Fischer died from a traumatic head injury sustained from a fall at Mount Field National Park. It appears that Ms Fischer may have crossed a safety barrier marking off unstable ground.

Gretel must be back in Germany now. At home, at rest. It should be sad, but Thea finds comfort in the thought. There are so many people who never make it home: bones slowly wearing down, never found, in a faraway place; or bodies buried under a headstone across an ocean, not in their homeland, but becoming part of new soil for their children and descendants.

Thea's told herself, over the years, that you don't need to sit beside a grave to remember someone, and that's true. Sometimes there isn't even a grave or a body, just a shard of something broken forever digging into you.

All Thea's dead are with her always. But she can't help thinking of her parents' grave, a rectangle of bright green grass on a gently sloping lawn. The homesickness pulls at her like gravity. It's as though her insides are being drawn in tight, the debris of life coming together like grains of iron sand on a magnet. She feels a yearning so intense, it's almost like thirst. She wants to go and sit with them. More than that, when her time comes, she wants to be buried somewhere near them. There's home, the place you live; and there's home, the place you're from. She loves Tasmania, but she can't imagine being buried there.

She thought she needed Chris. She thought they were the same. All their secrets, shame and guilt — and, yes, their sorrow

— bound them together. But with everything she's now said, and he's now said, she knows they're not the same. She can't stay with him. And if she can't stay with him, she can't stay here.

In the hours since they spoke, the truth has been seeping into Thea. The realisation came slowly at first; the incremental black-to-grey of dawn before the blaze and beauty of sunrise. It starts to loosen knots inside her, a little-by-little untying until suddenly she feels like she could fly up into the sky, free. No more secrets or lies to keep her here.

Then comes a more gentle lightening, when the radiant feeling of freedom fades to a flat white-blue. It's a sensation that could become an infinity of sorrow if she looks too long: pity for her younger self. It's not like she hasn't loved her life; these years in Tasmania have been rich with friendship and experiences. But she feels an ache for everything that girl went through, all the guilt she took on instead of talking to the people who cared — because there *were* people who cared, if only she'd been willing to look. A cold sense of shame has churned underground through all the years since that night on the mountain. It's a part of who she was, but it no longer has to be who she is.

There has been one word humming deep inside her for a long time, vibrating at the lowest pitch. The chant of *om*, the sound of the universe formed of a million glittering stars, the call of home. Now she's heard it, it's getting louder and more urgent.

She's going to leave one last time, but this time she'll run back to something, not away. She'll run towards wide open skies and black sand beaches, towards cliffs and volcanoes, towards everything she left behind. Building a life from bare ground, a home built on the foundations of truth, a life that is hers to live in.

There'll be a long list of things to do, things to pack, thirteen photos to take down and wrap, a Tasmanian tiger toy and a kiwi toy to squash into a box. But all that is yet to come.

She watches the clock as though the doors will fly open when it strikes six, as though with a single chime her world can change. As though it was always that simple.

After all these years, after all the words spoken and unspoken, there's one thing left to tell Chris: she's going home.

ACKNOWLEDGEMENTS

Sometimes people apply that old adage to writing books: it takes a village. In this case, it took a *pueblo*. And at least five cities and three countries. *The Stars Are a Million Glittering Worlds* owes so much to the mountains, lakes, trees, seas and skies of Aotearoa, Australia and Guatemala. So, first, thank you to the land and the landscapes, and to all the people of those places.

To my parents, Mike and Barbara Butson, my love and thanks for so, so much — not least, for whatever you did to make me believe that 'a writer' was a perfectly legitimate answer to the question 'what do you want to be when you grow up?' I miss you and your stories every day. (This is the time to acknowledge that there's a character in the book called Michael who bears no resemblance to my father, and nor was he meant to. The name just couldn't be shaken. Dad was never called Michael anyway.)

To Wynn Gemmell, thank you for showing so much interest

in this book, for being so proud of me, and for your love and kindness. It means a lot.

The Stars Are a Million Glittering Worlds is a work of fiction, but (to use another adage) truth is stranger than fiction. So . . . San Pedro La Laguna . . . To James Stephens and Angie Connell, this book clearly would never have been written without those months in Central America and those weeks in San Pedro, and I couldn't have written it without both of you. Thanks so much for all the stories and adventures. While this is most obviously and definitely not a book about us, I think you'll see some similarities to people — and places — we encountered. James: we made it all the way to Panama (wherever that is). I think one of the reasons it took me so long to write about Central America was that most of the stories I had felt like they were really your stories. Angie: while Sarah is very, very much not you, when I think of the best parts of her — her vibrancy, love for life and some of her style — I do think of you, my lovely friend. (To Mrs Connell, I would like to use this opportunity to apologise for my post all those years ago. It was made in jest, but with poor judgement and it gave you the wrong impression of me. All the same, I think perhaps you shouldn't read this book . . .)

The book began its written life as a short story, *Tajumulco*, written during a six-week Iowa Fiction Workshop at the International Institute of Modern Letters (Te Herenga Waka Victoria University) at the start of 2023. Thank you, Andrew Steiner, for facilitating workshops so well and for your insightful suggestions. Although the story changed over the following two years, some lines written during those wonderful weeks made it into the novel intact. Shaun Barnett, my classmate, who quickly became a friend, deserves acknowledgement for his enthusiasm as I expanded on the story, as well as particular thanks for providing Tasmania travel tips and suggesting routes up and down Ruapehu (to which I applied some creative licence. If you get lost on the mountain, the fault is mine, not Shaun's). Shaun, you had every reason to be more selfish with your time and energy, and I'm truly grateful for how you contributed to this book and for your friendship. How very much I wish you, me and Ashleigh (Young) could all catch up again for a beer and talk about our books.

Tajumulco became *Cumulus* a short while into my MA at the IIML. It quickly became apparent that *Tajumulco* wasn't really finished, and that I wanted to finish it more than I wanted to start the project I'd said I was going to spend the year writing. Thank you so much to my fellow MA students: Kate Twomey, Tōrea Scott-Fyfe, Gregory Reilly, Hannah Patterson, Amber O'Sullivan, Tara Leckie, Michelle Duff, Erica Challis and Shariff Burke. I feel so lucky to have been on the course with all of you and so very grateful for the time you gave my manuscript and the ways in which you helped shape the story. I will forever treasure that year of fantastic views, bread, hummus, sauerkraut and so many wonderful words and worlds. To Tina Makereti, who was our class convenor and my supervisor, I am in awe of your ability to see so quickly what needs to happen with a story, and to provide that feedback so patiently and kindly. I've learned so much from you, both during the MA year and after, and I know I have yet more to glean from the words of wisdom you imparted that year (forgive me, please, for the comma splices). To Laurence Fearnley, how very fortunate I was to have had you provide feedback on *Cumulus*. You have been so generous with your time and expertise and your encouragement. I truly appreciate it. Like Tina, you have made this a better book and me a better writer.

I'm grateful to the New Zealand Society of Authors for existing, but also specifically for arranging the Perfect Pitch Online opportunity. Via that process, *Cumulus* landed in the expert hands of the team at Allen & Unwin Aotearoa New Zealand and became *The Stars Are a Million Glittering Worlds*. Thank you to Michelle (Miff) Hurley, Leanne McGregor and all of the amazing team for treating my book with such care and attention. My book and I couldn't have been in better hands. I'm honoured to be part of your publishing whānau. Thank you for arranging for Sandy Cull to design the spectacular cover, for Megan van Staden to turn each page into a thing of beauty, and for the talented and astute Emma Neale to be my editor. Emma, your edits and suggestions — both big and small — have hugely improved the story and I'm so grateful to have had your input. It was an honour and a pleasure to work with you.

To my treasured Toi Stories writers' group — Wendy Cuthbert, Catherine Lavery, Fiona Mathieson and Cathy Tracey — your feedback on bits and pieces of all iterations of the story was so valuable. Thank you for letting me take up more than my share of our precious catch-ups talking about my writing.

To Sam Price, Jono Gardiner and Gareth Stiven, who have been not just tolerant but accommodating of having a creative writer in a team that favours spreadsheets over words: thanks for enabling my work life–writing life balance. Enjoy the correct use of semicolons.

Thanks to everyone who has shown continued interest in this book, despite my abysmal answer to the question 'what's it about?' Unfortunately, I can't list all the wonderful people in my life here, but since 'home' is a very important thread running through the book, I do want to give very special thanks to all the people who have made both Auckland and Wellington home for me. In particular, my beloved book club, whose existence means that a part of me will always be in Wellington and whose members I suspect will be among the most fervent promoters of my book; and the 'Pt Chev Commune', who, no matter how far I strayed or how long I stayed away, always made me feel that Auckland was still home.

Finally, a million glittering thank yous to the stars: the readers, the writers, the booksellers, the libraries and everyone else involved in the world of books.

AUTHOR PHOTOGRAPH BY EBONY LAMB

ABOUT THE AUTHOR

Gina Butson has worked as a lawyer and as an advisor in the public sector. She completed her MA in Creative Writing at the International Institute of Modern Letters (IIML) in 2023, and her short fiction has been published in *Newsroom*, *Salient* and *Turbine | Kapohau*. Gina won the Salient Creative Writing competition and was Highly Commended in the Sargeson Prize in 2024. She has been awarded a 2026 residency at the Robert Lord Writers Cottage.